DEC 13 2002

Hudson tried to boost the gain
on the distress signal.

7/03
2

STAR TREK®

THE BRAVE AND THE BOLD

BOOK TWO

KEITH R.A. DeCANDIDO

Based upon *Star Trek®*
and *Star Trek: The Next Generation®*
created by Gene Roddenberry,
Star Trek: Deep Space Nine®
created by Rick Berman & Michael Piller,
and *Star Trek: Voyager®*
created by Rick Berman & Michael Piller
& Jeri Taylor

POCKET BOOKS

New York   London   Toronto   Sydney   Singapore

This book is a work of fiction. Names, characters, places and incidents are products of the author's imagination or are used fictitiously. Any resemblance to actual events or locales or persons, living or dead, is entirely coincidental.

An *Original* Publication of POCKET BOOKS

POCKET BOOKS, a division of Simon & Schuster, Inc.
1230 Avenue of the Americas, New York, NY 10020

Copyright © 2002 by Paramount Pictures. All Rights Reserved.

STAR TREK is a Registered Trademark of Paramount Pictures.

This book is published by Pocket Books, a division of Simon & Schuster, Inc., under exclusive license from Paramount Pictures.

All rights reserved, including the right to reproduce this book or portions thereof in any form whatsoever. For information address Pocket Books, 1230 Avenue of the Americas, New York, NY 10020

ISBN: 0-7434-1923-5

First Pocket Books printing December 2002

10 9 8 7 6 5 4 3 2 1

POCKET and colophon are registered trademarks of Simon & Schuster, Inc.

For information regarding special discounts for bulk purchases, please contact Simon & Schuster Special Sales at 1-800-456-6798 or business@simonandschuster.com

Printed in the U.S.A.

For Terri

STAR TREK VOYAGER®

Part 3: The Third Artifact

2371

This portion of the story takes place several weeks
before the *Star Trek: Voyager* pilot episode
"Caretaker," and shortly before the
Star Trek: The Next Generation novel
Double Helix Book 4: Quarantine.

Chapter One

THARIA DIDN'T CRY when his three mates died.

It had been nine months, and not a single tear had run down his blue cheek.

He sat with two of his fellow Maquis rebels in a cave on some planet or other. Tharia wasn't even sure where they were, to be honest. He'd been too busy trying to repair one of the consoles to pay attention to wherever it was that they had crash-landed their shuttle. There had been four of them, but their pilot—a Bolian who had replaced Tom Paris after the imbecile Earther had gotten himself caught by the Federation—died in the crash. That left Tharia ch'Ren, Gerron Ral, and B'Elanna Torres.

"When's Chakotay supposed to get here?" Gerron asked in a whiny voice that made Tharia want to strangle him.

"He'll get here soon," B'Elanna snapped in a voice intended to intimidate. She didn't bother to look at Gerron. She was too busy keeping her eyes glued to her ancient tricorder, hoping it would tell her of Chakotay's imminent arrival with their ship, hoping it wouldn't tell her that Gul Evek or some other Cardassian had found them and was going to blast them into atoms.

At least their mission had been more or less successful. The shipment of grenades that Cardassian Central Command had earmarked for occupying forces on Dorvan V had been annihilated, first stolen from the freighter that was taking them to Dorvan, then destroyed an hour later in the shuttle crash. (Mercifully, the grenades hadn't been primed yet; had they been, more than the Bolian pilot would have been lost, and Chakotay would only have been able to find their remains with a tricorder—or tweezers.)

It would have been better if they had managed to keep the grenades intact and thus be able to add them to the Maquis's arsenal, but the important thing was that the Cardassians wouldn't be able to use them. Sometimes it didn't matter if you won, so long as the other side lost.

"It's going to be dark soon." Gerron, Tharia noted, sounded wholly unintimidated—which meant he was a fool, as B'Elanna's actions generally spoke louder than her words, and her words were fairly high in volume. "And with all our supplies trashed, we'll have to forage. I don't know if there's anything here we can even eat, much less—"

Tharia stood up, running a hand through his feathery white hair. "Oh, for Thori's sake, I'll go look for food." He looked down at Gerron. "If you want to make yourself useful, gather up some rocks that we can heat."

"Rocks?"

"Basic survival." Tharia sighed. "Did they teach you nothing on Bajor? You can use a phaser on rocks to heat them."

Gerron at least had the decency to look abashed. "Sorry. Forgot," he muttered.

Looking over at the half-Klingon, half-Earther engineer, Tharia said, "I'll be back soon."

B'Elanna only grunted, focused as she was on the tricorder. Knowing that was all the acknowledgment he'd get, Tharia headed outward toward the cave entrance in the hopes of finding something edible. Given that three— four, really, given B'Elanna's half-breed nature—species were represented in the cave, it would be a challenge. Andorians, Bajorans, Earthers, and Klingons didn't have similar eating habits, after all. But Tharia didn't care that much—he mainly needed to get away from Gerron before the young Bajoran drove him to anger.

Tharia preferred to keep his emotions in check.

His *zhavey* had cried, of course, back then. It took very little for her to cry, truth be told, and the deaths of her *chei*'s three mates was certainly more than a little. And several of his friends cried.

But Tharia didn't. Not when he found their broken, bloody bodies in the wreckage of their home on Beaulieu's World after the Cardassian bomb had destroyed it, not at the death rites held at the community center on Beaulieu's, not at the ceremony back home on Andor.

Ignoring the advice of his *zhavey* to stay on Andor, Tharia had returned to Beaulieu's after the ceremony. Once a Federation colony, Beaulieu's World had been one of many planets ceded to the Cardassians in a treaty intended to settle a border dispute. Unfortunately, the Federation colonists saw no reason to leave their homes, even if those homes were now in Cardassian territory. The Cardassians, in turn, saw no reason to let them live in peace. Tensions in the Demilitarized Zone that was created between Federation and Cardassian space became increasingly heated, incidents of harassment on both sides were reported, and the treaty intended to settle a dispute wound up setting off a powder keg.

A group of (now former) Federation citizens of the colonies, as well as a number of Starfleet personnel sympathetic to the cause, formed a group called the Maquis. Tharia had never been too clear on the etymology of the term, only that it was the same name as a similar group in Earth's pre-spaceflight days. It was also derived from one of Earth's secondary languages, so it was pronounced "mah-*kee*" rather than "*may*-kwiss," as Tharia had initially assumed.

Before the bomb struck his home, Tharia had been one of the more outspoken opponents of the Maquis. He didn't think their formation would gain the colonists anything but trouble. True, the Cardassians weren't exactly living up to their side of the bargain—hounding non-Cardassians, occasionally sending military ships into the Demilitarized Zone—but Tharia didn't see that as a reason to become terrorists.

The governing body of Beaulieu's had held an open forum in the community center on the subject of the Maquis, and Tharia had spoken against them there. "Sentient beings should be able to reason out their problems without having to resort to mindless violence," he had said. "Effecting change from behind a phaser bank is no true change, simply an imposition of will."

When someone in the audience had pointed out that negotiation was how they got into this mess in the first place, Tharia had said, "One poor example does not invalidate the method. And one does not compound an error by making a bigger one."

Tharia had been so passionate at that open forum that

tears came to his eyes, and all three of his mates congratulated him on his rhetorical skills.

Two months later, all three were dead, their home destroyed by a bomb of Cardassian make.

Three months later, Tharia sold the land on which the remains of their house stood to an Yridian developer who had been making overtures to them for over a year.

Four months later, he was part of a Maquis cell led by an Earther named Chakotay.

Five months later, he killed his first Cardassian, during a raid on a supply depot.

Tharia hugged himself in the bitter cold that greeted him at the cave mouth. In the two hours since the crash, the temperature had dropped by at least twenty degrees.

He hadn't cared what the name of the planet was, but now he found himself desiring to know it so he could avoid it in the future. He hadn't paid much attention when they crashed—he was more concerned with getting under cover—but now that he had a chance to look around, he realized that this place was what Tom Paris would have termed a dump.

When Thori in Her Greatness created this particular world, Tharia observed, She obviously was having a bad day. It was as if She couldn't be bothered to put together a proper ecosystem, so She tossed a few rocks and bushes around a flat, gray surface and hoped no one would notice. The sky was equally gray, and a limp wind blew, barely disturbing the minimal vegetation. Tharia's antennae quivered at—something, he couldn't tell what, exactly. All he knew for sure was that this world was dull and gray and he didn't want to be here any longer than he had to.

As Tharia walked across that hard, flat ground, he found no animal life, and the plant life was poisonous to all of them. Ironically, the plants were edible for Bolians. *Obviously,* he thought with irritation, *the wrong person died in the shuttle crash.*

After ten minutes, he gave up. His tricorder—a thirty-year-old Starfleet model that worked only sporadically at the best of times—was starting to lose power, and the temperature continued to drop. Tharia had never liked the cold. One of the reasons Beaulieu's had appealed to him when he and his family chose to move off Andor was because it was warm. And his antennae were quivering so fast he was sure they were vibrating on top of his head. It was time he went back to B'Elanna and Gerron.

You can do better.

Tharia whirled around. "What?"

You can do better. You don't need to settle for this. You can destroy them once and for all.

The tricorder had now completely lost power, but Tharia's antennae were now quivering with a purpose. The voice was coming from under one of the gray rocks.

He knew this mainly because the voice didn't sound in his ears or in his antennae, but in his mind.

Deducing that telepathy was at work, Tharia stopped walking. Only when he stopped did he realize that he'd been moving in the first place. He had been going toward the rock from which the telepathic voice had emanated, almost against his will. Tharia hated telepaths.

"What do you want with me?"

I want to help you achieve your goal.

"Really? Show yourself—and speak! I will not converse with a telepath who hides."

I am no telepath, and I'm not hiding. I'm but a tool that can give you what you desire.

Tharia made a derisive noise. "Can you bring my three mates back to me?"

No.

"Then you lie."

You misunderstand my purpose and my words, Tharia ch'Ren.

"Do I?" He didn't bother to question how the voice knew his name. Telepaths loved to show off how much they knew that was unspoken.

Yes. Getting your family back is a wish, not a goal. Items that can grant wishes are the purview of stories and myths. As I said, I'm a tool—and I can help you get—

"What I desire, yes, I see." Tharia felt foolish standing in the middle of the gray rocks talking to nothing, so he sat down. "So you can help me get rid of the Cardassians? Aid me in destroying them? Assist me in driving them from my home forever?"

Yes.

"And what do you get in return?"

I have lain unused on this miserable rock for thousands of lifetimes, Tharia ch'Ren. What good is a tool that gets no use?

Tharia leaned back, supporting himself on the rock with his arms. He could feel the emissions from this whatever-it-was more precisely now in his antennae. It was wedged in between two rocks amid the underbrush of a bush that stuck out between them.

"I will not be coerced. I can feel you trying to convince me with your mind games."

You are a wise man, Tharia ch'Ren. You are also a man with a mission. I can be a valuable aid on that mission. All you must do is hold me in your grasp.

Tharia stood up. "No. I refuse."

Images appeared in Tharia's head then.

He saw a humanoid of some kind, holding a small black box that glowed with an odd green hue.

He saw other humanoid figures kneeling before the figure holding the box.

He saw the figure walk outside into a day that was filled with sunlight, a sky with no clouds.

He saw the figure hold up the box.

He saw clouds appear seemingly out of nowhere, saw winds start to gust where the air had been still.

He saw the people cheer as rain came pouring down from the sky.

Then the vista changed: he saw the figure again—older this time—using the black box to start a blizzard. Then using it to melt a snow-filled region with intense, desertlike heat. Then causing a hurricane to tear through a residential area.

"Get out of my head!" Tharia was now screaming as he unholstered his phaser, his dead tricorder long since dropped to the rocky ground. He didn't even check to see what setting the phaser was on, he just activated it and fired.

The images continued to pour into his mind as he fired. As the amber phaser beam tore into the leaves of the bush, he saw the figure use the black box to wipe out a village with a tornado. As the phaser pulverized the branches, rain was brought to the desert. As the rocks blew apart, a fog rolled into a sky filled with air traffic, causing massive slow-ups and collisions.

"Enough!" Tharia cried as he finally stopped firing. He wrinkled his nose at the smell that emanated from the ground. Nothing remained of the two rocks and the bush but smoke and ash—

—and a black box with a greenish hue.

His mind was free of the images, but the voice remained. *You see what you can do if you wield me. All that is required is—*

"No!" Tharia raised his phaser to its highest setting and fired again, this time directly at the box.

The box seemed to simply absorb the phaser beam. The weapon had no effect on it.

Think what you can do with my capabilities. Think of the glory you can bring to the Maquis.

"I care nothing for glory! If you've seen into my mind you know that. I simply want—I want—to see the Cardassians—to get them—"

You want revenge.

Tears started to flow down Tharia's cheek. "Yes, damn you! I want revenge! I want them all destroyed! I want their heads ripped from their bodies!"

You want them to feel what you felt when you saw your mates' bodies in the wreckage of your home.

More images entered Tharia's mind, but they were not from the box. They were his own memories, suppressed for all these months when he refused to think about what had happened.

Athmin, impaled on a structural beam. Ushra, her head caved in by the ceiling. Shers, ripped to pieces by fragments from the Cardassians' explosive device.

Tharia fell to his knees. Pain shot through his legs as his knees collided with the hard ground, but he barely noticed. "I should have died with them," he said, his voice barely above a whisper.

But you didn't. As I said, I don't grant wishes. What I can do is make sure that those responsible pay for what they did to you.

He looked at the black box that sat on the ground, blurred by the months of repressed tears that now poured from his eyes. "Yes," he said in a whisper so quiet that Tharia himself could barely hear his own voice over the wind. "Yes, they must pay. All of them."

And they will. All you have to do is pick me up.

Tharia could not make his legs move properly, but somehow, he managed to crawl over to where the box sat, ignoring the pain of the superheated ground around it.

It was cool to the touch, which was impossible. He had been firing on it with a phaser at full, and the box had been absorbing the blast. He should have gotten third-degree burns just touching it. Yet he was able to cradle the box in his arms.

Everything you desire will be yours.

The moment he touched the box, Tharia noticed that the air around him got warmer. The chill that permeated the atmosphere was gone in an instant. It was now as warm on this despicable gray planet as it was on the most pleasant day back home on Beaulieu's.

"What did you do?" he asked quietly, wiping a tear from his cheek with his right hand as he cradled the box under his left.

Fulfilled a simple desire in order to show my ability to do so: I raised the temperature to one comfortable for you.

Tharia stood up. "Thank you."

It is the first of many desires I will fulfill for you.

It was another hour before Tharia finally made it back to the cave. B'Elanna and Gerron sat in the same spot, but this time they were on either side of a pile of rocks that had been heated by phaser fire. Still, even with that, it was cooler in the cave than it had become outside thanks to Tharia's new possession.

B'Elanna stood up quickly and barked, "Where the *hell* have you been?"

"I told you," Tharia said in a quiet, almost subdued voice. He had wiped his face dry, and carried the box—

the tool—the *weapon*—under his left arm. "I went out to search for food."

"And you put it in that box?" B'Elanna asked snidely.

"No. This place doesn't seem to have any native animal life, and the plants are all poisonous."

"Figures," Gerron muttered.

B'Elanna sighed. "Well, it doesn't matter—Chakotay's in orbit, and he'll be landing inside of fifteen minutes."

Nodding, Tharia said, "Good."

There was a momentary pause. "So what *is* in the box?" B'Elanna finally asked.

"I'll tell you all about it when Chakotay arrives," he said.

B'Elanna stood in front of the Andorian. Tharia could tell she was agitated by the way his antennae retracted in her presence. "I'm not letting you bring that thing on the ship until you tell me what it is, Tharia."

"It's a weapon. The only weapon we'll ever need. Trust me, B'Elanna. Have I ever lied to you?"

Knowing full well that he hadn't, B'Elanna could only let out a growl. "Fine. So what does the stupid thing do?"

For the first time in many months, Tharia smiled.

"I'll tell you when Chakotay arrives."

Chapter Two

CAPTAIN ROBERT DESOTO knew he was in trouble the minute he realized that his first officer was threatening his territory.

The extremely wide, almost disturbingly toothy smile of Lieutenant Commander Dina Voyskunsky flashed across the table of the *Hood*'s lounge at the captain as she placed a black stone down in a position that cut one group of his white stones off from the rest of his pieces. Suddenly, what seemed to be a solid, secure group of stones was now in serious trouble. Either it was going to wither and die, or he was going to have to struggle mightily to survive.

Regardless, it was quite possible that the move had cost DeSoto the game. And Voyskunsky knew it. The first officer had a thin face with a disproportionately wide mouth. She also had wide teeth that DeSoto, in his less charitable moments—like right now, when she was beating him at Go—thought would be more at place on a horse than a human.

"Your move, Captain," she said, leaning back in her chair.

DeSoto sighed, and gazed over the Go board. He could resign the game, of course—that was the proper thing to do when one was defeated and knew it. And DeSoto did know it.

Under any other circumstances, he would, of course, resign, but he wanted to at least try to get some of his own back, even though intellectually he knew better. It wasn't worthy of him—but what the hell, he was the captain, he could make an idiot of himself if he wanted.

Besides, there was a possibility, however slim. Thirty-five years in Starfleet had taught him that there were *always* possibilities. You just sometimes had to look *really* hard for them.

"I must once again thank you for teaching me how to play this game." Voyskunsky grabbed her glass of synthale, moved as if to take a sip, then realized it was empty and put it back down.

"Yeah, yeah, gloat all you want. You know I was the captain of the Academy team my junior and senior years? In fact, all four years I was there—"

"You won two out of four Federation championships," Voyskunsky said in a singsong tone. "You've only told me three times a day every day since I beat you the first time. That was, in case you've forgotten, eight months ago, and I've beaten you—"

"Regularly ever since," DeSoto said, taking some small pleasure in being the interrupter this time, "I know, I know." He ran a hand through his rapidly thinning brown hair. *I'm going to be as bald as old Jean-Luc soon,* he thought, referring to his old friend Captain Picard of the *Enterprise. Sooner if I keep playing Dina.*

DeSoto's mother, Captain Mirabelle Brodeur, had

been an amateur champion player of the ancient Earth game of Go, which dated back at least three thousand years. Originated in China, where it was called *Wei Chi*, the game was deceptively simple. One player got one hundred and eighty-one black stones and went first, the other got one hundred and eighty white ones and went second. The board was a grid of nineteen horizontal lines and nineteen vertical lines. Each player took turns placing a stone on an intersection, with the object being to secure the most territory. It was the precursor to many a tabletop war and strategy game, but where they had come and gone—and in some cases improved, particularly with the development of holographic technology— Go remained a vital and popular game. It also had remained all but unchanged over the millennia.

Brodeur's husband, Dr. Hiram DeSoto, a civilian physician, had never evinced any interest in the game, but their son did. By the time Robert DeSoto reached his teen years, he had become renowned—first at his local school, later at the Academy—as a championship-caliber player.

He couldn't get anyone on the *Hood* to play against him, though. The problem with being a such a good player, of course, was that you were far superior to most of those around you. This, along with the added awkwardness most had at the idea of playing against their commanding officer, left him with either the deeply unsatisfying notion of playing the ship's computer, or not playing.

Then Dina Voyskunsky transferred to the *Hood* from the *Excalibur,* and one day saw DeSoto playing against the computer. She asked what he was doing; he told her; she was intrigued, never having heard of the game; and he proceeded to take her under his wing as his mother had done with him.

A year later, he was deeply regretting that decision.

Voyskunsky had gone from a nine-stone handicap to playing even with him in six months, and now she was beating him with alarming regularity.

Then he saw it. There was indeed a possibility. It would require both of them to play brilliantly, and would probably still wind up with him on the losing end. However, he had to give it a shot. He had to do something to salvage the tattered threads of his dignity.

As he prepared to place one of his stones, he was interrupted by the beep of the communication system. *"Bridge to Captain DeSoto."*

It was the voice of Lieutenant Manolet Dayrit, the *Hood*'s security chief and current duty officer on the bridge. "Go ahead, Manolet," DeSoto said after tapping his combadge.

"Sir, you need to come up here. We're receiving a distress signal from the U.S.S. Voyager."

DeSoto frowned, then recalled a recent fleet memo about the newest *Intrepid*-class ship, which was supposed to incorporate bioneural circuitry that would facilitate navigation through the Badlands. With the growing Maquis problem—and with the Maquis increasingly making use of the plasma-storm-filled Badlands as a hiding place—Starfleet had decided to create a ship that could handle that navigation hazard more easily.

"We'll be right up," the captain said, standing. "DeSoto out."

Voyskunsky had once again employed her too-wide smile. "So what's your move?"

"We'll finish this later. Right now I'm more worried about that distress signal."

As they exited the lounge, Voyskunsky asked, "Why?" As they headed toward the turbolift, Voyskunsky reached to the back of her head to tie her long brown hair back into a ponytail. She wore it loose only off duty.

"Because *Voyager*'s supposed to be on her shake-down cruise. I don't know where that was supposed to be offhand, but I doubt it was this far out."

As they entered the turbolift, Voyskunsky said, "So it could be a very clumsily laid trap."

DeSoto nodded. "Bridge." The turbolift started to accelerate upward. "Or they really could be out here near the Cardassian border, in which case, I'd say the shakedown cruise went horribly wrong."

Dayrit had already moved from the command chair to the tactical station behind it when DeSoto and Voyskunsky entered the *Hood*'s small bridge. Ensign José Kojima stood at the operations console next to Dayrit, also right behind the captain, with Lieutenant Baifang Hsu at the conn at the bridge's fore. While DeSoto moved to the captain's chair, Voyskunsky stood between Dayrit and Kojima. "Report."

"The distress call does seem to be from *Voyager,* sir—the hailing language matches. We can be there in ten minutes at warp nine. But I checked—*Voyager* should be in Sector 001 on its shakedown cruise. The location of the distress call is only about an eighth of a light-year from the DMZ."

Voyskunsky looked down at DeSoto. "We have to check it out, Captain."

DeSoto nodded. "Agreed. Baifang, set course for that distress call, warp nine."

The young woman's long-fingered hands played across the conn. "Course plotted and laid in, sir."

"Hit it. José, the nanosecond we're in sensor range, I want a full scan on whatever's broadcasting that signal. Manolet, give me long-range—make sure there aren't any Maquis or Cardassian surprises waiting for us."

A pair of "Aye, sir's" came from behind him.

Ten uncomfortable minutes later, Hsu said, "Coming out of warp, sir."

Voyskunsky peered over Kojima's shoulder. "Reading the ship's ID beacon. It and the hull configuration match with NCC-74656, *U.S.S. Voyager.*" She turned to Dayrit. "Anything on long-range?"

Dayrit shook his head—an odd sight, as the Filipino security chief had no discernible neck, so his head seemed to swivel directly on his shoulders. "There's some activity in the DMZ, but it all seems to be interplanetary—and it's all civilian."

"As it should be," Voyskunsky said. "After all, 'demilitarized' means 'no military.' "

Kojima muttered, "And don't think the Maquis don't love that."

Turning back to the ops officer, Voyskunsky asked, "What was that, Ensign?"

"Nothing important, sir," Kojima said, straightening. "I just—well, if they allowed military ships in the DMZ, the Maquis might not be so much of a problem."

Snorting, Dayrit said, "No, instead we'd have Starfleet and Central Command ships baring their teeth at each other. Three minutes later, we have another Cardassian War on our hands." Something on the tactical console then caught Dayrit's attention. "Incoming call from *Voyager*—it's Captain Janeway."

Good, DeSoto thought. It was looking more and more like this call was legitimate.

"In visual range," Hsu announced from the conn.

"Put it on the viewer," DeSoto said.

DeSoto watched as the general vista of space was replaced with a side view of the *U.S.S. Voyager.* The ship had a more angular saucer section that made it more aerodynamic. Where that was an unnecessary consideration for most starships, the *Intrepid*-class ships like *Voyager* were designed to be able to land on a planet's surface. DeSoto appreciated the alteration to the standard design, though he couldn't help but think that it made the ship look like a garden spade.

Right now, the nacelles were dimmed, and only about half the ship's running lights were operational. If this wasn't a true distress call, they were certainly making a good show of it.

Standing up, DeSoto said, "Let's answer the hail, Manolet. Put Captain Janeway onscreen."

The view of *Voyager* was replaced with that of her bridge. DeSoto smiled at the sight of the other ship's much roomier control center. When his former first officer Will Riker had transferred to the *Enterprise* to be Picard's first officer over seven years earlier, DeSoto had joked that he was going to a luxury liner. While *Voyager* wasn't as grandiose as the *Galaxy*-class monster that Jean-Luc and Will served on, it still put the *Hood* to shame in its roominess. *You could run laps on that bridge and not disturb a single duty officer,* he thought with a smile.

In the center seat was a woman with features that managed to be both hard and soft, her brown hair tied into a bun at the back of her head.

"This is Captain Robert DeSoto of the *U.S.S. Hood.*"

"Captain Kathryn Janeway of what's left of the Voyager," the woman said dryly. *"Thanks for coming so quickly, Captain."*

"You're a little far from home, aren't you?" he said with a smile.

"No, we're a lot *far from home. The whole point of a shakedown cruise is to shake the ship and see what falls down. In our case, it fell right on our heads."*

"What happened?"

"Something's wrong with the new bioneural gel packs. First they supercharged the engines so much that our dash to Alpha Centauri at warp one became a crazed sprint to the Cardassian border at warp nine-point-nine-eight."

DeSoto whistled in appreciation mixed with horror.

"Now we're at ten percent power. We'd appreciate a boost, if you'd be so kind, Captain."

Voyskunsky said, "Bridge to engineering. Prepare to set up a power transfer between *Hood* and *Voyager*."

"On it, Commander," Lieutenant Czierniewski, the *Hood*'s chief engineer, said.

Janeway smiled. *"Thank you, Captain."*

"Happy to be of help."

"I'm afraid there's something else. My security chief discovered something before sensors went down. We need to verify it with you."

DeSoto shrugged. "Sure."

A tall, mahogany-skinned Vulcan lieutenant stepped forward from the tactical station at the aft of the bridge and addressed the screen. *"If you would please direct your sensors at coordinates 318 mark 15."*

"Scanning," Dayrit said, manipulating his console. His dark eyes then went wide. "What the hell—?"

"What is it, Manolet?" Voyskunsky asked.

"Weird energy reading is what it is. It's focused on one of the ships in the DMZ—hell, it's changing course. Heading is 211 mark 9, heading away from us. Can't get a solid fix on the ship." His dark face contorted into a grimace. "Damn, they changed course again."

Kojima spoke up. "Sir, I've determined what the energy reading is. It relates to General Order 16."

DeSoto turned around to look at Kojima. "Sixteen?"

"That confirms my suspicions," the Vulcan said.

"There is a ship in the Demilitarized Zone that is carrying one of the Malkus Artifacts from the Zalkat Union. Standard procedure would be to pursue that ship and confiscate the artifact."

Turning back to the screen, DeSoto said, "Yeah, well, standard procedure is also that Starfleet vessels don't enter the DMZ—or abandon ships in distress that they're in the middle of helping." He sat back down in the command chair. "Manolet, try to track that ship as best you can until it goes off sensors."

"It's already changed course four times, Captain."

"Understood. Keep trying anyhow." He looked at the viewscreen. "Captain, I'm familiar with what General Order 16 says but not why it says it. Since your security chief seems to know more about it, I suggest you beam over here so we can figure out the best way to retrieve it."

"I already have some thoughts about that, actually."

DeSoto smiled. "I'm sure. Meantime, I'll send a damage control team over to help your engineer out."

"Mr. Honigsberg will welcome the help." Janeway returned the smile. *"We'll be ready to beam over in fifteen minutes. Janeway out."*

Voyskunsky was checking one of the aft consoles. "Power transfer beam is active—reading stable. Power is increasing to *Voyager.*"

Nodding, DeSoto got up. "Great. C'mon, Dina, let's greet our guests. You have the conn, Manolet. Send all our sensor telemetry to Admiral Nechayev at Starfleet with a note that more will be forthcoming."

Dayrit nodded, which looked on him like his head was about to tumble forward and fall off.

As he walked toward the turbolift, DeSoto looked forward at Hsu. "Baifang, once the ship goes off sensors, project a course—take all their course corrections into account. If I'm going to talk Nechayev into letting us fly free in the DMZ, I'm going to need to know I have a course to follow."

Hsu nodded. "Aye, sir."

Voyskunsky's too-wide smile made a return as they entered the turbolift. "You're going to convince the Ice Queen to let you hop the fence?"

DeSoto grinned. "That's the plan."

"I guess the first question before us," DeSoto said as he looked around the table in the briefing room, "is what, exactly, are the Malkus Artifacts, and why is there a Starfleet General Order regarding them?"

In addition to himself and Voyskunsky, three officers from *Voyager* had come over for the briefing: Captain Janeway; her first officer, Lieutenant Commander Cavit; and the Vulcan security chief, Lieutenant Tuvok.

Janeway cut an impressive figure. She had what De-Soto had always thought of as the "captain's trick"—appearing to be the tallest person in the room even when he or she wasn't. DeSoto, who barely cleared a meter and a quarter, had never mastered the trick, which was why he had always cultivated a more relaxed style of command. People like Janeway or Picard could lead by their presence. Bob DeSoto knew he didn't have that, so he led his people in other ways.

Aaron Cavit had the look of a seasoned officer, though DeSoto found his round face almost as impossible to read as Tuvok's—from whom he at least expected it. DeSoto did, however, notice Cavit giving Voyskunsky an odd look as he entered. If DeSoto's first officer had any reaction to that look, she hid it well.

Tuvok, who was holding a padd, answered the captain's opening question. "There are, in fact, four Malkus

Artifacts, and they date back to the heyday of the Zalkat Union—an interplanetary governmental body that encompassed much of what is now known as the Alpha Quadrant approximately ninety millennia ago. For a period of indeterminate length, the Union was ruled by a tyrant colloquially known as 'Malkus the Mighty.' Two hundred and twenty years ago, an Earth ship discovered what is believed to be the homeworld of the Union on Beta Aurigae VII."

Voyskunsky snapped her fingers. "*That's* where I know the name. We used to vacation on Aurigae when I was a girl. We visited the museum there." She smiled. "I haven't been back there in *years,* though. As I recall, the ruins and artifacts found there were quite impressive."

"Indeed," Tuvok said, betraying only the slightest irritation at the interruption. He touched the display on his padd, and an image appeared on the briefing-room screen. It was a human woman in an old-style Earth space-service uniform and a Vulcan woman in a uniform that DeSoto didn't recognize. They were both wearing some kind of gloves and holding small objects that looked like old-fashioned optical chips. "Most telling was a chronicle that the officers of the Earth ship, aided by a Vulcan observer, were able to translate. It indicated that Malkus was able to enforce his rule with the aid of four devices."

DeSoto nodded. "The so-called Malkus Artifacts."

"Yes, Captain." Tuvok changed the display to one that showed a Vulcan Starfleet officer in a blue uniform holding a black box. The picture had to be at least a century old, based on the uniform, and after a moment DeSoto realized with surprise that he was looking at Ambassador Spock from his days serving in Starfleet. "Though all the artifacts look alike, each serves a particular function. One can exert telepathic control; one can manipulate weather patterns; one emits a beam of force; and one imparts a deadly disease. After Malkus was overthrown, the artifacts were removed from the Zalkatian homeworld and placed on distant worlds throughout the quadrant."

Janeway, who had been leaning forward in her chair, smirked. "But they didn't say which worlds, right?"

"No. It was feared that if any record was made of the artifacts' destination, someone of a less than scrupulous nature would seek them out and try to re-create Malkus's tyranny."

"Why not simply destroy them?" Janeway asked.

Tuvok's eyebrow shot up in that manner common to many Vulcans. "That was attempted, but the artifacts have proven resistant to brute force. They also give off a distinctive energy signature, which was encoded in the chronicles."

"I don't understand," Voyskunsky said. "If they wanted to hide them, why make them easy to find?"

"It's not a question of being easy to find," Cavit said with a level of annoyance out of proportion to Voyskunsky's question, "it's a question of knowing what you find if you stumble across it."

"Precisely," Tuvok said. "Thus far, two of the artifacts have been located. The first, as you can see from this picture, was found by the *U.S.S. Enterprise* and the *U.S.S. Constellation* during a mission to Alpha Proxima II to aid in curing a plague that had broken out on the surface."

"Caused by the artifact?" DeSoto asked.

"Yes." Tuvok changed the image again, this time to a starship shuttlebay. Once again a Starfleet officer held a black box, but this time the uniform was contemporary. And once again DeSoto recognized the figure: Benjamin Sisko, the commander of Station Deep Space 9. "The next was found four-point-five months ago on one of Bajor's moons by a terrorist known as Orta. This was the artifact that emits a beam of force. Orta was captured on the Runabout *Rio Grande* and incarcerated on the *U.S.S. Odyssey*. Both artifacts are presently being studied at the Rector Institute on Earth."

Cavit leaned back. "And it looks like the Maquis have found the third artifact. God help us if it's the mind controller, but even the weather controller would be devastating in their hands."

"There is one other concern." Tuvok changed the display once again, this time showing several identical sensor readings. Two were obviously from older Starfleet sensors, based on the style of the displays; the other four were modern starship displays. "These are the sensor readings taken of the artifacts. The first two are from the *Constellation* and the *Enterprise* a century ago, the second two from the *Odyssey* and the *Rio Grande* four-point-five months ago, the latter two the ones just taken from *Voyager* and the *Hood.* Notice the slight difference."

DeSoto squinted and realized that there was a slight variation in the energy pattern given off by the artifact in the DMZ. "That difference is pretty negligible."

"Indeed it would be, but for the fact that, according to the chronicle, the energy signatures should be precisely the same."

"And the signatures of the first two artifacts *were* precisely the same," Janeway added. "I doubt it's anything that significant, though."

"Perhaps not, but I thought it worth pointing out," Tuvok said archly.

Janeway smiled affectionately. "Of course you did."

DeSoto also smiled. *Obviously these two have served together a long time.*

"We need to go in," Voyskunsky said. "General Order 16 is pretty clear: we have to confiscate the artifact. Even if there wasn't such an order, Aaron's right—we have to keep that thing out of Maquis hands."

"An aggressive charge across the DMZ would be a mistake," Janeway said. "For one thing, it would alert the Maquis that we're onto them. Besides, you know full well that the Cardassians won't allow a Starfleet vessel to go in without an equivalent Central Command presence."

DeSoto sighed. "And that way lies madness."

"Definitely."

"What do you suggest, Captain?"

Janeway smiled. "I'm glad you asked. Tuvok?"

Tuvok changed the image on the screen once again. This time it was yet another familiar Starfleet face, though he wasn't wearing a Starfleet uniform. In fact, legend had it that he'd disintegrated his uniform with a phaser.

"Cal Hudson?" DeSoto asked, bemused. "What does he have to do with this?"

"Our first mission, once the shakedown is complete," Janeway said, "is to go into the Badlands to try to root out some of the terrorists that are hiding out in there—especially the Starfleet defectors like Hudson."

Tuvok steepled his fingers together. "Captain Janeway, Lieutenant Commander Cavit, and I have been formulating a plan whereby I would infiltrate the Maquis. Starfleet Intelligence has been able to trace Lieutenant Commander Hudson's movements, and we're reasonably sure that we can locate his cell. From there, I should be able to join them and gather intelligence about the organization."

Cavit added with a small smile, "We were kind of hoping to do this once *Voyager* was fully operational, so we'd be available to pull him out if need be, but with this . . ."

"The only alteration to Mr. Tuvok's mission would be that he would also be tasked with finding the Malkus Artifact and working to get it out of Maquis hands," Janeway said.

"And the only change in plan," Cavit added, "is to use the *Hood* instead of the *Voyager* as the backup ship, since we're out of action."

DeSoto tapped his finger on the desk. He certainly didn't have any problems with the idea in theory—he'd need to look at the plan the three of them had concocted, of course—but it would have been preferable for Tuvok's own ship to keep an eye on things.

"Dayrit to DeSoto."

The captain looked up. "Go ahead."

"Sir, Lieutenants Czierniewski and Honigsberg are requesting permission to beam aboard. They have a report they want to give you regarding Voyager."

"Send them down here, Manolet."

Within minutes, the short, rotund form of Tara Czierniewski entered, joined by the tall, lithe form of a human in a lieutenant's uniform—presumably Alexander Honigsberg, *Voyager*'s chief engineer. "Report," DeSoto said.

Honigsberg tossed a padd onto the table. "It's broken."

Janeway blinked. "Can you be a touch more specific, Mr. Honigsberg?"

"Oh, I'm sure I could spend half an hour breaking down all the specifics in a way that would sound really complicated, but it's all in the report," Honigsberg said, pointing at the padd. "And what it boils down to is that it's broken."

The smile Janeway hit Honigsberg with was as scary a sight as DeSoto had ever seen. "Try me, Lieutenant. I've used the occasional two-syllable word in my time. I think I can handle it."

Letting out a long breath, Honigsberg closed his eyes.

Then he reopened them and spoke. "The connections between the gel packs and the other systems are misreading the inputs. It's transferring power at a greatly accelerated rate, and we can't slow it down. It's not just improving response time like it's supposed to, it's increasing *everything*. And it's not a software problem. The only way to fix this is to go back to Mars and replace every single damn gel-pack unit—and every single gel pack, since the current ones are all burned out."

The smile became a sweet one, but no less scary for that. "See, Mr. Honigsberg, was that so hard?"

"How much time will we need at Utopia Planitia?" Cavit asked.

"We're talking weeks, Commander, at least. This is a major design flaw."

Czierniewski added, "But not unusual when you're playing with new toys. I mean hey, this is why you *have* shakedown cruises."

Cavit turned to DeSoto. "All the more reason why we need your help here, Captain."

Turning to his first officer, DeSoto asked, "Any objections, Commander?"

"Assuming the plan is sound, no. Aaron's plans do tend to work, though, so I'm pretty sanguine." She smiled. Cavit grimaced. "I still think we'd be better off going in full force, but sometimes the sneaky approach is better."

Remembering their latest Go game, DeSoto silently agreed, and turned back to Janeway. "All right, then, let's see what you've got. If we both back it up, I'm sure we can sell the changes in the plan to Nechayev."

Chapter Three

HAVING FINALLY CONVINCED DESOTO to resign the Go game—and gaining great satisfaction out of it, especially since she was able to counter his last-ditch maneuver—Dina Voyskunsky left the lounge and headed to the bridge while the captain headed for bed. Just as she arrived for the overnight shift, a communication came in from *Voyager.* Taking it in the captain's ready room, she was greeted by the smiling face of Lieutenant Honigsberg.

"Commander, it looks like we're as shipshape as we're going to be. We're back up to a hundred percent. I figure we'll only be at optimum power consumption for about six hours or so, but that's enough to get us home so we can beat this puppy into shape."

Voyskunsky returned the smile, remembering the glee of problem-solving from her own days as an engineer. "Looking forward to it, eh?"

"Nah, not so much," Honigsberg said with a slight tilt to his head. *"I want to get out into the field with this*

beast. I'm greatly looking forward to spending many years with these engines."

Chuckling, Voyskunsky said, "I'll have Czierniewski cut the power transfer, then."

"Fine. Thank her and her team for me, will you? The extra hands really helped. Oh, and Mr. Cavit wanted to talk to you."

"Put him on," Voyskunsky said with a smile, thinking, *I doubt that "wanted" is the right word to use. "Felt it necessary," maybe.*

The image switched from the happy face of a chief engineer to the dour face of a first officer. "You know," she said without preamble, "you didn't used to always look grumpy all the time."

Cavit closed his eyes, took a deep breath, then opened them. *"I was really hoping DeSoto would be on duty."*

"Nope, he's asleep," Voyskunsky said, reveling in his discomfort. "Went to bed after I whupped him at Go again."

Blinking, Cavit said, *"I couldn't have heard that right."*

"Heard what?" Voyskunsky blinked coquettishly, feigning innocence.

"It sounded like you said you beat Captain DeSoto at Go."

"That's because it's what I said." Voyskunsky got up and went over to the replicator in the ready room. If she was going to have a lengthy one-on-one talk with Aaron Cavit, she needed fortification. "Orange blossom tea, hot," she instructed the computer.

"When did you learn how to play well enough to beat him?"

"Captain taught me himself," she said, removing the tea from the replicator dispenser. The steam carried the lovely scent of oranges to her nose, relaxing her almost instantly. She retook the desk chair and faced Cavit. He looked more shocked than he had that time on Risa. *Now,* that *was a shore leave,* she thought with fond remembrance.

He snorted in a long-suffering manner. *"Doing your usual making friends and influencing people, I see."*

"Was there a point to this call, Aaron, or did you just feel like making up for lost time by cramming twelve years of verbal abuse into five minutes?" She took a sip of her tea. It was too bitter again. She made a mental note to talk to Czierniewski about it.

Cavit looked like he was about to say one thing; then he stopped himself, to Voyskunsky's annoyance. *"I wanted to tell you that Mr. Tuvok is ready to beam over. Have you taken care of everything on your end?"*

She'd been hoping to get a proper response out of him, but he was reverting back to professional mode. "I've updated all the records—as far as anybody's concerned, Tuvok's been serving on the *Hood* for three months and his family moved to Amniphon three years ago. I even got the authorities on Vulcan to change his wife and kids' records around so they're listed as having died on Amniphon last month, though I doubt the Maquis would be able to dig that deep." She smiled, then decided to take another shot. "I *did* tell you that I'd take care of it. You doubting my word now?"

"No, I just—" He sighed. *"Never mind. What was that crack about in the meeting, anyhow? About my plans 'tending' to work?"*

"They always did in my experience." She managed to keep her face straight. "When can we expect Tuvok?"

"At 0100 hours. Look, you don't have to make snide comments in meetings. If you want to—"

Voyskunsky rolled her eyes. This was not what she

was hoping for. She wasn't sure what to expect after twelve years, honestly, but this whining certainly wasn't it. "Enough of this. Look, Aaron, I wasn't going to bring a damn thing up. I didn't say anything in that meeting that was out of line with my duty as first officer of the *Hood*. Anything you choose to interpret is, frankly, your problem. Now, is there anything else?"

"*I—*" Cavit sighed. His dark eyes looked almost pleading, but she didn't want pleading, dammit, she wanted contrition. Or at least an emotional response of some kind that wasn't snarky. "*No, Commander, nothing else. We'll be getting under way shortly after Mr. Tuvok reports to you.*"

"Fine. And good luck."

"*Thank you.*" Cavit sounded like he wanted to say something else.

She decided to go for broke. "Look, Aaron, as far as I'm concerned, you've got a lot of gall copping an attitude when *you* were the one who never showed on Pacifica. Now unless there's anything else, I actually have work to do over here."

"*No, Commander,*" he said tightly, "*there's nothing else. Voyager out.*"

He cut the connection.

Damn, damn, damn, she thought. *Could've handled that more smoothly.* She started to sip her tea, then thought better of it.

She tapped her combadge as she exited the ready room, leaving the tea behind. "Voyskunsky to engineering. Cut the power transfer to *Voyager*." To the young night-shift ensign at conn, she said, "Set course for the Cardassian border. We'll implement at warp three once Lieutenant Tuvok reports on board."

"Aye, sir."

The viewscreen held the image of *Voyager,* a gray line seeming to connect it to a point just under the screen: the power transfer. Then the line blinked out of existence. All of the *Intrepid*-class ship's running lights were going at full bore; the nacelles glowed with their full blue luminescence. From what Honigsberg had said, that was a temporary condition, but at least they should be able to get back to Utopia Planitia and fix whatever was wrong.

"Transporter room to bridge. Lieutenant Tuvok and all his personal effects have arrived safely, Commander."

Voyskunsky smiled. "Hit it, Ensign."

The following morning, Captain DeSoto found his first officer in the main shuttlebay along with Lieutenant Tuvok. The former was holding a tricorder, the latter a phaser rifle, and both were standing near the Shuttlecraft *Manhattan.* The shuttle had seen better days: phaser scars marred several parts of the hull. As the captain entered, Voyskunsky said, "Now fourteen centimeters up and six centimeters to the right."

Tuvok fired the phaser at the hull of the *Manhattan* without bothering to take any measurements. DeSoto had no doubt that the resultant phaser blast was right where Voyskunsky instructed it to be in relation to another phaser scar.

"How goes the deception?" DeSoto asked.

"Almost finished," Voyskunsky said. "Next one should be across the port bow, say a forty-five-degree angle."

Tuvok turned to look at the lieutenant commander. "That would not be consistent."

"I beg your pardon?"

DeSoto smiled. "Let me guess, Mr. Tuvok—you're about to point out that the next logical phaser blast would be across the starboard bow, as that would be the standard Starfleet tactical procedure when firing on a small vessel taking a standard evasive course, yes?"

"That is correct. If we wish the Maquis to believe that I stole this shuttle from the *Hood*—"

"Then the phaser scarring should match the pattern that we'd follow. Not everything in the field is by the book. Commander Voyskunsky, Lieutenant Dayrit, and I sometimes improvise these things. Besides, we'd know that you, logical person that you are, would follow a textbook evasive course."

"And we're the kind of people who like to throw people off by reading the book backward," Voyskunsky added with a smile.

"The Maquis would not necessarily be aware of your—proclivity for improvisation." Tuvok hesitated briefly, and DeSoto suspected the Vulcan was searching for an appropriately diplomatic way of putting it.

Voyskunsky nodded. "Maybe. And it's true, there are no known Starfleet defectors in the Maquis who served on this ship. A testament, I'm sure, to our fearless leader's ability to inspire loyalty," she said with a nod to DeSoto.

"If you're trying to suck up after last night's game, Commander, it won't work," DeSoto said with a chuckle.

"Noted, Captain." Her face growing more serious, Voyskunsky continued. "On the other hand, for all we know they have informants in Starfleet, and even here on the *Hood*—or at the very least, someone I may have served with on the *Excalibur* or that Manolet served with on the *Discovery*. I'd rather we erred on the side of personal consistency."

"And if Lieutenant Commander Hudson or one of the other Maquis examine the *Manhattan* and question this anomaly?"

DeSoto shrugged. "Then you tell them the truth. Adds

versimilitude to an otherwise bald and unconvincing narrative."

Tuvok raised an eyebrow. "Let us hope that, unlike Pooh-Bah's, my narrative is believed."

Laughing, DeSoto said, "I wouldn't have pegged you for a Gilbert and Sullivan fan, Lieutenant."

"I am not. However, during my first tenure in Starfleet, I served under Captain Sulu on the *Excelsior.* He was—inordinately fond of *The Mikado,* and there were several performances of it on the ship during my time there." Tuvok spoke with as much distaste as he could muster.

"In any case," Voyskunsky said, "if you'd be so kind as to fire across the port bow at an angle of forty-five degrees?"

"Of course, Commander."

As Tuvok took aim, Voyskunsky tapped the tricorder against her chin. "That raises an interesting question. Legend has it that Vulcans never lie."

"Extreme generalizations are not logical," Tuvok said after firing the phaser, "as it only takes one counterexample to disprove them. However, deliberate falsehood is frowned upon, yes."

"And yet you're going to have to tell the Maquis that your family was among those lost in that rockslide on Amniphon. Now, the rockslide itself destroyed most of Amniphon's computer records—in fact, that's the biggest argument that it was artificially induced by the Cardassians rather than natural, since the damage was *so* specific—but the fact is, your wife and children didn't die there. Are you going to be able to say they did?"

Tuvok lowered the phaser rifle and regarded Voyskunsky. DeSoto noticed no change in his attitude or demeanor—*but then, I probably wouldn't.* According to

Tuvok's file, during the time between his two tours with Starfleet, he had undergone the *Kolinahr* ritual. DeSoto didn't know all that much about Vulcan disciplines, but he did know that *Kolinahr* resulted in a much deeper repression of emotions than even the Vulcan norm.

"My first duty, Commander, is to Starfleet. You can be assured that I will follow that duty wherever it may take me. Now then, if you please," he said, once again raising the rifle, "what is the next shot?"

Before Voyskunsky could answer, the intercom beeped. *"Bridge to Lieutenant Tuvok."*

"Go ahead."

"You have a personal message from Vulcan, sir."

Tuvok looked at DeSoto. "May I take this in the shuttle, Captain?"

"Of course."

Setting the rifle on the deck, Tuvok moved toward the shuttle hatch, opened it, entered, and closed it behind him for privacy.

Voyskunsky grinned. "Speak of the devil and the devil calls you on subspace—assuming that is his wife or one of his kids calling."

"Probably. I take it you're concerned with Tuvok's cover story."

"Just want to make sure. We've had enough legitimate defections that he should be able to blend in fine. And we certainly created enough of an isolinear trail that any checks the Maquis do will turn up fine. I'm worried about two things: whether or not he can sell the cover story, and whether or not he won't be one of those defections."

DeSoto blinked. "Why are you worried about that?"

"Tuvok left Starfleet once already, some seventy-three years back. I don't want to risk a repeat performance."

"I wouldn't worry," DeSoto said, putting a reassuring hand on Voyskunsky's shoulder. "His record is spotless. I'm sure he'll do his job and do it well."

She nodded twice. "You're probably right, sir—I just want to be sure."

"Understandable. By the way—is there something going on between you and Commander Cavit that I should know about?"

"That you should know about? No, sir."

DeSoto smiled. *Nicely handled,* he thought. *An honest answer without actually giving any information.* "If you say so."

The shuttle hatch opened. Tuvok stepped out and picked up the rifle.

"Was the news good, bad, or indifferent, Lieutenant?" DeSoto asked with a smile.

"The news was personal, Captain. I would prefer not to go into any more detail."

"Of course," DeSoto said. "Carry on, you two. Let me know when you're ready to leave."

Gul Eska hated rain.

As he left home for his usual morning walk to the office, he found himself suddenly pushed by a heavy wind and pelted with enough rain to soak his garments and hair in seconds.

One of the reasons he had fought hard for the assignment to Nramia was that it had mild weather—rain was a rarity in the capital city of this Cardassian colony near the Federation border. No, Nramia was a planet that had nice, hot weather. The red sun beat down on the planet like a lover's embrace. It was paradise.

For months, Eska had supervised the military installation on Nramia as well as the six hundred thousand colonists who lived peaceably on the surface. *Krintar* grew on Nramia, a rare plant that was the primary ingredient in *halant* stew. No replicator had ever been able to match the exquisite flavor of natural *halant* stew, and people would pay through the neck for *krintar* roots, so by administrating Nramia, Eska was sitting on a latinum mine.

Some pointed out that he would have been better off taking on a few shipboard assignments, but as much as Eska hated bad weather, he hated no weather even more. The idea of spending his time trapped inside a duranium can with nothing but recycled, sterile air to breathe filled him with loathing. True, many lived their whole lives in artificial environments, whether on ships or on planets with unbreathable atmospheres, but that didn't mean Eska had to live that way. He could barely call that living. No, he wanted the dirt of a planet beneath his feet and the warmth of a real sun beating down on his face.

On Nramia, he had that.

Until the day it started raining.

Eska had heard that the Federation could actually control the weather, to a degree, on their planets. While Cardassia had nothing quite that sophisticated, their ability to predict the weather was near absolute. The meteorological system on Nramia had never been off by more than a few degrees in temperature here, a bit off in the speed of the wind there.

Never had the system neglected to predict a rainstorm.

Certainly, not this kind of rainstorm. Oh, it rained periodically in this area of the continent, but nothing like this.

It was coming down in sheets, a heavy wind blowing hard enough that the rain seemed to be coming at him sideways.

Eska's home was only a five-minute walk from the

office complex where he had his seat of power. Picking up the pace, he ran the rest of the way, covering the distance in less than a minute. Grateful for his Central Command training, he wasn't even winded when he reached the door.

When Eska had taken over the administration of Nramia, he had had the military headquarters moved to this building. Though it was considered an eyesore by most—it was from a period in Cardassia's architectural development that many considered negligible, and indeed most examples of it throughout the Union had long since been demolished—Eska rather admired it. The entire façade was made of one-way transparent aluminum. Nobody could see in, obviously—that would be a security threat—but every room in the building had a glorious view of the capital city. Better still, throughout the day they could see the sun providing its glorious warmth.

Except for today, of course. Today, all they saw were the streaks of rain on the windows.

Eska was greeted at the door by his two aides with a towel and a refresher. Inside the lobby of the complex, the staccato rhythm of the rain pounding on the transparent aluminum was a constant undercurrent. It reminded Eska of being on board a ship. Whenever he traveled, the thrumming engines always seemed ridiculously loud and made concentration difficult. He never understood how anyone could grow accustomed to such constant noise. Now, with the even more intrusive noise of the rain, he wondered again.

The taller of the aides, Glinn Coram, shook his head and smiled. "Were we transported to Ferenginar without anyone telling us, sir?"

"I'm starting to wonder," Eska said, toweling his ears. They were so waterlogged that Coram had sounded like a staticky subspace comlink. "Find out what's going on. Get in touch with the meteorological center. This—" He was interrupted by a massive thunderclap of a type he hadn't heard since he was stationed on Chin'toka IX during monsoon season. "—should not have happened," he finished in a harder voice.

"Yes, sir."

To the shorter, fatter aide, he said, "Doveror, do a full sensor sweep of the entire planet. Tie in to the satellites. I want a *full* picture." He had to raise his voice even higher, as the rain was growing more intense by the minute. No longer staccato, the rain was a virtual wall of sound slamming against the building.

"Yes, sir," Glinn Doveror said in his squeaky voice. Most found him irritating and difficult to listen to, but he was also a most efficient aide, so Eska put up with it.

"And call Gul Evek and tell him to get a ship over here, just in ca—"

Eska's words were interrupted by another thunderclap, but this time it was immediately followed by an earsplitting shattering sound, as an entire section of the transparent aluminum collapsed, shards flying through the air, propelled by the wind and no longer held in place by the structure of the building. Even as his ears cleared of that noise, it was replaced by exclamations of pain ranging from quick shouts to lengthy screams. Shards of transparent aluminum were all over the floor of the lobby, and probably elsewhere in the building.

Then Eska felt like he was being pelted with stones. The rain had turned into hail and was now coming into the building. Raising his arm to protect his eyes, Eska ran toward the turbolift bay at the inner portion of the building. He didn't even bother to look to see if Doveror or Coram followed.

As it happened, they did, which he knew only because they entered the turbolift with him. "Operations," Eska said as the door closed. "Something is wrong."

"The weather is certainly a bit aberrant," Doveror said gravely.

"Aberrant!?" Eska almost grabbed Doveror by the neck ridges. " 'Aberrant' is a few extra centimeters of rain per year. The first hailstorm in the recorded history of this continent is not 'aberrant.' Thunder intense enough to shatter our allegedly unbreakable windows is not 'aberrant'! Someone is attacking us, and I want to know who."

Coram fixed his commanding officer with a dubious glance as the turbolift doors opened. "Attack? That seems unlikely, sir."

Eska stepped out of the lift into the large room. Consoles lined three of the walls, and a large round desk sat in the center. The fourth wall was taken up with a viewscreen. Currently on that screen was an image of the capital city, which was a chaotic jumble of snow, sleet, freezing rain, hail, and wind. "Weather patterns don't develop like this naturally," Eska said, pointing to the viewscreen, "and they certainly don't develop out of a cloudless sky."

One of the glinns sitting at the main operations table said, "Sir, we're picking up—something in orbit."

Eska threw his towel angrily at Doveror, who fumbled to catch it, and approached the table. "Define 'something,' Glinn."

"I'm afraid I can't, sir," she said. "We can't get a firm fix on it. It's probably a ship, but—" Her eyes widened. "Sir, it's firing on the orbital defense satellites!"

"Return fire!" Then Eska frowned. "Why didn't the satellites challenge that ship immediately?"

"Not sure, sir—best guess, the indeterminate readings

were too anomalous for the computer to register as a threat. Honestly, sir, I probably wouldn't have bothered reporting it to you if not for everything else that was happening—and because the weather changes matched when the reading appeared in orbit." She peered at her display. "Sir, all orbital defenses are down!"

Eska was about to say that that was impossible, that one anomalous reading shouldn't be able to take out six satellites, but he was interrupted by the shaking of the entire room. Loose items fell to the floor, and several people followed the objects. Eska was not among those, as he gained purchase on the edge of the center table even as his footing was momentarily lost.

When the ground settled, he turned to the glinn. "That was a lightning strike, sir," she said in a very small voice.

"*That* was lightning?" Eska obviously needed to revise his estimates on what was impossible.

"Yes, sir." She peered down at her console, then looked back up at Eska. "The subbasements are still structurally sound, but the infrastructure of the above-ground portion of the building is compromised."

"Evacuate the building immediately."

"Sir, I don't think they'll be any safer out there. The winds are now at two hundred—"

Eska's head swam. "They're still safer in the open than inside a fifty-story building that's about to collapse!"

"Yes, sir."

He whirled to face Coram, who was now at a communications console. "Get me Evek!"

"Waiting for his reply now, sir," Coram said in a surprisingly calm voice. It made Eska realize just how hysterical he was starting to sound.

Eska turned to the viewscreen. People, both civilians and Central Command soldiers, were running out of the building. You could tell the difference only by what they were wearing, as they all had the same panicked look as they dashed about madly. The building itself was quite literally a shell of its former self. Its roginium superstructure was all that was left—the transparent aluminum had been blasted away, as had the plastiform that made up the interior walls.

If this place is collapsing, Eska thought with horror, *then the rest of the city's buildings will be dust before this is over. And we have no defenses. . . .* Eska silently cursed whoever was responsible for not assigning any ships to Nramia. He could hear whichever idiot Central Command bureaucrat it was now, going on about how the orbital defenses were *more* than sufficient for the job. . . .

"Sir," Doveror said, "reports are coming in from all over the planet. This peculiar weather is not limited to the capital. The polar regions are registering temperatures several orders of magnitude hotter than usual. The ice up there is melting, and computer projections are calling for dangerous floods within a day or two. The tropical regions are suffering blistering heat with no humidity, the desert regions are getting massive rainfall—"

"I get the idea," Eska muttered.

Then, to Eska's relief, the image of Gul Evek came on the screen. Cardassian heads tended to be rather rectangular, but Evek's countenance was downright boxy. *"What can I do for you, Eska?"* Evek said distractedly, looking down at some readouts even as he spoke.

"We need to evacuate Nramia."

Everyone whirled toward Eska at that. Eska couldn't blame them, as he was as surprised as any of them at the words that had come out of his mouth, but it was the only sane course of action.

Evek looked up sharply at that. *"Excuse me?"*

"Something in orbit has wiped out our defenses and is causing deadly weather all over the planet."

Smiling an unkind smile, Evek said, *"You want us to evacuate because of the weather, Eska?"*

The building chose that moment to shake again. "Another lightning strike, sir," the glinn said.

"That was lightning?" Evek was frowning now.

"Yes, Evek, *that* was lightning. And we're in a subbasement in the most structurally sound building on Nramia. Our polar ice caps are melting, our jungles are drying out, our deserts are flooding, and here in the capital, we're being subjected to deadly hail and gale-force winds."

"Don't you have ships of your own?"

Eska rolled his eyes. *Save me from spacefaring types.* "Yes, of course we do. And at present, they're all on the planet. With conditions as they are, none of them would be able to achieve orbit before being torn to pieces."

The building shook again for good measure.

"I'm diverting the Sixth Order to Nramia now," Evek said. *"We'll be in orbit within three hours."*

Eska grimaced. "I hope we live that long."

"If you don't, the Maquis will pay for your deaths, rest assured."

"The Maquis?" It never occurred to Eska that the Maquis would be responsible—not because they weren't philosophically capable of it, quite the opposite, in fact, but because they were a ragtag group of terrorists whose ships were held together with little more than stem bolts and happy thoughts. Nothing in any of the intelligence reports Eska had read indicated that they had any kind of weaponry that could do *this*. He said as much to Evek.

"Perhaps you're right. But this fits their mode of operation, even if it is beyond what we know of their capabilities. Still, remember that there are far too many

former Starfleet personnel in the Maquis, and they are distressingly resourceful." With a bitter smile, Evek added, *"Besides, whether they are responsible or not doesn't mean we can't blame them."*

"I'm thrilled for your ability to milk this for political gain, Evek," Eska said through clenched teeth, "but I'm a bit more concerned about the people of Nramia."

"I've done all I can for now. I will contact you when we arrive."

With that, Evek's face faded, replaced once again with the image of ever-more-panicky Cardassians in the street of Nramia's capital.

"Sir," Coram said, "the anomalous reading has disappeared. If it was a ship, I would guess that it has left orbit."

"Let's hope the weather improves, then."

But it did not. By the time the Sixth Order—five *Galor*-class ships, including Evek's command, the *Vetar*—arrived at Nramia, fully a quarter of the population were dead, most were injured to some degree or other, the capital was flooded under several meters of rainwater, and the polar ice caps had started to melt, with icebergs starting to roam in the oceans. Computer projections estimated that Nramia would be uninhabitable within a day.

As Eska was beamed up to the flagship of the Sixth Order, he thought, *I really really hate rain.*

Chapter Four

As Cal Hudson read the report from the Maquis infiltrator on Deep Space 9, he felt queasy.

He was tempted to mention this to his second-in-command, Darleen Mastroeni, presently sitting next to him in the cramped bridge of the *Liberator*. Indeed, the word "bridge" bespoke a grandeur it hadn't earned. It was more like the cockpit of an old airship. Hudson and Mastroeni sat side by side in chairs they barely fit in, surrounded by controls on either side of them and lining the bulkhead in front of them—excepting the tiny viewscreen, of course. A third person on the bridge would have been a physical impossibility.

However, if Hudson did share his gastrointestinal discomfort at the report with Mastroeni, the shorter woman would probably just make a comment about how his precious stomach, having been raised on safe and easy replicated food, wasn't used to the home cooking favored by most Maquis—mainly because replicator power was not the near-infinite resource it was on a Starfleet vessel, and needed to be rationed for other uses.

But it wasn't the badly prepared hamburger he'd had for lunch that was making him ill right now. It was the report from Michael Eddington, newly appointed head of Starfleet security for DS9, and Maquis agent.

Getting Eddington onto the station had been quite a coup for the Maquis. DS9 was, after all, the most important strategic post in the sector thanks to the Bajoran wormhole that led to the Gamma Quadrant. Many ships went through there, and having an agent on-station would be invaluable—even if that agent was someone who pretty much told a lie every time he put on his Starfleet uniform.

But it wasn't even the use of a Starfleet officer to aid the Maquis cause that irked Hudson. He, too, had turned his back on Starfleet and the Federation—but given how shabbily those two organizations had treated their citizens with this idiotic treaty, he had no compunctions about that. If Michael Eddington had no trouble reconciling his duties on DS9 with his dedication to the Maquis, then Hudson had no trouble using him.

No, the true source of Hudson's queasy feeling was that he was doing this to Ben Sisko.

Hudson and the DS9 station commandant had been friends since their Academy days. They had gotten into trouble with each other, they had participated in each other's weddings, they had consoled each other when they lost their respective wives.

Now they were on opposite sides of a war. Ben had brought Hudson his Starfleet uniform, and Hudson had made a show of phasering it into oblivion in front of him. And now Hudson had put a viper in his friend's midst.

"Cal, we're picking something up," Mastroeni said. She looked up and touched a control over her head. "It's a Starfleet distress call, but with a Maquis call sign."

"Really?"

Mastroeni snarled. Her face had never formed a smile in the six months that Hudson had known her. "An outdated call sign. It isn't one of ours—probably some Starfleeter trying to lure us into a trap. Permission to blow it to atoms."

Hudson sighed. The unfortunate thing was, Mastroeni was dead serious. However, Hudson wasn't so cavalier. He checked the sensor readings. "Reading a type-3 shuttlecraft—call sign indicates it's the *Manhattan*, presently assigned to the *U.S.S. Hood*."

"I'm not picking up the *Hood* on any scans—or any other Starfleet vessel," Mastroeni said. "So if we destroy them, no one will know."

"She's also damaged," Hudson continued, ignoring her. "Those are phaser hits—*starship* phaser hits."

"Now we're being hailed. I assume I should ignore it and fire phasers?"

Turning angrily at Mastroeni, Hudson said, "I'm not about to fire on a ship in distress, Darleen."

"You're not in Starfleet anymore, Cal."

"You're right—and I haven't joined Central Command, either. If we start firing on ships that ask for help, we're no better than the Cardassians."

"I don't give a good goddamn about being 'better' than the Cardassians!" Mastroeni said, slamming a hand on the arm of her chair. "I just want them *and* Starfleet gone from my life."

A beep from the console sounded before Hudson could reply. It was a repeat of the hail from the *Manhat-*

tan. Hudson reached over and answered it rather than ask Mastroeni to open the channel.

"This is the Federation Shuttlecraft Manhattan *to any Maquis ship within range. This is Tuvok of Vulcan, former lieutenant in Starfleet. I request asylum with the Maquis. Please respond."*

"Good thing he identified himself as a Vulcan," Hudson muttered. "That's the only thing to explain how calm he is." Louder, he said, "Mr. Tuvok, this is the Maquis." He wasn't about to identify himself by name over an open channel. "We've got you on sensors. What happened?"

"I absconded with this shuttlecraft when Starfleet refused my request for a leave of absence following the deaths of my wife and children on Amniphon."

Hudson looked sharply at Mastroeni. The rockslides on Amniphon had killed thousands. They still hadn't even begun to properly catalogue the dead.

"So you left Starfleet."

"Affirmative. The Hood *naturally tried to pursue, but they would not enter the Demilitarized Zone without authorization. However, that authorization may come soon. Therefore I would request that you beam me aboard and then destroy the shuttle."*

Hudson rubbed his chin. "Mr. Tuvok, I'd love to accommodate you, but I've got a first mate here with an itchy trigger finger. She'd like to just destroy your shuttle without bothering to beam you over first. I'm gonna need a good reason to hold her back."

"Your attempt to play the human game of 'good cop/bad cop' is somewhat transparent, sir. However, I do understand that you will require a gesture of good faith. I was the chief of security on the Hood, *and can provide you with intelligence and current access codes that might prove beneficial to the Maquis."*

Mastroeni lined up a shot with her phasers. "Like we need *him* for that. C'mon, let me—"

"In addition," Tuvok added, *"I have information on how to detect a weapon that is currently within the confines of the Demilitarized Zone. It is an artifact of tremendous power that might tip the balance of power in favor of the Maquis. And Starfleet Command is not presently aware of it."*

"He's lying." Mastroeni's eyes almost rolled back in her head.

"Maybe." Hudson rubbed his chin again. "And maybe not. I'm willing to look into it." He smiled at Mastroeni. "We can always kill him later."

She just snarled again in response.

"Prepare to be taken in tow, Mr. Tuvok."

"I would not recommend that course of action. As long as the Manhattan *is intact, the* Hood *will be able to track it. Starfleet has recently improved the security measures on their shuttlecraft. One such attempt by a potential Starfleet defector to deliver a shuttle into Maquis hands resulted in the officer's incarceration. I would prefer to avoid Ensign Lestewka's fate."*

"I don't believe him," Mastroeni said.

Hudson frowned. "There was an Ensign Lestewka who served on the *Tian An Men*. Reports were that he was favorable to our cause, but he was caught trying to defect. I always assumed he just got caught 'cause he was stupid, though."

"Only," Tuvok said dryly, *"if you consider not paying attention to security briefings 'stupid.' The choice is, of course, yours, but it would be safer for all concerned if you destroyed the shuttle. If nothing else, it denies me my best avenue of escape and leaves me wholly at your mercy."*

"You already *are* at our mercy, Vulcan," Mastroeni said, now locking phasers on target.

"Hardly. Although damaged, this shuttlecraft could still hold its own in a firefight—especially against a sub-standard Mishka-class raider with a malfunctioning phaser array."

At that, Hudson laughed.

"What's so funny?" Mastroeni asked.

"He's good. All right, Tuvok, have it your way. Stand by for our signal to beam you aboard. Out." Then he opened an intercom channel. "Mindy, you there?" Mindy McAdams was supposed to be on duty in the transporter room.

"Yeah, Skip. And I overheard your tête-à-Vulcan. I'll get Schmidt in here with a couple of rifles and bring him on board."

"Good." Hudson had long since given up discouraging McAdams from calling him "Skip," short for "Skipper." He turned to his copilot. "Once he's on board, blow up the shuttle. Then let's start doing some digging. I want to know everything there is to know about Tuvok of Vulcan, security chief of the *U.S.S. Hood.* See if Eddington can call up his service record and get it to us."

"Fine, whatever you say."

Hudson sighed and fixed his first mate with an encouraging expression. "Look, Darleen, if even the slightest thing is off-kilter with what we find, we'll kill him. I promise."

"I'm holding you to that, Cal. Because we're going to regret having that Vulcan on our ship, mark my words."

"Are you out of your mind?"

Tharia heard Chakotay's words, but did not acknowledge them. He was busy trying to figure out what his next target should be.

Chakotay's ship—which he had christened the *Geronimo,* after some Earther freedom fighter or other—had been salvaged from a Tellarian depot a year earlier. Tharia admired the bridge design: a U-shaped, two-level room at the fore of the ship. The upper level extended from the back wall about halfway into the room, and contained the command center. Generally, Chakotay, Seska, and Tharia sat there; they were there now, plus Torres. The front part of the lower level had the navigation and engineering consoles, with all other systems controlled from consoles under the command center, which was accessible via a ladder.

Most impressive of all was that the *entire* front wall was a viewscreen. Right now, it showed Nramia. Normally appearing bright green and yellow from orbit, now the planet was shaded in darker greens and blacks, giving it an almost sinister look. Inset into the huge screen was a sensor reading that showed the abnormal weather patterns throughout the world.

Weather patterns that Tharia had caused.

Chakotay was pointing at those sensor scans. "This was *not* part of the plan, Tharia. We were just going to target the military headquarters, not wipe out the entire population."

From below, Chell said, "Uh, actually, they may not all die. I'm reading a fleet of *Galor*-class ships. Registers as the Sixth Order. My guess is that they're here to handle some kind of evacuation or other. At least, that'd be my *guess.*"

"Evek," Chakotay muttered. Then he said to the Bolian, "Get us out of here, Chell. Maximum warp."

"No!" Tharia screamed. "We can't! Not yet! They have to all die first!"

Chakotay grabbed Tharia by the shoulders. "Get ahold of yourself! I don't know what you think you're doing, but it stops now."

"What's the big deal, Chakotay?" B'Elanna asked.

With a vehemence that might have surprised Tharia if he bothered to care about such things anymore, Seska replied. "There are civilians down there, B'Elanna. Military's one thing—they swore an oath to die for the Central Command, and they knew what to expect. But the civilians aren't responsible for the treaty or for the actions of the government, any more than we are—or than my people on Bajor were when the Cardassians subjugated them." Turning to Tharia, she added, "They certainly don't deserve *this*. At this rate, unless you reverse what you did, the planet's entire ecosystem will tear itself apart within a few months. The flooding alone will cause incalculable damage."

"We're not giving him the chance," Chakotay said. "Engage at warp six, Chell."

Tharia said, "We have to make sure they all die!" at the same time that Seska said, "We can't just leave them!"

Chakotay, ever the calm presence, first looked at Seska. Tharia knew that the two of them were lovers, and he wondered if he'd still be so calm if he found her broken body destroyed by Cardassians. "We can't stick around so Evek can pound us to a pulp, Seska. B'Elanna's right—these are Cardassians, and I have no problem with tying them up in a rescue mission and with the military outpost here being history." Then he turned to Tharia. "I *do* have a problem with the scale—and with my orders being disobeyed. I want you to turn that box of yours over to me *right* now."

"You don't understand," Tharia said.

"You're right, I don't. And I don't care, either. Dalby," he called down to the lower level, "escort Tharia to his barracks and retrieve that box of his."

Tharia paid no attention to anything anyone was saying, or to Kenneth Dalby, who came up the ladder and practically yanked Tharia toward the doorway. "C'mon, ch'Ren," he said, "let's get this over with."

He paid no attention because he was turning his thoughts to his next campaign. It was obvious that Chakotay was no longer to be trusted. *There's one warp-capable shuttlecraft left,* he thought. The *Geronimo* had two originally, but they had crashed one on the planet where Tharia found his gift.

As soon as he and Dalby reached the cabin Tharia shared with Hogan, Ayala, and Bendera, the Andorian reached out with his mind to the weapon. In turn, the weapon reached out to the ship's environmental controls.

The traitors cannot be allowed to stop me, he thought.

"C'mon, ch'Ren, get a move on," Dalby said, pushing Tharia toward his bunk.

As the temperature in the room lowered, Tharia turned and leapt through the air, tackling a surprised Dalby. While he lay stunned on the floor, Tharia ran to his bunk, grabbed the weapon, ran back toward the door, grabbed Dalby's phaser, kicked him in the ribs for good measure, then headed toward the shuttlebay.

The temperature continued to lower to near-freezing levels, but Tharia only really noticed it on an intellectual level—he didn't feel anything except for his burning need to make the Cardassians pay.

By the time he got to the shuttlebay, he reckoned, it would be down past freezing. Then he would raise the temperature to the boiling point as he left the *Geronimo*. The hull would start to rupture under the stress.

In his mind's eye, he started plotting a course for the Slaybis system. *The traitors there will die just as the traitors here will.*

Chakotay and the others had been his comrades. But they could not see the truth. The Cardassians *all* had to pay, whether civilian or military. They *all* had to die. Seska was Bajoran, she should have understood that.

Since she did not, she would die when the hull buckled.

Ayala and Henley were doing some kind of maintenance on the shuttle when Tharia came in. Without hesitating, he shot them both. He had no idea what setting the phaser was on—the fact that they fell to the deck in a heap meant it wasn't set to disintegrate, but that still left half a dozen possible settings—nor did he much care. If they weren't dead now, they would be soon.

He boarded the shuttle, entering an override code. The bridge systems were probably literally freezing up by now, so there was no way Chakotay or Torres would be able to stop him.

"Bridge to shuttlebay. Whoever's in there, get back here now!" Chakotay's calm voice had finally broken into a shout. Tharia also could hear a shiver in his voice.

Tharia cut off the communication as he exited through the shuttlebay doors.

Once he was clear of the *Geronimo*, he set course for the Slaybis system. There were more people there who needed to die.

About his comrades, he didn't spare a thought.

He was thinking about the broken bodies of his mates. And the broken bodies of the Cardassians who died on Nramia.

It wasn't enough. Not yet.

I will help you achieve your goal.
Soon . . .

Cal Hudson sat in his quarters and read through the data on the optical chip Tuvok had provided. Half-remembered Academy classes in galactic history came back to the forefront of his mind as he read it. *So many of those damn ancient civilizations,* he thought, *they all blend. The Zalkat Union, the Iconians, the Tkon Empire . . .*

He remembered sitting in that class, bored out of his mind. Ben Sisko was in the class with him, and they'd spend most of their time the first few weeks trying to get the other one to do something stupid that would get the (negative) attention of the professor. It was childish, but they were first-year students who were eager to explore strange new worlds. A class about dead civilizations didn't interest either of them.

Eventually, they settled down, of course—if they hadn't, they wouldn't have made it through the Academy in the first place. *Those were good times,* Hudson thought with momentary sadness.

Exacerbating the painful nostalgia was the fact that the artifact that Tuvok had found with the *Hood*'s sensors while on the night shift at ops—and, according to the Vulcan, had then wiped from the ship's records—was one of four. Two others had been discovered, one only a few months ago on one of Bajor's moons. Ben was involved in that mission. *So if I do chase this thing down, it'll be another connection to Ben. Seems we can't get away from each other, even when I try. . . .*

Hudson shook his head. Thinking about Ben led to thinking about Ben and Jennifer, which led to thinking about Gretchen. He shook his head, forcing himself to pay attention to the data in Tuvok's chip.

Tuvok himself was currently under guard in the mess hall. The *Liberator* didn't have a brig—prisoners weren't often a consideration in their line of work—so Hudson stuck him there while he went over the data and sent Mastroeni to check out his story.

The door chime rang. "Come on in," he said. The door opened to the short, compact form of his second-in-command. "What do you have for me, Darleen?"

As the door closed behind her, Mastroeni let out another of her snarls. "I hate to say it, but everything checks out. Eddington went over the records on DS9, and Tuvok was recently assigned to the *Hood* and the *Hood* has been patrolling the Cardassian border lately. His family is listed as having lived on Amniphon at the time of the rockslides."

"What about his requests for leave?"

She shook her head. "DS9 doesn't have records that complete about officers not actually assigned to the station, and he couldn't really dig that deep without arousing suspicion. However, I got Quiring to hack into the Vulcan central net."

Hudson's eyes widened and he rose from his chair. "What!? Are you out of your mind? Darleen, you don't hack the Vulcan net!"

Mastroeni almost smiled. "Quiring did. At least a little. He got out before anyone caught on to him, but he was in long enough to verify that T'Pel and all the little Tuvok-lets moved to Amniphon three years ago. What about the stuff he gave us?"

Sitting back down, Hudson glanced at the small viewscreen on his desk. "Well, the codes he gave us aren't anything we haven't gotten from Eddington, but Tuvok wouldn't know that. If nothing else, it worked as a good-faith gesture. And this artifact thing he found *could* be damn useful."

"You're not sure?"

Tilting his head, Hudson said, "It depends. It's one of two possible artifacts left over from a ninety-thousand-year-old empire."

A snort escaped from Mastroeni's lips. "And it's still supposed to work?"

"Two others have been dug up, and they both worked just fine." *Too fine,* he thought with a shiver, having just read the reports of the epidemic on Proxima a hundred years ago, and the near-destruction of one of Bajor's moons only a few months ago. "One possibility is that it can manipulate weather patterns."

Mastroeni's eyes widened. "That has all *kinds* of entertaining possibilities."

"I agree." Hudson leaned back in his chair and fixed Mastroeni with a serious look. "The problem is, the other possibility is that it's a telepathic weapon that enables the user to control other people's minds."

It woud be inaccurate to say that Mastroeni's face darkened, given her near-permanent scowl, but that scowl did appear to deepen. "If it's a telepathic weapon, I don't want a damn thing to do with it."

"Neither do I. But—"

Slamming a hand on the wall, Mastroeni said, "I *mean* it, Cal. I won't have us going that way! I'll destroy the thing!"

"Good luck." Hudson chuckled. "Those things are apparently indestructible. That's why they're still intact and working after ninety millennia. Anyhow, it doesn't matter—point is, we need to track this thing down, and Tuvok's given us the energy signature. I think we ought to follow it. *And* I think we need to keep Tuvok alive. He's earned at least that much."

With obvious reluctance, Mastroeni said, "I agree— but *only* that much. So far, he's done everything right, but he's also done everything I'd expect a Starfleet infiltrator to do. I want a phaser pointed at his head every minute of every day."

Hudson sighed, knowing that she was serious, regardless of the impracticalities of such a plan. Still, he figured it would probably be wise to assign McAdams to Tuvok, at least for the time being. Unlike Mastroeni, she would keep a clear head, and was much less likely to fire without provocation or orders.

He got up and proceeded to the mess hall, Mastroeni right behind him. McAdams and Schmidt were on opposite sides of the room—McAdams's lithe form leaning against the wall near the door, Schmidt's massive body crammed into one of the mess-hall chairs across the hall, both of them with phaser rifles conspicuous. Tuvok sat placidly in the middle of the room, his elbows resting on one of the tables, his fingers steepled together near his forehead. *Probably something vaguely meditative,* Hudson thought.

At the new arrivals' entrance, McAdams straightened up. "He's just been sitting there, Skip. I don't think he's even blinked since he sat down." She grinned. "Better check, make sure his eyes haven't gone all crusty."

Hudson smiled and approached the prisoner.

Tuvok looked up. "My suspicions were correct, I see."

Frowning, Hudson said, "What suspicions, Mr. Tuvok?"

"Your voice over the comlink sounded sufficiently similar to the voice on record as belonging to a former lieutenant commander in Starfleet named Calvin Hudson. Your face matches that record as well. It is therefore reasonable to deduce that you are he."

McAdams grinned. "Well, if he does wind up joining, he can fill Sakona's old role of class pedantic."

Mastroeni shot the other woman a venomous look, no doubt angry that McAdams used the name of one of their fellow Maquis, but Tuvok said, "If you are referring to the woman who was captured on Deep Space 9 last year, it is my hope to prove more useful to you than she was." He turned his impassive gaze on Hudson. "You have investigated the data?"

"We have." Hudson rubbed his chin. "So far, it looks promising—but I don't see any good reason to trust you. On the other hand, I have half a dozen reasons to shoot you on sight."

"I will assume, since you have not shot me on sight, that you're willing to give me the benefit of the doubt for the nonce."

"For the nonce," Hudson said with a nod. "We'll enter these energy readings into the computer, see if we can track it down."

"I will join you on your bridge," Tuvok said, standing up.

Hudson smiled. "I'm afraid that won't be possible, Mr. Tuvok. Our bridge doesn't have much walking-around room. We'll keep an open channel down here." He pointed to the viewscreen on the side wall. "I'll tie that in to the main viewer so you can see what we see. Let us know if we do anything wrong."

Dryly, Tuvok said, "I will assume that request is limited to anything you might do in relation to the Malkus Artifacts."

Mastroeni raised her phaser. "*Good* assumption, Vulcan. You've been living on borrowed time since you first

61

entered the DMZ, and it's only a matter of time before someone burns your head open with a phaser."

Tuvok seemed unmoved by the threat. "All mortals live on 'borrowed time,' madam. Concerning oneself overmuch about the nature of how one gives that time back, so to speak, would be an illogical waste of resources."

"Darleen!" Hudson barked just as Mastroeni raised her weapon.

After a moment, Mastroeni calmed down and lowered her weapon. "Don't push me, Vulcan."

Tuvok continued to look unimpressed.

Hudson grabbed Mastroeni by the arm and led her out, giving both McAdams and Schmidt nods as he left, indicating that they were to remain on guard. As soon as the door closed behind them, he spoke. "Will you stop that, please? I know you don't trust him, but we're *not* killing him if we don't have to, and if he *is* legit, I don't want him expecting a phaser in the back from you." As they approached the door to the bridge, which was on the same deck, he added, "Unless, of course, you're just trying to intimidate him, in which case you're wasting your time. He's obviously one of the more imperturbable types."

Mastroeni snarled again. "I just don't like him." With that, she opened the door to the bridge.

Hudson sighed and followed, settling into his chair. He entered Tuvok's chip into one of the slots in the console in front of him, then called up the energy signature. Not for the first time wishing like hell they had a ship with a *working* voice interface, he manually fed the signature into the ship's sensors and then did a long-range scan.

"I think this is a waste of time," Mastroeni said. "We're not going to find anything. We should just shoot him and then get as far away from—"

The sensor alarm beeped. "We've got something,"

Hudson said with a certain amount of satisfaction. Mastroeni's caution was understandable, of course, but there was enough of the Starfleet officer left in Cal Hudson that he didn't feel comfortable with a first mate who insisted on shooting a person down in cold blood.

"That's in Cardassian space," Mastroeni said, peering at the sensor display in front of Hudson. "Right over the border."

"Nearest planet is Nramia." Hudson pursed his lips. "That's on the list."

Mastroeni shot Hudson a look. He didn't need to explain any further. The Maquis had a list of planets that were viable targets. Hudson knew that one of the other cells—though he did not know which, nor would he know—had targeted Nramia, a colony that had a military outpost.

Hudson hesitated at first. He didn't want to barge in on someone else's operation—but if one of the Malkus Artifacts was on Nramia, he had to find it sooner rather than later. They certainly couldn't risk the Cardassians getting their hands on it.

Besides, there was no timetable for the attack on Nramia that Hudson was aware of. So for all he knew, whoever was attacking wouldn't be doing so for weeks yet.

"Set a course for Nramia, Darleen. Warp six."

They made their way toward the Cardassian border in silence. Hudson took advantage of the time to finish reading the report from Eddington that he'd started. What got his attention in particular was the *Defiant*. Hudson remembered Ben Sisko talking about the ship— a warship originally designed for use against the Borg— when the latter was assigned to Utopia Planitia. The ship had been outfitted with a cloaking device, on loan from the Romulan Star Empire with the proviso that it be used only in the Gamma Quadrant.

I wonder if there's any way we can get our hands on that. . . .

"Cal, we've got a problem. Actually, two."

Hudson looked up. "What?"

"I'm not reading the energy signature anywhere near Nramia anymore. However, I *am* picking up five ships bearing down on the planet, and they're all *Galor*-class."

Hudson immediately called up a long-range scan of Nramia itself. Something didn't look right.

Tuvok's voice sounded suddenly over the intercom. *"Those readings should not be accurate. Nramia's northern continent is mostly desert and should not experience such extremes of precipitation as are being shown in that scan. In addition, the polar ice caps are melting at an alarming rate, one that would, in the normal course of time, take decades. The logical deduction is that the Malkus Artifact in question is the weather controller, and it has already been used."*

"Gee, all that from a long-range scan," Mastroeni said, rolling her eyes.

"I would also surmise—"

"This ought to be good," Mastroeni muttered.

Tuvok continued as if Mastroeni hadn't spoken. *"—that the artifact is already in the hands of fellow Maquis."*

Hudson smiled. *Nice touch,* he thought, *referring to them as "fellow."* "It's possible the Cardassians have it."

"Unlikely. If that were the case, we would still be reading the artifact's emissions. I recommend that we abandon our course to Nramia and attempt to relocate the emission."

"Much as I hate to agree with our—guest, he's right," Mastroeni said.

Hudson nodded. "I agree, too. Those Cardassians'll have itchy trigger fingers, and they'll probably blame the Maquis whether or not we're actually responsible. Change course back into the DMZ. I'll try to reacquire the emission."

"Changing course 284 mark 9." Mastroeni then frowned. "We're picking up a weak distress signal at 173 mark 6." She looked up. "It's a Maquis call sign—a current one this time."

"Go," Hudson said, then looked down at his readout as the sensor display beeped. "I've got the artifact emission."

"Good. We can pick it up after we check out the distress call," Mastroeni said.

Hudson grimaced. "It'll be sooner than that. The emission's at 173 mark 6."

Mastroeni looked up sharply.

"Warp eight, Darleen. I've got a nasty idea about what's happening."

To her credit, Mastroeni didn't hesitate, even though the maximum safe cruising speed for the *Liberator* was warp seven-point-three.

Then Hudson tried to boost the gain on the distress signal. "*—otay of the* Geroni—*mayday, we need imme—ance. Repeat, this is Chakotay of—nimo, we need immediate assista—*"

That was followed by the sound of wrenching metal.

A shiver went down Hudson's spine and he froze in his chair. Anyone who had ever lived on a starship, as Hudson had most of his adult life, learned to fear that sound, because it meant that the hull—your lifeline, the only thing separating you from the unforgiving vacuum of space—might well be buckling.

"I lost the signal," Mastroeni said.

"Warp nine."

Mastroeni didn't even look up, trying as she was to regain the distress call. "That's crazy, Cal, we can't—"

"I said warp nine!"

This time she did look up. Cal Hudson rarely raised his voice—but he wasn't in the mood for an argument, and he wasn't about to let Chakotay and his people suffer any more than they had to. He didn't know Chakotay well, only that he too was ex-Starfleet, that he was from Trebus, and that he had already carved out a good reputation among the Maquis for both efficiency and fairness. But even if he were a total stranger, he would not allow him to suffer the agonies that awaited him if the *Geronimo's* hull ruptured.

"Fine, warp nine," she said. "I just hope our hull doesn't go the way of theirs."

Chapter Five

ROBERT DESOTO WAS NOT LOOKING forward to this impending conversation.

About two hours after Tuvok left, he had put in a formal request to Starfleet Command to enter the Demilitarized Zone. He then awaited the call back from Admiral Nechayev denying the request. All according to plan. If Tuvok was able to find the artifact, or if the artifact made its presence known in some more overt manner, the plan might change, but for now Tuvok needed a clear path to get on the Maquis's good side.

Instead, Nechayev's small face with its even smaller features appeared on the screen on the desk of his ready room and informed him that she needed to get back to him, and she would contact him again in one hour on a secure channel, along with Gul Evek.

Voyskunsky had been in the ready room with him when Nechayev's call came in. She frowned. "That wasn't part of the plan, was it?"

DeSoto shook his head. "What's the old saying? The plan of action is usually abandoned three minutes into the mission?"

"Something like that, though my experience says that estimate is often generous."

Smiling, DeSoto said, "Obviously the board has changed shape somewhat."

The captain decided to take the second call alone in the observation lounge. A secure channel from Alynna Nechayev meant captain's eyes only—he'd judge afterward how much Voyskunsky needed to know, though his instinct would be all of it. It was never a good idea for a captain to have to keep things from his first officer.

The more spacious observation lounge, with its viewscreen on one of the walls, gave DeSoto more room to walk around, which he had a feeling he was going to need. Since this promised to be a long talk—Evek and Nechayev both were overly fond of the sounds of their respective voices—he wanted room to move to disguise the fidgeting.

One hour and twenty-five minutes after Nechayev said she'd get back in touch in an hour, Dayrit said, "Incoming transmission from the *U.S.S. Nimitz.* It's Admiral Nechayev—priority alpha."

Voyskunsky grinned toothily. "Nice to know that the admiralty's reputation for promptness remains nonexistent."

Merely rolling his eyes in reply, DeSoto got up from the command chair. "Pipe it through to the observation lounge, Manolet, and make sure it's secure on our end, too. You have the bridge, Dina."

Still grinning, Voyskunsky said, "All our hopes and dreams go with you, sir."

DeSoto snorted. "That makes it *all* worthwhile."

As soon as he arrived in the observation lounge, De-Soto activated the viewscreen. It revealed a split screen, with Admiral Nechayev's pinched features on the left and the rectangular head of Gul Evek on the right.

"Thank you for waiting, Captain," Nechayev said.

DeSoto came within a hair of saying something off-hand about needing the nap, but with Evek on the line, he needed to present the front of the outraged ship captain who'd lost an officer to the Maquis. "I didn't have much choice, Admiral."

"I understand. But I hope you understand that this is a delicate matter—even more delicate than you might realize. Captain Robert DeSoto, may I present Gul Evek of the Sixth Order."

"From what Admiral Nechayev tells me, Captain," Evek said without any kind of preamble, *"the catastrophe on Nramia relates to this artifact of yours."*

DeSoto's head swam. Technically, he wasn't supposed to know anything about an artifact, since Tuvok's cover story had the information wiped from the *Hood*'s sensor logs. Conveniently, he also had no idea what Nramia was or what manner of catastrophe was involved. So his confusion was genuine when he said, "Excuse me?"

"My apologies," Evek said, sounding completely unapologetic. *"I had assumed the admiral briefed you."*

"That was the purpose of this call," Nechayev said primly. *"Captain, it seems that another one of the Malkus Artifacts has surfaced. You're familiar with them, of course."*

"Of course," DeSoto said.

"Apparently, the Maquis have discovered a third artifact. And it's capable—"

Evek shifted in his seat. *"It's capable of destroying a planet, Captain. Right now, my entire fleet is engaged in rescue operations to evacuate Nramia because your terrorist friends warped the weather patterns sufficiently to make it uninhabitable. I can assure you, our response will be appropriate."*

Nechayev said quickly, *"They're not our 'friends,' Gul Evek."*

"Not hardly," DeSoto said, trying to sound bitter. "They abandoned Federation citizenship. Admiral, I've already requested permission to enter the DMZ to pursue Lieutenant Tuvok. If a Malkus Artifact is in Maquis hands, that's two reasons. General Order 16 is very clear on the subject."

Before Nechayev could speak, Evek said, *"The general orders of Starfleet are of little interest to Central Command, Captain. What we want is revenge for the indignities—"*

"What you want is to escalate the situation," DeSoto said, "and start a war."

"You surprise me, Captain. The Maquis declared war on us when they blew up the Bok'Nor *at Deep Space 9 months ago. It will end when they're all dead."*

DeSoto didn't like the direction this conversation was taking. "Admiral—"

"Don't worry, Captain," Nechayev said quickly. *"We don't plan to escalate this situation. Right now, I think it's in the best interests of both Central Command and Starfleet to send one ship from each fleet into the zone to try to locate the Malkus Artifact and confiscate it."*

"I don't agree," Evek said sharply, then softened. *"But I have been overridden. The* Vetar *will join you in the Demilitarized Zone in three days, once we have finished overseeing the evacuation of Nramia."*

"Gee, Evek, I thought you were in a rush to get revenge." Despite DeSoto's tone, he was glad to see that the Cardassian was putting saving the lives of those on Nramia over vengeance. That kind of attitude was the only way there was to be any hope of peace along the Cardassian/Federation border right now.

"I think we all agree that safeguarding lives is of utmost importance," Nechayev said before Evek could respond.

"Bridge to Captain." That was Voyskunsky's voice.

"Hold on a second, please, Admiral, Gul." DeSoto then muted the video and audio feed to Evek. Nechayev's face now took up the entire viewscreen. "Go ahead, Dina."

"Captain, we've reacquired the emissions from the Malkus Artifact." Now DeSoto was glad he'd muted Evek. The use of the word "reacquired" would not have jibed with the cover story they'd given the Cardassians. *"It's in motion, heading for the Slaybis system."*

DeSoto turned to Nechayev's image with a questioning look. "Why do I know that name?"

"There are two Class-M planets in that system. One is a Cardassian colony. The other is a human colony." Nechayev hesitated.

"Slaybis IV," DeSoto said, finally putting it together with a Starfleet Intelligence dispatch that he and Voyskunsky had read as part of their briefing prior to being posted to the Cardassian border. For that matter, they had shared the contents of that briefing with Tuvok prior to his departure. "SI has an operative there, doesn't it?"

Nechayev nodded. *"Obviously, this information should not be shared with Gul Evek."*

"Yeah, but the artifact going to Slaybis should. This might be just what we need to give him a kick in the tail." He brought Evek back up on the screen. "Gul, that was my bridge. They've detected a signal that matches the records of the Malkus Artifact—and it's heading for the Slaybis system. I believe there's a Cardassian colony on the second planet?"

Evek spoke with a sarcastic disdain. *"After a fashion. The colonists on Slaybis are a group of fanatics, Captain. Cultists who think that technology has ruined their lives. They flew to Slaybis in a spaceship that they proceeded to dismantle and now live a peaceful, agrarian lifestyle unsullied by the evils of replicators and other such equipment."* Evek hesitated. *"Captain, do you mean to tell me that those murderers of yours are headed for Slaybis II?"*

"We don't know where they're headed, just that they're on course for that star system."

"They're not even a formal part of the Cardassian Union! They've rejected any form of aid from the government—it's funded by a few rich eccentrics." Evek spoke in a tone of voice that told exactly what he thought of oddball projects funded by wealthy civilians.

"That makes it less likely to be a target, if there's no military value," DeSoto said. "Of course, there's a human colony there, too."

"I think we can safely rule out a Maquis attack on a human colony, Captain. If the Maquis are targeting a completely unmilitary—one might even say antimilitary—target, then—"

DeSoto saw an opening. "Then, Gul Evek, we need to go in *now*. We can't afford to wait three days for you to finish your evac. Let the *Hood* go to Slaybis—we can be there within twenty-four hours."

Until this moment, DeSoto had never seen a Cardassian grit his teeth. It was not a pretty sight. *"Captain, the term 'demilitarized zone' means a zone with no military. The treaty—"*

"—can be flexible up to a point," Nechayev said.

"We cannot allow a Starfleet presence in the zone

without an equivalent Central Command presence." Evek's words were sure, but his tone was weakening. DeSoto tried not to smile. His white pieces were surrounding Evek's black ones oh so slowly but surely.

"What if we promise to share all intelligence we gather on the Maquis?" Nechayev said.

Evek leaned back in his chair and folded his arms. *"What assurances do I have that you'll share all your data gathered?"*

Nechayev's lips moved only infinitesmally, but it definitely qualified as a smile. *"I never said we'd share all our data, Gul, only that we'd share our intelligence on the Maquis. You won't have unexpurgated access to Captain DeSoto's logs, but you will be provided with useful intelligence. And all we ask in return is for one ship to go unescorted into the DMZ just long enough to save a planetful of Cardassian cultists."*

Unfolding his arms, Evek glared at the screen. DeSoto once again had to keep himself from smiling. The gul was making a show of thinking about it, but DeSoto knew when the other player was ready to resign. And, as little as Evek might have thought of the people who formed the colony on Slaybis II, it would be politically unwise to condemn them to death over a technicality in the treaty.

"Very well—but I expect a complete sharing of intelligence on the Maquis. I am determined to make sure this ragtag group of terrorists are wiped from the face of the galaxy once and for all!"

Evek punctuated his outburst by cutting off the communication at his end.

"Very dramatic."

Nechayev actually chuckled. *"I'm surprised. Evek doesn't usually go for those kinds of histrionics. But this is a difficult situation."*

"True. If that's all, Admiral, we need to get the lead out." DeSoto moved as if to cut the connection.

"One thing, Captain." DeSoto's finger hovered over the control. *"The most important thing right now is retrieving the artifact. We can't afford to let it fall into Maquis or Cardassian hands. It's far too dangerous."*

"We'll get it back for you, Admiral. *Hood* out."

As he walked out to the bridge, he shook his head. *Gee, Admiral, thanks* so much *for explaining to me what I already knew.*

"Dina," he said to Voyskunsky as she vacated the command chair for him, "if I ever turn into a hidebound desk-jockey type, please don't hesitate to shoot me in the head."

"Noted and logged, sir."

"Anyhow, we've got our free pass in the DMZ. Baifang, set course for the Slaybis system, warp nine. José, keep an eye on those readings. If the artifact changes course even a micrometer, I want to know about it. Manolet, arm phasers and load torpedo bays." He gave Voyskunsky a small smile. "We're the lone white piece in a sea of black pieces."

A chorus of "Aye, sir's" flew about the bridge.

Hsu added, "Course plotted and laid in, sir."

"Hit it."

When the *Liberator* came out of warp, Cal Hudson was surprised to see an intact hull.

"Pull in to forty thousand kilometers," he told Mastroeni, and then did a full scan. The sensors explained the seeming discrepancy between the hull-buckling sounds in Chakotay's distress call and the image on the viewscreen: Hudson was reading severe damage to the *inner* hull, and also extreme temperature variations throughout the small vessel. "Looks like Tuvok's weather controller got loose inside the ship."

"The emissions are still in motion, about two light-years ahead and traveling at warp three." She looked over at Hudson. "Their course takes them right to the Slaybis system."

"Slaybis?" Hudson racked his brain, and then came up with a match. "There's a human colony on the fourth planet and a bunch of Cardassian farmers on the second. Neither of them's much of a target. Why would whoever has the artifact be heading there?"

"You can ask Chakotay himself," Mastroeni said, looking down at her console. "He's hailing us."

A dark face appeared on the tiny viewscreen. The captain of the *Geronimo* had determined features, accented by a featherlike tattoo over his left eye, and close-cropped black hair. *"This is Captain Chakotay of the* Geronimo. *You must be Captain Hudson."*

"Cal is fine," Hudson said. He'd left ranks behind when he quit Starfleet, and being referred to as a captain—particularly given that he was "only" a lieutenant commander when he resigned—just brought back bad memories.

Chakotay smiled grimly. *"Normally, I'd be wary of the two of us talking like this."* Maquis cell leaders deliberately avoided contact with each other as a security measure.

Returning the smile, Hudson said, "Hey, if you want us to turn around . . ."

"That's quite all right. We've got thirty-eight people here and a ship that's buckling at the seams. My engineer tells me we'll implode inside of fifteen minutes."

"You can give me the details once we get you settled over here. Hudson out." He then instructed the transporter room to start beaming Chakotay's people over, as well as whatever cargo the *Liberator* had room for. There turned out to be very little of that; most of Chakotay's people's personal belongings were in a safe place that Hudson didn't want to know the location of.

It only took ten minutes to complete the transfer. From the transporter room, Chakotay said, *"If you've got the weapons to spare, Hudson, I'd like you to destroy the ship. I'd rather a stray Cardassian didn't come across any useful remains."*

"Understood." Hudson nodded to Mastroeni, who loaded the torpedo bays. Within two minutes, the *Liberator*'s photon torpedoes had reduced the *Geronimo* to components far too small to be of any use.

Hudson then joined Chakotay in the cargo bay, where thirty-five of his people were gathered. The other three had been taken to sickbay—a small room that consisted of two beds, a medical tricorder, and a mishmash of medikits. Two had been stunned by phaser fire, and the other had three broken ribs.

"The ship's been scuttled," Hudson said. "I'm sorry we had to do that."

Chakotay nodded. "That's all right—it was my fault, really, for giving her that name. The real Geronimo fought the good fight, but came to a bad end. Next time, I'll think more carefully."

"So what happened?"

Quickly, Chakotay summarized his rescue of three of his people from a desolate planet in the DMZ, with the added bonus of a black box of some kind—the Malkus Artifact. The *Geronimo* then attacked Nramia, but what Chakotay had ordered as a strike against the capital city turned out to be a planetwide disaster.

"This Tharia person," Mastroeni said, "doesn't normally act like this?"

Before Chakotay could reply, a Bajoran woman stepped forward. "Like a complete lunatic? No, he doesn't. That damn box must've done something to him."

A woman with Klingon-like features spoke up. "He could've just cracked. The man lost his entire family."

Hudson flashed on a mental image of Gretchen, which he forced out of his mind. "What happened?"

"His three mates died in a Cardassian attack," Chakotay said. "He took it fairly well—maybe too well. Sometimes it just takes a little longer to grieve—or to fall apart."

"Or maybe just the right tool," the part-Klingon woman said. "This weapon is incredibly powerful."

Hudson nodded. "We saw what it did to Nramia. In fact, it's why we found you." He then quickly filled Chakotay in on his own reasons for being here, and on their prisoner and potential recruit in the mess hall.

"I'd like to meet this Tuvok," Chakotay said.

"Of course." Hudson was about to lead Chakotay to the mess hall when a Betazoid stepped forward.

In a soft voice, the dark-eyed man said, "Excuse me, sir, but there's something I think you should know."

"What is it, Suder?" Chakotay asked.

The Betazoid hesitated. "It wasn't anything I could put my finger on, but—well, since you rescued Tharia, B'Elanna, and Gerron, there's been something—"

"Spit it out," Chakotay said impatiently. This Suder person spoke very quietly, and Hudson could see how his roundabout way of talking—unusual for a telepath—could be irritating.

"Tharia's mind has been—different. It isn't anything specific, but—you know that I'd never pry into your minds without permission, sir. But—Tharia was definitely changed, subtly, by that thing he found."

Chakotay started to say something, then stopped.

Hudson suspected that the large man was going to up-braid the Betazoid for not speaking up sooner—it's what Hudson might have done under the same circum-stances—but then he thought better of it. After all, there was little to be gained by recriminations now.

Instead, he simply said, "Thank you, Lon. Seska, B'Elanna, come with me. The rest of you, stay here. Hudson?"

Hudson and Mastroeni led the trio to the mess hall, where McAdams and Schmidt still stood guard. To them, Hudson said, "You two report to the bridge until Darleen and I report back."

Nodding, the pair departed. Chakotay, meanwhile, gazed upon the Vulcan. "Hudson says you know about this artifact."

"Yes. I am Tuvok of Vulcan. My family was killed at Amniphon, and I have come to the Demilitarized Zone in order to join the Maquis. The information about the Malkus Artifact that I provided to Mr. Hudson was by way of—"

"Letting us think you're legitimate, fine," Chakotay said quickly. He obviously wasn't interested in the prelim-inaries. "One of my most trusted comrades has gone from a sane, steady presence to a homicidal maniac thanks to this thing, Vulcan. I have a Betazoid who says that his thought patterns have changed. Can you explain that?"

"One of the Malkus Artifacts is reported to have the ability to control thoughts, but that is separate from the artifact that affects weather patterns."

Hudson frowned. "What about the other two people who wielded the artifacts?"

Tuvok's eyes almost seemed to turn inward for a half-second as he recalled the records of the artifact. "One was a citizen of a human colony. She was a disaffected civil-service worker named Tomasina Laubenthal, and had no history of mental illness prior to finding the artifact. However, she had recently gone through a life change that was believed to be the reason for her using the artifact to commit attempted mass murder. The second artifact was used by the Bajoran terrorist Orta."

The Bajoran woman—Seska—snorted at that. "I've heard of him. He isn't a model of mental health at the best of times."

Tuvok steepled his fingers together. "However, the artifacts do not have any visible controls. They must function by reacting to the thoughts of the wielder."

"Tharia seemed to simply will the device to do what it did," Chakotay said.

"It may therefore be logical to postulate that the transfer of psionic waves works both ways, as it were—that the artifacts are capable of, in essence, forcing the possessor to utilize them. This hypothesis is supported by a telepath noticing a change in thought patterns." One of his eyebrows rose. "In the case of Ms. Laubenthal, it probably would have taken very little to convince her to do so, given the life change she had undergone."

"In Orta's case, it wouldn't have taken any convincing whatsoever," Seska said.

Nodding, Tuvok said, "It is an intriguing hypothesis."

"It's also pretty irrelevant." That was B'Elanna, the part-Klingon woman. "We need to find Tharia—that shuttle can't go higher than warp three. I assume this tub can do better?"

Mastroeni gave the woman one of her lesser snarls. "We hit warp nine to rescue you."

"Tharia was headed for Slaybis. He's got a head start, but we should be able to beat him there at warp nine."

Hudson shook his head. "We can't maintain it that

long. But I'm not sure why he'd want to go there. The only Cardassians there are a bunch of civilians."

Chakotay hesitated. "Actually, Slaybis IV was on our list."

"That's a human colony!" Mastroeni said angrily.

To Hudson's surprise, it was Tuvok who responded. "However, it is a human colony with a Starfleet Intelligence operative working on it." He turned to Chakotay and again raised an eyebrow. "Logically, that is the only possible reason why Slaybis IV would be a legitimate Maquis target."

Hudson also turned to Chakotay. "Is this true?"

Slowly, Chakotay nodded. "We got word that one of our couriers, a young man named Elois Phifer, was working for SI."

Tuvok added, "Lieutenant Phifer is, in fact, an SI operative, sent in six months ago to gather intelligence on the Maquis, though his information has been sporadic and less than useful to Starfleet."

Rubbing his chin, Hudson turned to Mastroeni. Her face was unreadable, which told Hudson all he needed to know. Tuvok gave up an SI operative before Chakotay had a chance to—that was a major point in the Vulcan's favor.

He tapped an intercom. "McAdams, set course for the Slaybis system, warp seven-point-five." He turned to B'Elanna. "I can't risk going any faster than that—we already strained our engines to get to you as fast as we did."

B'Elanna smiled. "Let me get a look at your engines. I'll coax warp eight out of them at least."

"Let her do it," Chakotay said. "She's the best. In fact, she's better than the best."

Chakotay didn't strike Hudson as the type given to hyperbole. "Darleen, take her to engineering."

Mastroeni fixed Hudson with a glare, but did so without comment.

"All right, Mr. Tuvok, I think you've shown plenty of good faith," Hudson said. "I'm still not completely convinced that your desire to join the Maquis is legitimate, but I'm content to not shoot you for the time being. Right now, the main thing is to get that artifact back from Tharia. We'll figure out our next move after that."

"Agreed," Chakotay said.

Tuvok nodded. "Thank you."

"First thing we're doing is getting you out of that uniform. It won't go over well around here." Hudson smiled. "I think I've got something in my footlocker that'll fit you."

Tuvok's eyebrow practically climbed off his head. "That estimation may be optimistic." The Vulcan had a tall, lithe form, completely unlike Hudson's own bulkier frame. Tuvok's torso could practically fit in one of Hudson's shoulders.

"We'll figure something out. C'mon."

"*Cal.*" It was Mastroeni over the intercom.

"Go ahead," Hudson said, looking up.

"*I've got good news and bad news. Tell Chakotay he wasn't kidding about this Torres woman. We've got warp eight-point-five.*"

"The bad news?"

"*Tharia's still going to beat us to Slaybis by about two hours.*"

Chakotay muttered a curse in a language Hudson didn't recognize. "With that weapon, two hours is a lifetime."

"It will surely be the remaining lifetime of Lieutenant Phifer," Tuvok said dryly.

Whirling on Tuvok, Chakotay said, "I don't give a damn about the life of a Starfleet infiltrator, Vulcan. He knew the risks when he went undercover. But Tharia can't tell what a legitimate target is anymore. He's lashing out at everything in his way. He's spent the last nine months pretending that the deaths of his mates didn't affect him, and now he's making up for it by killing indiscriminately."

As calm as Chakotay had been intense, Tuvok said, "Then logic dictates we do everything we can to stop him."

Chapter Six

A SMALL SHIP FLEW THROUGH THE REGION between star systems in a sector that currently was designated 22402 by the United Federation of Planets. Its registry was the *Sun,* though it was, truthfully, not registered to any particular planet, only to its owner, a woman named Aidulac.

Various and sundry ships piloted by Aidulac and named the *Sun* had wended their way throughout the galaxy for millennia, with but one purpose: to find the Instruments of Malkus the Mighty. The four Instruments that she herself had helped create millennia ago. The four Instruments that Malkus had used to cause untold death and destruction. The four Instruments that the rebels who overthrew Malkus hid throughout the galaxy.

The four Instruments that Aidulac swore to destroy if it took her the rest of her life. And, since she was functionally immortal, the rest of her life was as long as it needed to be.

It was, for the most part, a tedious existence. But Aidulac persevered.

The universe, naturally, didn't make things easy on her. Perhaps it was its revenge for her having pried into so many of its secrets. Or perhaps she just hadn't noticed the universe's vicious sense of humor before. But for an obscenely long time, nobody unearthed the Instruments, and so she never found the wave pattern that would identify them. She went through hundreds of ships—all of which she named the *Sun,* after the vessel that had given her freedom from the Zalkat Union—and waited.

No one knew of the Instruments, even when questioned under Aidulac's irresistible mental charms. So she waited some more.

At one point, bored with waiting and insane with loneliness, she went to a world now called Pegasus Major IV and used her abilities to take on many lovers and bear many children. Her mental charms had lessened over the years, to her annoyance. Nowadays she could truly affect only males. But that was sufficient. She thought she wanted the company of children while she waited.

But she grew bored with that, too, and resumed her wandering ways.

And her waiting.

Finally, the universe gave her hope. She detected an Instrument on a human colony belonging to a governmental body that had taken over many of the worlds once ruled by the Zalkatians: the United Federation of Planets. They called it Alpha Proxima II. However, by the time she reached the world, two Starfleet ships had already arrived, and they would not permit her to land on the planet to take the Instrument—ironically, because the planet was quarantined thanks to the Instrument's virus, which had infected thousands.

She might have been able to convince the two Starfleet commanders, Decker and Kirk, to let her take the Instruments, but many of her descendants on Pegasus Major IV had inherited her persuasive abilities. They had been nicknamed "Sirens" after some human mythological creature and gained a reputation—one that Decker and Kirk had used against her.

The second Instrument had proven just as elusive, again because of the interference of Starfleet. This time it was the energy weapon, which had been discovered on a moon of the planet Bajor.

Now, only a few short months later, she had been thrilled to find that the third Instrument—the weather controller—was in a region of space between the Federation and the Cardassian Union. Best of all, the region was demilitarized—there was no chance of interference from Starfleet.

The Instrument was in transit to a star system that the locals referred to as Slaybis. Aidulac put the *Sun* on course for that world.

This time, she thought, *I will not fail.*

"So what's your story?" Darleen Mastroeni asked B'Elanna Torres.

Torres had just finished rerouting some of the power relays to coax some more speed out of the warp engines without straining the *Liberator* hull or shorting out its structural-integrity field. Mastroeni had been worried about the latter, since the SIF had taken a beating after their last throw-down with the Cardassians, but everything seemed to be functioning well. Torres was obviously *very* good at the type of seat-of-the-pants engineering that was required to survive in the Maquis, and Mastroeni had decided that she was going to do

Keith R.A. DeCandido

what she could to recruit this prodigy away from Chakotay.

"Story?" Torres asked as she checked over the readings.

"C'mon, everybody in the Maquis has a story."

Smiling, Torres said, "Oh yeah? What's yours?"

"You ever hear of Juhraya?"

"Of course," Torres said with a nod.

"Did you know that the first contact between humans and Cardassians was on Juhraya? Most people don't know that."

"I certainly didn't," Torres muttered. "Is there somewhere I can get a drink on this boat?"

Mastroeni nodded and led the way toward the mess hall. "Sure. Follow me." Tuvok wasn't there anymore, so Mastroeni could go there to relax. "Anyhow, a Cardassian ship crash-landed on Juhraya about fifty years ago. Some people say it was a Starfleet ship that made the first contact—some kind of silly diplomatic thing—but that's typical of their propaganda. It was us, and everyone who matters knows it."

Torres laughed. "No love for Starfleet, huh?"

Snarling, Mastroeni said, "Not remotely. A bunch of arrogant prigs with no conception of how the galaxy actually *works*."

As they entered the mess hall, Torres said, "You won't get any argument from me. I went to that penal colony they call the Academy for a year and a half."

Mastroeni nodded. "They kicked you out."

"Let's just say we all agreed that it wasn't the place for me."

"Well, that agreement turned out good for us. Coffee?"

Torres nodded, and Mastroeni approached the food replicator and ordered two coffees, black.

"How'd you know I took my coffee black?" Torres asked as she removed her steaming mug from the slot.

"You're an engineer. Haven't met one yet that didn't drink it black."

"Very observant." She took a sip. "Anyhow, you've now heard most of my 'story.' I grew up on both Kessik IV and Qo'noS."

"So you *are* part human?"

"Half and half," Torres said with a nod. "My father's human, but he left when I was a kid. After that, my mother and I moved to Qo'noS."

"Which did you like better?" Mastroeni asked the question mostly by way of trying to find out what Qo'noS was like. She knew very little about the Klingons, but she always imagined that she would like it on their homeworld.

"I hated both of them pretty much equally, actually. Kessik was too pastoral for the Klingon side of me, and Qo'noS was too rough-and-tumble for my human side to deal with." She laughed. "Or maybe I was just rebelling. Who knows? I was a dumb kid who resented her parents, like most dumb kids. So I went to the Academy, figuring they'd take just about anybody, and I hated that, too. Came to live out here and actually liked it until the treaty messed everything up, so I joined Chakotay."

"Who is now a man without a ship," Mastroeni said, grateful for the opening.

Torres shrugged. "He'll pick up another one. Probably some junk heap I'll have to beat into shape, like usual."

"You know, we could use a good engineer here. The *Liberator* obviously likes your touch."

"I don't think it'd work." Torres grinned. "Chakotay and Hudson on the same ship would just get ugly."

Mastroeni started to ask why they needed Chakotay, but she cut herself off. Torres had thought the offer was being extended to the entire cell. "Yeah, that would," she said slowly. "Of course, you could just come over yourself."

Before Torres could answer, the door opened to reveal Tuvok. The Vulcan had changed into a shirt that was tailored for a person twice his size—*probably one of Cal's,* Mastroeni thought—and pants that had been rolled up at the ankles. On anyone else such garb would have looked foolish, but, much as Mastroeni hated to admit it, Tuvok wore it with dignity.

Her hand automatically went to her phaser. "What do you want, Vulcan?"

"I was seeking out Ms. Torres. Ms. McAdams informed me that she would be here."

"We're having a private conversation," Mastroeni said.

"That's all right," Torres said, setting down her mug and walking over to the Vulcan. "What is it, Tuvok?"

Cursing, Mastroeni set down her own mug and also walked over to the Vulcan, who was holding a padd. Obviously, her attempt to recruit Torres had failed. Still, she didn't trust the Vulcan—and she wasn't at all happy that he was gallivanting around the *Liberator* unescorted. She made a mental note to talk to Hudson about that later.

"I have been perusing the data on the Malkus Artifacts from the Rector Institute—where the first two artifacts are being studied," he added at Torres's quizzical look, "as well as sensor data from the *Odyssey, Rio Grande, Enterprise,* and *Constellation.*"

Frowning, Mastroeni asked, "You got all that from the *Hood?*"

"Before I departed, yes, I made copies of all that data."

"You expect me to believe that Starfleet ships carry around sensor data from hundred-year-old missions?"

"Of course," Tuvok said as if such a colossal waste of

computer storage were the most natural thing in the galaxy.

Torres nodded. "He's right, actually. You never know when you may need a piece of information from an old mission. And Starfleet computers have a *lot* of storage space."

Mastroeni still thought it a waste, but at this point she was staring a gift horse in the mouth. This information might help them deal with this crazed Andorian and his weapon. "What've you found?"

"The sensor data that the ships have been able to accumulate—combined with the usual advances in sensor technology—means that we might be able to get a transporter lock on the artifact when we find it."

Tuvok handed Torres the padd. She studied the data on the screen, but shook her head. Mastroeni looked over her shoulder and saw that the screen had several different sensor readings on different sections of the viewing area, including recent readings from the *Liberator*'s own scans.

"These readings are too scattershot. Maybe—maybe—if you got the thing onto a transporter pad, then the two consoles working together could get a lock, or if you put some kind of homing device on the thing, but that's the only way to do it."

"My combadge could easily serve such a function," Tuvok said.

Mastroeni snorted. That combadge was currently in Hudson's possession, surrendered to him when Tuvok changed clothes. She had been suspicious that he had left the device on—it was the easiest way for Starfleet to track him down—but simply said, "What does this mean in plain words?"

"I had hoped that we would be able to get a transporter lock on the artifact when we arrived at the Slaybis system and simply confiscate it that way. Unfortunately, as we have seen, this will not be possible."

A thought occurred to Mastroeni. "Wait a minute, why don't we just lock in on those distinct emissions of yours? Isn't that how we know it's there in the first place?"

"Unfortunately, those emissions cannot be traced to the precise location of the artifact. A transporter lock requires a precise coordinate fix, and thus far the energy signature given off by the artifacts has not been able to provide that."

Torres looked up suddenly. "We might be able to do something sneakier than a combadge. Tharia's not stupid. I doubt we'd be able to sneak a combadge or a pattern enhancer or anything like that onto it. But I might be able to put together a mini-transponder." She turned to Mastroeni. "Mind if I paw through your parts? I know I've got some of what I'd need in my footlocker, but I'll need some molybdenum, some bits of ODN cable, and a solenoid transtator."

Tuvok's eyebrow came dangerously close to flying off his forehead. "I fail to see how a solenoid transtator would be of any use."

Grinning widely, Torres said, "Watch and learn, Tuvok."

I have simply got to get this woman to join our cell, Mastroeni thought as she led the pair of them to the parts locker. *Anybody who can make a Vulcan—especially that particular Vulcan—look that nonplussed is someone I want to keep around.*

Chapter Seven

As soon as the *Liberator*'s long-range sensors started picking up readings from Slaybis IV, Cal Hudson knew they were too late.

For starters, sensors were picking up the distinctive emissions of the Malkus Artifact on the planet itself, with no immediate sign of the *Geronimo*'s shuttlecraft in orbit.

Then Mastroeni gave her report on what sensors were picking up on the planet: "Temperatures in the equatorial regions are below freezing, with snow and ice storms. Temperatures in the polar regions are close to fifty degrees *above* freezing, with severe flooding. I'm picking up hurricanes on the coasts and tornadoes inland." She looked over at Hudson with as grave a look as he'd ever seen on her face. "It's Nramia all over again."

Hudson shook his head. "Prepare to come out of warp and plot a standard orbit."

"Sure, I—" Then something caught her eye. "Uh, better make that an orbit of the third moon. I'm picking up a Starfleet ship, heading for Slaybis at warp eight." Again she turned to Hudson, but this time the grave look was replaced by fury. "It's the *Hood!* That goddamn Vulcan betrayed us!"

"We'll deal with that in a minute," Hudson said, more concerned with their immediate safety than the long-term—or even short-term—consequences of the *Hood*'s presence in a demilitarized area. "Get us to the moon without their seeing us."

"I know what to do," she said through clenched teeth. It was risky, but they could wait until the last possible second to come out of warp and slide right into orbit of the moon—currently on the far side of the planet. It involved dumping a lot of velocity in a short amount of time, and was difficult for any ship to pull off—a ship with a sufficiently small mass to be able to dump velocity that fast sometimes wasn't structurally sound enough to survive the maneuver, and a larger ship simply couldn't decelerate that quickly. Usually space was large enough for a huge margin of error when it came to dropping speed, but a standard orbit decreased that margin considerably.

"Decelerating—now!" Mastroeni said as she performed the maneuver. Alarms went off all around Hudson. Most were warnings of problems that could be tabled, or fixed quickly—except for the one that indicated the failure of the structural-integrity field.

"Engineering," he yelled, tapping the intercom, "McAdams, we—"

Then the alarm stopped. SIF then read at one hundred percent. The lights did dim, however.

"McAdams, what just happened?"

"This is Torres. I was able to divert power from life-support to the SIF."

Hudson blinked. "Are you out of your mind? Life-support—"

"—*is nonessential in the short term. Just the air we've got will last us a day or two, and we can live with low lights for a while. We'll be able to get the SIF running on its own long before there's any kind of problem.*"

"Uh, fine," Hudson said, nonplussed. He wanted to rebuke Torres, but he found he had nothing to say that was in any way recriminatory. "Carry on." He turned to Mastroeni. "Any way we can steal her from Chakotay?"

Mastroeni almost smiled. "Working on it."

It figures. Hudson shook his head and put his mind back to immediate business. "Did you read any Cardassian ships?"

"No. And I'm still not."

"What about the *Hood?*"

"Not reading them either, but that's because we've got a moon and a planet between us—and it also means they can't see us, either. Hopefully they didn't pick us up. If they stay on course, they'll be in orbit in five minutes."

Hudson checked his status board and saw that repairs were already under way on the lesser systems that had given out. He nodded, appreciative of his team. Then the comm systems indicated some traffic on the Starfleet channel. "The *Hood*'s sending a message."

He put it on the speaker. "*Slaybis IV Control, this is the Starship* Hood. *Respond, please.*" A pause. "*This is the U.S.S.* Hood. *We have been given special dispensation by Starfleet and the Cardassian Central Command to enter the Demilitarized Zone unescorted in order to comply with General Order 16. Please respond.*"

"Hudson to Tuvok."

"*Go ahead,*" came the Vulcan's calm voice a moment later.

"Mr. Tuvok, the *Hood* has entered orbit around Slaybis IV. They claim to have gotten special dispensation to come here in order to confiscate the artifact. I'm wondering if they're here for another reason."

"You suspect me of leading them here."

"The thought had crossed our minds," Mastroeni said sharply.

"A reasonable supposition, but erroneous. I have no reason to lead the Hood *here. It was inevitable that they would eventually detect the Malkus Artifact even after I wiped the sensor logs as long as it stayed in use within the Demilitarized Zone. It is good that we destroyed the* Manhattan. *As it is, Captain DeSoto will no doubt use this excursion as an excuse to try to take me back."*

Hudson muted the intercom and shot Mastroeni a look.

She shrugged. "He's saying all the right things, but I don't like it."

"They say Vulcans don't lie," Hudson said with a wry smile.

Mastroeni snorted. "Yeah, but it's mostly Vulcans who say that."

"Good point." He de-muted the intercom. "All right, Tuvok, we'll—"

"Cal, I'm picking up readings from the surface," Mastroeni said suddenly. "The capital city is coming into range. According to our records, there should be a very large building that houses the government in the center of the city." She looked up. "According to the sensors, there's a pile of rubble in the center of the city."

"This is Tharia ch'Ren," said a voice over the comm channel, in response to the *Hood's* hail, *"representing the new face of the Maquis."*

Hudson and Mastroeni exchanged a glance. "I don't like the sound of that," Hudson muttered.

Yet another new voice came on. *"Mr. ch'Ren, this is Captain DeSoto. What has happened to the government of Slaybis IV? We haven't been able to raise them."*

"That is because they're all dead, Captain. As is the traitor, Elois Phifer. As are several dozen other people. And they're only the first."

"You said you're the 'new face' of the Maquis. What does that—"

"What it means, Captain, is quite simply that we have been gentle—quiet. Until now. You have called us 'terrorists,' but you have not seen true terror before. The citizens of Nramia know the meaning of terror now, and those who dwell on Slaybis IV will do likewise—followed by the farmers on Slaybis II, and everyone else in the Demilitarized Zone."

"Mr. ch'Ren, do you intend to—"

"We intend to exterminate all life in this sector, Captain. And if you stand in our way, we will exterminate you as well."

"Well, I don't like the sound of that," Dina Voyskunsky muttered from behind DeSoto. She stood between Dayrit and Kojima. The captain silently agreed with her assessment from his vantage point in the command chair.

The image of an Andorian was on the main viewer. Tharia ch'Ren's feathery white hair extended to the small of his back, and his antennae stood straight up out of his head. His watery yellow eyes seemed almost empty, which made his words all the more disturbing to DeSoto.

Ch'Ren had kept his end of the transmission tight on his face. Based on the sensor readings of the Malkus Artifact and the triangulation of the communication, he was in the capital city, and based on the fact that he wasn't being rained on, he was indoors—according to Kojima, the capital city had gotten its entire average annual allotment of rainfall in the past two hours—but beyond that, there were no clues as to his precise location.

Dayrit whispered, "Captain, I have something."

"Hold on a moment, please, Mr. ch'Ren, while I consult with my senior staff."

The Andorian simply inclined his head.

DeSoto stood up and made a throat-cutting gesture. Once the transmission was muted, he said, "Report."

"I'm picking up the wreckage of a shuttlecraft in the capital city. It doesn't match the registry of any of the ships in the Slaybis port—but it does match the configuration of a Maquis shuttle that attacked a Cardassian freighter a couple of days ago and made off with a weapons shipment. Central Command claimed the grenades were for a supply depot in the Chin'toka system, but SI was pretty sure they were earmarked for Dorvan V. It also matches the type of shuttlecraft that would be used on the vessel that attacked Nramia."

Voyskunsky let out an annoyed breath. "Dorvan's one of the Cardassian worlds in the DMZ. Captain, if Manolet's right—"

"And he usually is," DeSoto added with an appreciative smile at his tactical officer. Dayrit inclined his head in response.

"—then ch'Ren may have crashed his ride here. We're not reading any other ships in the area—maybe we can use it as a bargaining chip."

"Let's hope so." He sat back down in his chair—it gave him more of a sense of security. Besides, standing was a sign of respect, and DeSoto wasn't feeling especially respectful for the person responsible for the carnage on Nramia, or the similar carnage the *Hood*'s sensors were picking up now.

"I'd like to avoid extermination if at all possible, Mr. ch'Ren," DeSoto said slowly when ch'Ren's face reappeared on the viewer. "Perhaps we can discuss a solution that is mutually beneficial to us both."

"I see no reason to negotiate with you."

"Right now, I've got four phaser banks and a dozen photon torpedoes trained on your location. I also have a means of getting you off-planet—we know your shuttle crash-landed. Besides, I've read up on your new toy. It has limitations. My guess is that you can't do any further damage to the planet for a while. Until it recharges, you're vulnerable. I don't want to use force, but I will if I have to."

"Do you expect me to believe that Starfleet would commit murder?"

"Do you expect me to believe that I won't respond to your threats? You've already expressed a willingness to attack my ship—I've now expressed my willingness to respond in kind. Still, given a choice I'd rather talk this out like two intelligent beings." He leaned back. "Of course, within a couple of days, the *Vetar* will be here, and I can assure you that Gul Evek will stop at nothing to destroy you after what you did to Nramia."

"Your attempts to frighten me are pointless, Captain," ch'Ren said in a hiss. *"I have no fear of Gul Evek, nor of any other Cardassian. Do not mistake a minor vulnerability for weakness."* A pause. *"However, I am willing to meet with you to discuss terms. I will transmit coordinates to you."*

DeSoto looked up at Kojima, who nodded.

"The room where we will meet will be encased in a forcefield that will prevent any communication signals from penetrating. You will not be able to summon rein-

forcements, nor transport out of the room. You will come alone, Captain. If you send surrogates or bring others, I will destroy your ship. And if you doubt my ability to do so, I challenge you to find the Maquis vessel christened the Geronimo—*or, rather, its twisted hulk.*"

With that, ch'Ren cut the signal.

Voyskunsky came around to the middle of the bridge to face DeSoto. "You're not beaming down alone."

"You heard him, Dina—if I don't, he attacks. Maybe he was bluffing, maybe he wasn't. If he's willing to talk, maybe he isn't as far over the edge as he looks."

She frowned. "You shouldn't put yourself—"

"—in danger, I know. You're not the first first officer to give me this song and dance," DeSoto said, remembering an incident almost a decade earlier on this very same bridge with Lieutenant Commander William T. Riker. "But right now, I don't have a choice."

Voyskunsky's wide lips pursed. "All right, but if you turn up dead, I'm putting you on report, sir."

DeSoto grinned. "Noted."

"Do you really think this is the 'new face' of the Maquis?"

Shaking his head, DeSoto said, "Doubtful. Especially if he's telling the truth about the *Geronimo.* My guess is he's gone rogue, and is using the Maquis name to make a bigger stink."

"Sir?" Dayrit said. "I've got something."

Both DeSoto and Voyskunsky walked around to the tactical console. With a pudgy finger, Dayrit pointed at a sensor reading. "I'm reading the forcefield that ch'Ren's using. It *is* proof against communications—but not against transporters. The problem is, getting a lock would be difficult. But a standard-issue transponder should be able to penetrate with no problem. If we program it to send a constant low-level signal, I doubt that ch'Ren will pick it up—it should read as background comm traffic, especially with the additional EM activity from all the thunderstorms he's been cooking up down there."

DeSoto put a hand on the security chief's shoulder. "Good work, Manolet. Have one ready for me in Transporter Room 3."

"Yes, sir," Dayrit said with a rare smile.

Turning to the ops officer, Voyskunsky said, "José, I want you tracking that transponder signal every second. If *anything* happens to the signal—it changes, it modulates, and especially if it goes away—beam him out of there immediately."

"Will do," Kojima said with a nod.

"Let's hit it," DeSoto said. "The bridge is yours, Dina. I hope to be back soon. I still want a rematch of that Go game."

Voyskunsky grinned her huge smile. "You're on, Captain."

Hudson gathered Chakotay, Tuvok, Mastroeni, Torres, Seska, and McAdams in the mess hall. Tuvok stood against one of the walls by the door, and both Chakotay and Hudson stood with their backs to the rear bulkhead. The other four sat around the largest of the tables. Torres had a padd in her hand, while Mastroeni's hand hovered near her phaser. Hudson noticed that Mastroeni had made a point of sitting where she could keep an eye on Tuvok.

"Your friend," Hudson said to Chakotay, "has gone over the edge."

"And he's going to take the rest of us with him," Mastroeni added.

"These two colonies are peaceful—they're not affiliated with the Federation, Cardassia, *or* the Maquis. If we let him—"

Chakotay interrupted Hudson. "We're not going to 'let' him do anything. We have to get the artifact back. If we don't, the Maquis will lose whatever sympathy we have in the Federation. Starfleet and Central Command will come out in force against us."

Tuvok added, "In addition, such a radical departure from the usual methods will divide the Maquis itself. From what I have seen, the organization is already relatively fractious—in part by design. By committing genocide in the Maquis's name—"

"We know what'll happen," Torres snapped. "Chakotay's right, we have to get the artifact back."

Mastroeni shook her head. "The nanosecond we come out from behind this moon, the *Hood*'ll be all over us."

Seska nodded. "She's right. I for one have no interest in spending the rest of my life in a Federation prison."

"Actually, we won't have to leave our hiding place," Torres said. "I can boost the gain on the transporter so we can get to the surface from here. We'll have to go down one at a time, but I can do it."

Chakotay nodded. "Good. Then we can go in, get the artifact, and get out before DeSoto even knows we're there."

"Even if he does know we're there, it won't matter much," Seska said. "You heard his deal with Tharia—he's going down alone. Starfleet captains are usually just stupid enough to actually live up to promises like that."

Chakotay snorted in what Hudson supposed was agreement, then turned to Torres. "Have you finished that mini-transponder to put on the artifact?"

Torres nodded. "I made four of them, just in case." She grinned. "Amazing what you can do with a few solenoid transtators."

"I have an additional suggestion," Tuvok said.

"As if we care," Mastroeni muttered.

Hudson shot Mastroeni a look, then said, "What's your thought, Tuvok?"

"We do as Captain Chakotay suggests—but turn the artifact over to Captain DeSoto."

"We're *not* giving that thing to Starfleet!" Mastroeni said.

"Starfleet has a general order in place that compels them to confiscate the artifacts. If we take possession of it, then we become a target. The *Hood* will not leave the Demilitarized Zone until they have completed their mission: to retrieve the artifact." He turned to Hudson and Chakotay. "In addition, it will show Starfleet that Tharia is, in fact, a rogue who does not speak for the Maquis as an organization."

Chakotay looked at Hudson. Unlike Mastroeni—or Torres or Seska, for that matter—Chakotay had, like Hudson, worn a Starfleet uniform. The Federation might have betrayed the people of the DMZ, but Hudson knew that, in some matters, Starfleet could be trusted. Hudson assumed that Chakotay felt the same.

"Much as I hate to admit it, Starfleet's better equipped to handle that thing than we are," Chakotay said after a moment. "They've already got two of them, and knowing them, they'll probably dig up the fourth one before long. And frankly—I don't want it. It's already turned one of my trusted comrades into a psychotic killing machine. And Tuvok's right about something else—Tharia's done tremendous damage to the cause with what he just said to DeSoto. We have to nip that in the bud before the *Hood* reports back to Starfleet that we've all turned into maniacs. I think capturing the artifact and then handing it to DeSoto will accomplish that." He smiled wryly. "Besides, I get the feeling we may have to rescue the good captain from Tharia before the day is out. Starfleet captains may be stupid sometimes, but they also usually are properly grateful."

Hudson considered. Then he looked at Mastroeni and McAdams. The latter nodded quickly. "Darleen?" he prompted.

Predictably, she snarled. "I don't want to do anything to help Starfleet."

"I don't see that we have a choice here."

For the first time since he'd met her, Darleen Mastroeni smiled. "Oh, there's *always* a choice, Cal—just a question of making the right one or not." She then sighed. "All right, fine. We do it this way. I'm in."

Chakotay gave his own people the same look.

"I'm in," Torres said with no hesitation.

"We should just destroy the thing," Seska said.

"It has been attempted," Tuvok said.

Undaunted, Seska said, "Then I say we attempt it again."

"And when we fail?" Chakotay asked.

Seska folded her arms. "Then we give it to Starfleet."

"All right," Hudson said. "Chakotay and I will beam down, along with Tuvok." He cut off Mastroeni before she could object. "I know you don't trust him, Darleen, but he knows these artifacts better than any of us." He turned to the others. "We'll each wear one of Torres's mini-transponders so she can pick us up again. The fourth'll go on the artifact, just in case we need to confiscate it for a while." Looking at Chakotay, he said, "I want to keep my options open."

"Agreed. Let's do it."

Chapter Eight

THE FIRST TIME CAL HUDSON went through a transporter, he was four years old and he thought it was the most wonderful sensation in the world. One second he was standing on an indoor transporter platform, the next he was in the middle of Central Park in New York City. His father had promised young Cal a ride on the famous carousel, but the four-year-old boy had found the mode of getting to the attraction more exciting. The entire time he sat going around on the artificial horses, he was waiting for it to end so he could go through the transporter again.

In the intervening years, he had tried to keep that same sense of wonder about this mode of travel, though years in Starfleet—where transporters were used almost as often as turbolifts—had dulled it somewhat. Still, he always loved that feeling of moving instantly from one place to another place, watching the world dissolve and re-form.

Beaming down to Slaybis IV from the *Liberator*, however, was more like watching the world dissolve and then dissolve further.

Rain pelted his face while intense wind slammed into his chest. Instinctively, his right arm went up to protect his eyes. Within seconds, his clothes were soaked through, sticking to his flesh. He was almost afraid to open his mouth to speak.

He squinted under his upheld arm—which was doing precious little to protect his eyes—and saw Chakotay and Tuvok in a similarly bedraggled state.

Just as he was about to scream out if there was shelter nearby, the wind started to die down and the rain lightened.

Hudson lowered his arm. "That Malkus Artifact doesn't do things halfway, does it?"

Chakotay looked up just as the clouds started to clear. "This is definitely not natural."

Within seconds, Hudson had to raise his arm again, this time to shield his eyes from the rays of Slaybis that now beat down on its fourth planet's surface. "I hate to think what this is doing to the planet's ecosystem."

"Nothing good, I can tell you that."

"I just wish Torres could've put us down indoors."

"Look around, Hudson," Chakotay said, indicating the area with one arm. "There's not much indoors left."

Following Chakotay's gesture, Hudson took stock of his surroundings. He saw no evidence of habitation—whether people were dead or evacuated was impossible to tell—but plenty of evidence of damage. None of the nearby buildings were especially tall, but all were distressed to some degree or other: broken windows, scarred façades, missing doors and parts of roofs. What especially concerned Hudson were the cracks in many of the buildings' superstructures. Assuming they were constructed from the usual building materials—plastiform, rodinium, and the like—they shouldn't have cracked like that. *Yeah,* Hudson thought after a second, *and the* Geronimo's *hull shouldn't have buckled from the inside, either.*

Chakotay turned to Tuvok, who had taken out his Starfleet tricorder. "Can you get any readings?"

"Give me a moment, please," Tuvok said as he peered down at the instrument. "I'm afraid the tricorder's response time is not what it was."

Hudson smiled, but made no apologies. When Tuvok came on board, Mastroeni had confiscated the tricorder, and wouldn't give it back to the Vulcan until after McAdams had literally taken it apart to look for bugs, transmitters, or anything else that could be used against the Maquis. It turned out to be clean, and McAdams—a moderately skilled tinkerer—had managed to put it back together, but apparently not at one hundred percent.

Sweat was now intermingled with the rainwater on Hudson's brow. Amazingly, there was very little humidity in the air, given the recent precipitation, but the temperature had shot up. Where moments ago he had felt like he was in the tropics during monsoon season, now he felt like he was in the middle of the desert.

"I am not reading any Andorian life signs in the immediate vicinity."

"Damn," Chakotay muttered. "Did he move?"

"Unlikely. I am also not picking up any Starfleet combadges in the vicinity—however, there is other evidence to suggest that both Captain DeSoto and Tharia ch'Ren are present. I am receiving the emissions from the Malkus Artifact, as well as a low-level signal from a Starfleet transponder. Both are emanating from an area that has no life readings—or any other significant readings of any kind." He looked up. "The logical deduction would be that Tharia is, as promised, using a forcefield. However, while the forcefield is able to keep out the relatively passive signals generated by bioreadings and combadges, it cannot deter the more active signals of the artifact or the transponder."

Chakotay nodded. "DeSoto probably brought the transponder so his ship can keep in touch with him. Smart move."

"Yeah." Hudson turned to Tuvok. "How far are they?"

"Approximately half a kilometer northwest of here."

"Let's get to it, then, before the weather changes again," Hudson said as he started to walk northwest.

That hope was in vain. Before they'd gone ten meters, the temperature plummeted and the skies clouded up. The sweat and rainwater cooled against Hudson's skin. Within two more steps, the snow started.

"I suggest we take shelter until this passes," Tuvok said.

Hudson started to say that they couldn't afford to wait, but then the snow reached the intensity level of the rain—as did the wind. He also found that he couldn't speak because his teeth were chattering. So instead he simply ran toward the closest structure: what looked like a residential building.

The front door slid open about halfway, then made a screeching noise.

"The metal has been warped," Tuvok said.

"G-g-get ins-side," Hudson said, squeezing between the door and its frame. Chakotay and Tuvok did likewise—both were smaller of build than Hudson, so they had an easier time of it—and then the door shut. The building's lobby was a utilitarian affair: a square room with walls painted beige. The back wall was lined with a series of turbolifts; a few hideous paintings sat dolefully on the two side walls, broken only by a computer interface that no doubt allowed visitors to communicate with residents. A plush beige carpet took up the entire floor. Hudson decided it was the most boring room he'd ever been in.

"W-wish we'd beamed down a medikit," Hudson said, trying to warm himself with his arms and failing miserably. His hair felt odd—no doubt the water there from the rain had frozen into ice—and his skin felt like one giant goose bump. "We'll get pneumonia at this rate."

Tuvok checked his tricorder. "It is a possibility—unfortunately, this is not a medical tricorder."

Nodding, Hudson turned to Chakotay. "Have you given any thought to what we might have to do today?"

"I'm not sure what you mean," he replied stoically, not looking at Hudson.

"Yes, you do."

"All right, so maybe I do," Chakotay snapped, turning toward Hudson, his jaw set. "If I have to, I'll kill him, but I'd like to avoid it if I can."

"I know that," Hudson said, grateful that he was now warm enough that he could talk normally without forcing himself to enunciate without stuttering from the shivers. "But it's never easy to take up arms against your comrades—or your friends." He hesitated. "Last year, right after we started the Maquis, I had to face off against my oldest friend—my best friend. He was in a runabout, I was in the *Liberator*—and I realized that I might be put in a position where I'd have to kill my friend."

"What happened?"

Chuckling, Hudson said, "Actually, it was never an issue. Ben won the fight. I was in bad shape, turning tail and running." Hudson looked at Chakotay. "The funny thing is, Ben *did* have the opportunity to fire on me. He could've disabled me, destroyed me—but he let me go. He faced the test and couldn't do it. Funny thing is, I wasn't sure I would've done the same thing in his place."

"There's a big difference," Chakotay said. "I assume that 'Ben' is Commander Sisko of Deep Space 9?"

Hudson nodded.

"He's not a freedom fighter—he's just a soldier. He was doing his job, nothing more. You were fighting for a cause." He smiled. "Besides, Starfleet's always been big on the lost cause. There's no problem they can't solve—so they let you live, because they think you can be 'cured.'" Chakotay sighed. "I wish they were right, most of the time."

Hudson found he had nothing to add to that, so he turned to the Vulcan. "You picking up any life signs in the building?"

"Negative."

"Hm." He walked over to the computer interface, his clothes and hair dripping water onto the carpet. He touched the black surface, and it lit up.

"Computer, was this building evacuated?"

"Please identify yourself."

"Calvin Hudson. I'm a visitor to Slaybis IV."

There was a pause while that information was processed. *"The municipality of Slaybis Central is in a state of emergency. All citizens have been evacuated. Your presence in this building is unauthorized. Please depart immediately or this unit will alert Law Enforcement."*

Tuvok looked up. "The temperature is once again rising, and the snow has stopped. I would suggest that we follow the computer's directive."

"Yeah." As Hudson moved toward the door, he pointed at Chakotay's phaser. "Let's hope you won't need to use that—or make that choice."

The door to the building didn't open any further than it had before, but they managed to get through. At least now they knew why the capital city—*Slaybis Central? What bureaucrat thought* that *was a good name for a town?* he wondered—seemed like a ghost town: it was.

Again, the heat of the sun bore down on the city streets, melting the snow that had already started to accumulate. Now, however, the humidity had *not* died down. "This," Hudson said, "is getting tiresome."

"Isn't there an old joke about how if you don't like the weather, wait five minutes?" Chakotay said with a small smile.

"The quote is often attributed to a human author named Samuel Clemens, who wrote under the name Mark Twain," Tuvok said without hesitating. "It was an attempt to humorously convey the inconsistent weather patterns of San Francisco—illogical, as that city has an unusually even climate for an Earth city."

"Twain was big on illogic," Hudson said with a grin. "C'mon, let's move."

Why are you talking? You must destroy!

"Get out of my head," Tharia muttered.

"Excuse me?" the Starfleet captain said, a frown on his face.

"Nothing," Tharia said quickly. "There is nothing to say."

"Then why am I here?"

"Not—never mind."

Tharia started pacing across the room. The device continued to whisper in his mind. But he was having doubts.

It had all seemed so sensible at first. The Cardassians had to die, he knew that now—*knew* it, with a clarity he'd never had regarding anything in his life.

From there, he knew that all the traitors had to die: Chakotay and his stupid limitations, Elois Phifer—whose corpse he had been sure to identify—for betraying them, the people of Slaybis IV—

Why did they have to die?

Everyone must die. They must all pay for letting your mates die.

Tharia had been sure of that. At first.

No, more than sure. Certain. He had no regrets about what he did on Nramia.

. . . bodies broken, lying in the street . . .

(Don't think about it.)

Nor did he regret what he did to Chakotay and the others. They deserved it for trying to stop him. Chakotay upbraiding him—Seska actually *criticizing* him for killing Cardassians! And her a Bajoran, how could she do that?

But the people of Slaybis IV. Not to mention those farmers on Slaybis II, where he planned to go next. What of them?

What of them? Just think about revenge. That's all that matters.

"Yes. Revenge—it's all that matters."

"Revenge against who, Mr. ch'Ren?"

Tharia looked up suddenly. He had actually forgotten about the Earther captain. What was his name? Whoever he was, he had come and asked to talk—the alternative was for them to fire on him and kill him and destroy his gift.

They can't destroy me. Every method was attempted to destroy me. They failed. I am indestructible. Nothing can stop me.

"The Cardassians," Tharia said, trying to ignore the voice. "They killed my mates—took our land, betrayed us at every turn. They have to be stopped, Captain. All of them must pay for what they've done."

"I can understand your feelings, Mr. ch'Ren, but—there aren't any Cardassians here."

"No, no, there was something worse than a Cardassian here—there was a traitor. Phifer claimed to be one of us, but he betrayed our cause. He needed to be stopped, don't you understand? It's because of traitors like him that the Cardassians felt free to destroy our home! Athmin, Ushra, Shers—they're all dead because of them!"

"I understand your anger," the captain said in a maddeningly calm voice—as calm as Chakotay had been when he dared to criticize Tharia on the *Geronimo*. "But there are thousands on this planet who did not betray you. They're civilians. They're not a part of this."

He's lying. Don't listen to him. He must die with the others.

"No—no, you don't deserve to die, Captain."

The captain half-smiled. "I'm relieved to hear that. Especially since I'm the only way you can get off this world."

Tharia frowned. "Don't be insane. I've a ship."

"Not anymore you don't." The Earther gave him a quizzical look. "It was destroyed. Don't you remember?"

"We landed without incident, Captain. I will tolerate no more lies from you!"

"I haven't lied," the Earther said quickly. "Check for yourself—the shuttle you came down on was wrecked."

He is lying. Kill him.

Ignoring the voice, Tharia went to the computer from which he had contacted the Earther's ship earlier. He ordered the sensors to train in on the area where his shuttle had landed.

His antennae stood up straight on his head. A building had collapsed nearby—no doubt the victim of Tharia's own doings with the gift as he had used it to wreak havoc on this world as he had on Nramia—and horribly damaged the shuttle some time after he had taken over this building.

Tharia was no engineer. He could operate a computer with the best of them, make it do whatever he wanted it to, but he had no skill with actually putting the pieces together. That was B'Elanna's job.

But B'Elanna was probably dead now, destroyed with the *Geronimo*.

He was trapped here.

No. You can go anywhere you want, be anything you want. I can help you achieve your goal.

"It seems you're right, Captain. What do you propose?"

No! Do not negotiate! Kill him now! You can take his ship!

The Earther said, "If you turn yourself and the artifact over to us, I'll make sure that you get a fair trial."

"I can't do that. The Cardassians must—must be—be destroyed." *Yes, they must be destroyed.* "I can't allow you to take my gift from me." *Together, we will achieve your goals.*

"But there aren't any Cardassians!" the Earther said. "And you have no way of getting off this world."

"Yes, I do, Captain." Of course. It all made sense again. This Earther had to die so Tharia could take over his ship. It was simple. Why didn't he see it before?

Together, we will triumph.

Tharia unholstered his phaser.

"Drop it, Tharia."

Whirling around, Tharia saw Chakotay, along with two others, an Earther and a Vulcan, whom he did not recognize. In fact, he barely recognized Chakotay—his clothes were in disarray, his hair was wet and sticking out in all directions, and he had mud smudged on his face. He was also pointing a phaser at Tharia, as was the other Earther. The Vulcan only had a tricorder.

"You're dead," Tharia said. "You can't be real, I killed you."

"Not quite."

The Earther captain stepped forward. "Who are you?"

"My name is Chakotay, Captain DeSoto. Tharia's my problem, not yours. Your best bet is to stay out of this."

Smiling, the Earther said, "It became my problem the minute your friend started killing people. I can't just walk away from that."

"Shut up, all of you!" Tharia cried. He pointed his phaser at Chakotay. "Why aren't you dead?"

The other Earther said, "I saved him."

"Now we want to save you," Chakotay said. "The artifact changed you, Tharia. Turned you into something you aren't. I *know* you—you'd never kill indiscriminately like that. You'd certainly never leave your comrades for dead." He stepped forward. "You have to let that thing go."

Don't listen to him. He just wants me for himself.

"Shut up! You're not real!" Tharia himself was not sure to whom he directed the comment—the gift or the shade of Chakotay.

If shade it truly was. It was possible that the *Geronimo* was rescued. Yes, of course it was.

No! Kill him! Kill him now, before it's too late!

Thunder rumbled, shaking the building. The room they were in had no windows, but Tharia could hear the rain now pounding against the transparent aluminum of the windows in the outer rooms.

Tharia mentally instructed the gift to lighten up the rainstorm. He needed to think, and this noise wasn't helping.

The rain did not let up. In fact, it grew louder. The next wave of thunder was intense enough to knock all five people in the room to the floor.

"Stop it!" Tharia cried. "I command you to stop!"

"You don't give me orders, Tharia," Chakotay said.

"Not you!"

The Earther captain's face fell. "He's lost control of it."

If you will not do what needs to be done, I will do it instead.

Tharia screamed. "No! You will obey me! You're mine to command!"

"Chakotay," the other Earther said in a tone that sounded like a warning.

"Dammit, Tharia, stop doing this," Chakotay said.

"I'm not doing anything," Tharia said, running to the back of the room. He threw open a cabinet that was lodged under the computer console to reveal the gift. It still glowed green. "You have to stop doing this!"

. . .

"Why won't you obey me?"

. . .

It took Tharia a moment to realize the truth—the gift had gone silent. Whether he had lost control or not didn't matter. It had been taken away from him.

Just as Athmin, Ushra, and Shers were taken away from him.

Just as his life was taken away from him.

"Step away from it, Tharia."

The building shook again, but this time it wasn't just

from thunder outside—it was from lightning inside. A bolt smashed through the ceiling and struck the floor not two meters from where Tharia stood.

The noise from the accompanying thunder was deafening. Tharia could feel the increase in EM activity in his antennae. The noise from both filled his very being.

He looked over at the Earther captain, who had stumbled to the floor.

Then he looked over at the other three—the ones with Chakotay were fellow Maquis, probably. One of them—the Earther he didn't know—was on the ground, a wound in his head. The Vulcan had maintained his footing.

Chakotay was struggling to get up.

Rain started to pour in through the hole the lightning had made in the ceiling.

Tharia stared at Chakotay. His captain. His friend. His comrade.

His recruiter. The one who had convinced him to join his cell.

The one who told him he could get his revenge on the Cardassians by joining the Maquis.

If it hadn't been for the Maquis, this would never have happened.

The Cardassians attacked Beaulieu's World because of the growing threat from the Maquis.

Athmin, Ushra, and Shers died because of the Maquis.

Tharia found the artifact because of the Maquis.

Because of Chakotay.

"Because of *you!*" he cried, and fired his phaser at his erstwhile captain.

He fired again. And screamed again. And fired again. And kept firing and screaming. He had no idea if he hit anything or anyone, he just kept firing.

It all made sense now. There was only one way to make everything right. Only one way to end all the pain, all the suffering, all the death.

For the first time, he realized the truth—the *real* truth. Everyone didn't need to die to avenge his mates. He didn't need to join the Maquis.

For the last time, he fired his phaser.

But this time, he had it pointed at his own chest.

Still, he kept screaming for as long as he could.

He no longer felt the rain on his chest, even though he felt the pain of the phaser hit. His antennae and ears had both fallen silent. He could no longer hear his own screams.

The one thing he could feel was his sense that at last—after doing so many things wrong—he had done the right thing.

I should have died with them was his final thought before he found he could no longer see, either.

And in his mind, he could hear screams, but they were not his own. . . .

DeSoto stood upright and straightened his uniform. *Well, this has been something less than a howling success.* While he had been grateful for the arrival of Tuvok, Hudson, and the other one—since ch'Ren seemed likely to shoot DeSoto—things deteriorated pretty quickly.

He looked across the room to see rain pounding in from a hole in the ceiling. Ch'Ren, Hudson, and the third Maquis were all on the ground, getting progressively wetter. The Andorian looked dead. Hudson had a gash on his head that probably had rendered him senseless, and the other Maquis looked like he'd taken a phaser hit as well. Both humans' chests were rising and falling, at least.

That left DeSoto and Tuvok. Neither of them were armed—DeSoto had come down unarmed, per ch'Ren's instruction, and Tuvok no doubt hadn't earned enough of the Maquis's trust for them to issue him a weapon.

"Good work, Mr. Tuvok," DeSoto said. The captain noted that the Vulcan was moving closer to the cabinet that held the artifact. "Uh, what, exactly, are you doing?"

"Ensuring our safety." He seemed to toss something at the artifact.

DeSoto didn't like the sound of that. "Whose safety?"

"That of the Maquis, of course."

"The Maquis?" DeSoto *really* didn't like the sound of that. "Don't tell me you've actually gone over to these traitors? How could you, of all people, do such a thing?"

"I respectfully submit, Captain, that you do not know me well enough to make such a judgment of my character."

"We'll discuss this later. Right now, I'm taking you, your new friends, and the artifact back to the *Hood.* You'll all be taken into custody." DeSoto started to move closer to Tuvok ever so slowly—and also toward Hudson's weapon, which lay on the floor about two meters from where the former Starfleet officer had fallen.

"I cannot allow that, Captain. You are welcome to take the artifact—it is too dangerous to be allowed in the hands of any but the researchers at the Rector Institute. But you will not take us in."

DeSoto knew that Tuvok was much closer to ch'Ren's weapon than he himself was to Hudson's—and that Tuvok was a Vulcan, and therefore much faster than a human. But words were not going to win this conversation; Tuvok had either truly gone over to the Maquis, or was making far too good a show of his infiltration. Either way, DeSoto couldn't take any chances.

"Watch me," he said, and then suddenly dove toward the weapon, grabbed it, and rolled over. The idea was to then rise to his feet on the upward roll, but he wasn't as young as he once was, and he stumbled twice as he rose.

He found himself facing the barrel of ch'Ren's phaser, held by Tuvok.

"It was worth a shot," DeSoto said with a smile. "So now what, Mr. Tuvok? You shoot me?"

Tuvok looked down at the floor. "That won't be necessary."

DeSoto couldn't help but follow Tuvok's gaze, especially once the Vulcan pointed his phaser at the same spot on the floor.

He saw his transponder about twenty centimeters from his foot. DeSoto had placed it in his boot, but it obviously had dislodged when he rolled over to pick up the phaser.

Oh, crap.

Tuvok fired at the transponder. It disintegrated in an instant.

For the first time, DeSoto cursed his crew's efficiency. Not a second later, he felt the familiar tinge of a transporter beam as José Kojima—reading the destruction of the transponder—followed orders and had the transporter room lock on to where the transponder had been and beam anything there up.

In less time than it took him to complete the realization that he was being transported, he found himself on the *Hood*'s bridge. Voyskunsky got up from the command chair just as he yelled, "Beam me back!"

"What happened?" Voyskunsky asked.

"I'll explain later." DeSoto was yelling. *Of all the times...* "Beam me back, *now!*"

Kojima said, "Sir, the Malkus Artifact emissions have disappeared from the surface."

DeSoto blinked. "Dammit. Pick it up, José."

"Trying, sir."

Voyskunsky smiled her toothy smile. "Still want to beam back down?"

Glowering at her, DeSoto said, "You're between me and my chair."

"Mine 'umblest apologies, sir," she said, stepping aside and indicating the command chair with a flourish.

As he sat down, DeSoto said, "Manolet, can you get a life-sign reading from where I was beamed out?"

Dayrit shook his head. "Not reading anything, sir. The forcefield's down, by the way—but there are no indications of life." A pause. "We're being hailed."

DeSoto frowned. "By who?"

"It's a ship in orbit of the third moon—they're just coming into sensor range."

"Sir," Kojima said, "I've picked up the artifact—it's now in orbit around the planet's third moon."

Voyskunsky let out a breath. "Gee, I wonder who *they* could be."

"Baifang, intercept course for that ship, half impulse," DeSoto said in a tight voice.

"Aye, sir."

"Shields up, red alert, all hands to battle stations. Arm phasers and load torpedo bays. Can you identify them, Manolet?"

As the bridge was plunged into red lights and the alert klaxon started to sound, Dayrit said, "Configuration matches one of the ships that engaged Commander Sisko and his forces at Bryma last year."

DeSoto nodded. "Hudson. He was one of the Maquis I met down there, along with another human—and Tuvok." He sighed. "Put the Maquis on screen."

To DeSoto's complete lack of surprise, Tuvok's face

appeared on the viewer. He appeared to be standing in a mess hall that looked fairly generic. No one else was with him—a wise precaution, as it meant that no one aside from Hudson and that other human could be identified. *"My apologies for forcing your exit, Captain, but I could not allow you to take me or my allies into custody."*

" 'Allies,' huh?"

"I would have thought, Captain, that my theft of the Manhattan *made my intentions clear enough. Since it has not, let me officially tender my resignation now. I am a member of the Maquis."*

"Good. That's another charge I can add when I arrest you. We in range, Manolet?"

"Yes, sir."

"Fire phasers on the Maquis ship."

Two seconds passed, and no phasers fired. "Sir, I've lost weapons control. And shields are going down!" Dayrit slammed his hand against the console. "Dammit! I've been cut off."

Hsu said, "I've lost helm control."

"Internal and short-range sensors functioning," Kojima said, "but long-range is offline."

"Again, my apologies, Captain," Tuvok said. *"It would have been wise to change the* Hood's *prefix codes after my departure."*

DeSoto gritted his teeth. They hadn't changed them because they hadn't expected Tuvok to use that knowledge against them, or give it to the Maquis.

"Something's being transported into Cargo Bay 2," Kojima said. "Sensors are reading an explosive device!"

Dayrit tapped his combadge. "Security to Cargo Bay 2."

"Is anybody in there?" Voyskunsky asked.

Kojima shook his head. "No, the bay's empty." Then an alarm sounded. "Explosion in Cargo Bay 2! Hull has been breached; forcefields sealing it off. And sir—now I'm picking up the Malkus Artifact in the cargo bay."

"I attached a small explosive to the artifact, Captain," Tuvok said. *"I told you that Starfleet was welcome to the Malkus Artifact. That was the truth. Tharia ch'Ren did not speak for the Maquis. We have no interest in attacking civilian targets such as the two planets in the Slaybis system—or Nramia, for that matter. Nor do we have any interest in a weapon that would have such a corrupting influence."*

"You expect us to just let you go?" DeSoto said.

"Yes, sir, I do. Going to warp with a hull breach would be ill advised."

Hsu turned to look at DeSoto. "They're moving out of orbit, preparing to go to warp."

"Czierniewski to bridge. I'm negating the override of the prefix codes."

"They're going to warp," Hsu said.

Voyskunsky shook her head. "Too damn late."

Tuvok said, *"I suggest you examine the artifact, Captain. You may find it educational. Tuvok out."*

The Vulcan's face disappeared from the viewer, replaced by the Maquis ship, which went into warp.

"Czierniewski to bridge. You should have full functions now."

"Helm control active," Hsu said.

Kojima added, "I've got long-range."

Voyskunsky waked around to the ops console. "Can you pick the Maquis up?"

He shook his head. "They're not on the same heading."

DeSoto sighed. "They beat us."

Bitterly, Dayrit said, *"Tuvok beat us."*

Voyskunsky raised an eyebrow. "I'm not sure he did. He went out of his way not to do any permanent damage to us. He had access to our systems, so he knew Cargo Bay 2 would be empty. He did enough damage to keep us from going to warp after him, but that's it. And he did all of it while consolidating his cover, because I'm sure that right now his Maquis buddies think he's the bee's knees."

Dayrit said, "Commander, they'd also think that if he really did join them."

"There's one way to find out," DeSoto said, standing suddenly. "Tuvok specifically told me to check out the artifact. Has your security team reported, Manolet?"

Checking his status board, Dayrit said, "Yes, sir. The cargo bay's secure—and there's a black box sitting on the deck near the hole in the wall."

"Good. You have the bridge. C'mon, Dina," DeSoto said, moving toward the turbolift. "Let's see if he really did leave us a message."

Within minutes, they arrived in the cargo bay. DeSoto tried not to look at the big hole in the hull that made it look like the bay was exposed to space. Right now, a forcefield was all that kept that look from being the truth.

Two of Dayrit's people, Weiss and Hayat, were also present, going over the room with tricorders.

Weiss said, "It's all secure, sir—but, uh, there's something attached to the artifact."

"Looks like some kind of mini-transponder," Hayat added.

"Is that what it is?" Weiss frowned. "I'm reading a solenoid transtator. Who the hell still uses transtators?"

Voyskunsky's wide smile split her face. "Maquis who have to scrounge for parts." She knelt down by the artifact and found a small, flat, circular object no more than a centimeter in diameter. It came off the black box with no difficulty.

Hayat's eyes widened. "I'm reading an ODN chip in there."

"How much you want to bet that's Tuvok's message?" Voyskunsky said with her trademark smile.

DeSoto returned the smile. "No bet."

As they turned to leave, the artifact suddenly gave off a brief discharge of green light. DeSoto had to blink spots out of his eyes. "Report," he quickly said.

Both Weiss and Hayat examined their tricorders. "No indication of anything harmful, Captain," Weiss said.

"But the artifact's now reading inert," Hayat added.

Voyskunsky indicated the artifact with an inclination of her head. "Look, it's not glowing anymore, either. Just a plain black box." She scratched her chin. "Come to think of it, I think the same thing happened to the other two after they were separated from their users. But there wasn't anything in the records about ill effects suffered by the people involved with their mission."

Blowing out a breath, DeSoto said, "Probably just some kind of shutdown procedure." To the security guards, he said, "Stow that thing somewhere safe." Then, to his first officer, he said, "C'mon, Dina, let's see what Mr. Tuvok has to say."

Chapter Nine

CAL HUDSON FOUND CHAKOTAY SITTING in the mess hall of the *Liberator*. He was nursing a cup of tea that had gone cold and staring at the bulkhead. Hudson was standing halfway across the room from him, but he could smell the dirt and grime on his clothing even from there.

"I've gotten a request from the crew, Chakotay," Hudson said after a moment. "They've asked me to drag you—kicking and screaming, if necessary—to the cargo deck so you can get out a change of clothes."

Chakotay shook his head, as if coming out of a daze, and looked over at Hudson. "I'm sorry?"

"Your clothes, Chakotay. You haven't changed since we beamed up from Slaybis. And, after the multiple weather offerings we got, the ones you're wearing are pretty ripe. People want to eat in here, but thanks to you, they walk right out with a lost appetite."

"I'm—I'm sorry, I'll change, of course. It, ah—it hasn't been at the top of my list."

Hudson smiled. "Wasn't at the top of mine, either. But then, I was unconscious. Last thing I remember was a piece of wall falling on my head—then I'm lying on my bunk with a bandage on my head." His hand involuntarily went up to the electronic bandage that still sat over the wound the debris had made when the lightning had shattered part of the building on Slaybis.

"That's a better excuse than mine," Chakotay said with a small smile.

"I'm not so sure about that. I assume you're thinking about Tharia."

Chakotay snorted. "Gee, how'd you guess?"

Deciding to brave the olfactory gauntlet, Hudson walked across the mess hall and sat across from Chakotay. The smell was almost overpowering, and Hudson wondered how Chakotay could stand it.

"I keep going over what happened in my head," Chakotay said, "trying to figure out some way I could've changed things. If I'd just stunned him as soon as we walked in the door—"

"And if you'd missed?"

"Then I'd have fired again." Chakotay went to take a sip of his tea, realized it was cold, then put it back down. "We could've stopped him."

"And when he woke up?"

"I don't know, but he didn't have to—" Chakotay cut himself off. "I'm sick of death, Hudson. Every time I turn around, I see people dying—more to the point, *family* dying. My family on Trebus, Tharia's family on Beaulieu's, hell, even Tuvok's family on Amniphon. And it's only going to get worse."

Hudson nodded. "I know. I lost my wife, Gretchen, not long ago—not to the Cardassians," he added quickly, "but—well, I wonder sometimes if I would've done what I did if she were still alive."

Chakotay stood up just as the door to the mess hall opened again. "We should've been able to save him."

"Perhaps," said the new arrival: Tuvok. "But we were not. It is illogical to dwell on that which we cannot change."

"Maybe, Tuvok," Chakotay said, "but it's just as illogical to ignore the past when you can learn from it."

"True. However, my concern is not with the past, but with the future."

Smiling, Hudson said, "You want to know if we're going to let you join or shoot you down where you stand?"

"I had assumed the second alternative to be somewhat less dramatic than you describe, but you are essentially correct."

Hudson had, in fact, been considering that very thing since he woke up. The *Liberator* was currently on course to the Badlands in order to make sure that they had truly shaken the *Hood;* then it would proceed to a Maquis safe house to off-load Chakotay's people. Torres had made noises about having to scrounge for another ship, but her grumbling had been good-natured—she seemed to enjoy the challenges of taking clapped-out old ships and making them work. Of course, Mastroeni hadn't stopped her attempts to recruit the half-Klingon woman, but Torres was apparently having none of it.

That left the question of what to do with their apparent new recruit.

"We can't deny," Hudson said after a moment, "that you kept your word—and you definitely fought for our side."

"He and DeSoto were in the room alone together. That was a perfect opportunity to turn both of us in, and he didn't take it. Instead, he did everything he could to make sure we got away from the *Hood* safely—and gave them that damned artifact while he was at it." Chakotay gave a lopsided smile. "It's not like Starfleet isn't chomping at the bit to get both of us into a prison cell, after all. They tend to get self-righteous about people who 'betray the uniform.' "

"Betray, hell," Hudson said, his expression sour. "I've done more to uphold what Starfleet's *supposed* to stand for since I joined the Maquis than I ever did as one of their officers."

"It is my hope," Tuvok said in a quiet voice, "to do likewise."

"I hope so, Mr. Tuvok, because unless Captain Chakotay here has an objection, I think you'd be a welcome addition to the ranks."

Chakotay shook his head. "No objections here. In fact, I'd like to offer you a place with me. After all, I—" His voice caught. "I just lost a hand at operations, and I think it'd be nice to have someone in that position who was less—volatile than he was." He turned to Hudson. "Unless *you* have any objections?"

"No, that's fine. I don't really have an open slot here—in fact, I'm looking forward to getting you people off here so we have some *space* again—and I don't think Darleen's ready to serve with our Mr. Tuvok just yet."

Tuvok nodded. "I would tend to agree. Therefore, Captain Chakotay, I accept your offer."

"Bridge to Hudson," said Mastroeni's voice over the intercom. *"We're entering the Badlands. Still no sign of pursuit."*

"Good. I'll be right up." He turned to Chakotay. "Speaking of space—will you *please* go change your clothes so people don't have to stand three meters away from you?"

Tuvok added with as much emphasis as he was ever likely to use, "A most apt suggestion."

Laughing, Chakotay said, "Fine, fine, I'm going." He moved toward the door, then stopped and turned around. "By the way, when we make it to the safe house, I want to have a service for Tharia. I think it's the least we can do. Will you join us?"

"Of course," Hudson said.

"Thank you." With that, Chakotay left. Hudson's nose was relieved.

He turned to the Vulcan. "You realize there's no going back, Mr. Tuvok."

"I can assure you, Mr. Hudson, I am fully cognizant of the consequences of what I have done today. The only regret I have is that we were not able to save Mr. ch'Ren. In retrospect, I should have realized that suicide was a danger. The first person to find the artifact also took her own life when confronted with the possibility of capture."

"Even if you had anticipated it, I doubt we'd have been able to get the phaser out of Tharia's hands before he turned it on himself. Don't tell me you're having the same doubts as Chakotay?"

Tuvok's eyebrow raised. "Doubts? No. As I said, it was merely a regret. And, as I told Captain Chakotay, dwelling on regrets is illogical. If you will excuse me, Mr. Hudson."

"Of course," Hudson said.

That man's going to make an interesting Maquis, Hudson thought.

Captain DeSoto had already watched Tuvok's recording, so he instead watched Kathryn Janeway's reaction as she watched it.

They sat in the conference lounge on the *Hood,* the latter ship having returned to Sector 001 after a quick and fruitless search for the Maquis ship. *Voyager* had made it safely back to Utopia Planitia and was now undergoing repairs. Janeway had taken a shuttle to rendezvous with the *Hood* at Earth, where Voyskunsky, Dayrit, and a security detail had been tasked with delivering the Malkus Artifact to the Rector Institute. In addition, Admiral Nechayev had sent a sufficiently edited account of the mission to Gul Evek, thus keeping the Federation's side of the bargain that allowed the *Hood* access to the DMZ.

Tuvok's message was being delivered in the corner of what appeared to be a cargo bay. *"While it is true that there would be short-term benefits in turning Lieutenant Commanders Hudson and Chakotay over to Starfleet, it is my opinion that more information on the Maquis can be gathered in a long-term infiltration than any attempt at questioning the lieutenant commanders—who would not, I believe, part with any useful intelligence. In addition, with the death of Lieutenant Phifer, we have lost a long-term operative. I am the logical replacement for him, especially given the level of trust that I believe I have engendered with the Maquis. I will attempt to make regular communications to Deep Space 9 to apprise Starfleet of my progress. Lieutenant Tuvok out."*

Janeway smiled and shook her head as Tuvok's face faded from the screen. "Typical."

"What?" DeSoto asked.

"All of it. Everything Tuvok does is proper and logical—even by Vulcan standards. Notice how he referred to Hudson and Chakotay by the rank they each had when they quit Starfleet? Not to mention calling himself 'Lieutenant Tuvok.' That's his way of reassuring us—or me, at least—that he hasn't abandoned us."

"Either that or he's putting up a *very* good front."

Shaking her head, Janeway said, "No chance of that, Captain."

"Please," DeSoto said, "it's Bob. After over ten years in the center seat, I've gotten sick of the word 'captain.'"

"All right, Bob," she said with a small smile. DeSoto noticed that the smile didn't change her face all that much—Janeway always seemed to be alert, her eyes always probing. "And I'm Kathryn."

"Not Kate?" he said with a smile.

The smile widened, and this time it *did* change her face to a mischievously vicious expression. "Not twice."

"Kathryn it is."

"In any case, Bob, I've known Tuvok for a long time—he wouldn't betray the uniform."

DeSoto leaned back. "I hope you're right. 'Cause I gotta tell you, he certainly had *me* fooled."

"Then he's doing his job right," Janeway said. "In any case, thank you for showing me this. Once *Voyager*'s back up and running, Tuvok should have gathered enough intel to make the mission a success. Then we can start solving the Maquis problem once and for all."

Remembering the chaos on Slaybis IV, DeSoto said, "I hope so, Kathryn. I truly hope so. This whole mess has gone on too long as it is." He smiled. "When are you due back?"

"Tomorrow."

"In that case, can I interest you in a tour of the ship—maybe some coffee, a meal, even a friendly game of Go?"

Janeway laughed. "Nice try, Bob, but I'm not about to get hustled by a champion Go player. Besides, I haven't played in *years*. And even at my best, I wouldn't stand a chance against you."

Shrugging, DeSoto said, "Well, you can't blame a guy for trying."

"Besides," Janeway said, standing up, "since I am back on Earth, there's someone I have to go see."

DeSoto recognized the glint in Janeway's eye. He saw it in the mirror every time he was able to get back to the Rigel colonies where his wife lived. Also rising from his chair, he offered his hand. "Well, have fun, Kathryn. Once my people report back, we're going to be heading off to Starbase 96 in order to take some supplies to Brackin's Planet. But I hope to get some progress reports from you on how Mr. Tuvok's doing."

Accepting DeSoto's handshake vigorously, Janeway said, "I'll do my best. Oh, and say hi to Commander Ju'les for me when you reach the starbase."

"I will."

With that, Janeway departed the lounge. DeSoto sighed. *I was really hoping to get her into a game of Go. Need to find someone besides Dina to go up against . . .*

Dina Voyskunsky returned to her quarters after she and the security team had beamed back up from Earth. The people at the Rector Institute had been thrilled to see them—except, of course, for the wizened old Vulcan woman T'Ramir, who simply nodded. She had apparently been studying the Zalkat Union all her life, and had been trying (mostly in vain) to learn more about the Malkus Artifacts since the first one was brought back to Earth by the *Enterprise* a century earlier.

Voyskunsky had hoped to visit her aunt Irina in Estonia before they had to ship out again, but she only had time to send a quick message. Dayrit had expressed a similar regret regarding his sister in the Philippines.

As she entered, she asked the computer for any personal messages. She was off duty, so any official communiqués could wait.

"You have two personal correspondences. One from Irina Voyskunsky and one from Lieutenant Commander Aaron Cavit."

She blinked. Then she smiled and sat down at her desk. "Put the message from Commander Cavit on screen."

"Dina, it's Aaron." The look on Cavit's face was one Voyskunsky hadn't seen in a very long time: contrition. *"Look, I'm sorry about how I behaved. I wasn't expecting to see you again, and I—"* He hesitated. *"You were right, it was my fault. I'm the one who got cold feet on Pacifica. I guess I just wasn't ready to deal with what it might mean for both of us, for our careers, if we kept going the way we were going and good God, listen to me, will you?"* He suddenly burst into a smile. *"I've been in bad holonovels that weren't this overdramatic. Let me try that again."* He looked right at the viewer. *"I'm sorry. I made a mistake. Forgive me."* The smile came back. *"How's that?"*

"Better than whining," Voyskunsky muttered with a smile.

"Unfortunately, I'm stuck at Utopia Planitia for at least a few more weeks, and my sources tell me the Hood's off to Starbase 96. And once we're done here, we'll be off to the Badlands to ferret out the Maquis. But once that's done, I've got some leave time coming. The way these things usually go, it probably won't be for another month or three, but maybe we can get together—on Pacifica or somewhere else—and see if we can make up for lost time." He grinned, a facial expression she wouldn't have credited him with being capable of based on his last visit. *"Or, failing that, at least catch up on*

the last twelve years. I seem to recall your being an excellent dinner companion. What do you say? Let me know. I'll be on Mars for quite some time."

The screen went blank.

Voyskunsky stared at it for several seconds.

Part of her was sorely tempted not to respond. *Let him twist in the wind the way I did on Pacifica. Three days I waited for him to show up . . .*

Then she decided that she was too old for such pranks. Besides, much as she hated to admit it, she missed Aaron Cavit, and wouldn't mind finding out what he'd been up to.

"Computer, reply to message from Lieutenant Commander Cavit. Simple text message: It's a date."

Aidulac piloted the *Sun* through the Demilitarized Zone.

For the third time, she had failed. Again, Starfleet had managed to get there before her. She had no idea how or why the *Hood* had been able to enter the DMZ unmolested, but there it was.

At least her biggest fear—that the people who found the Instruments would use them to re-create Malkus's tyranny—were unfounded. Starfleet had, at least, managed to confiscate the Instruments before the damage they did was too extensive. Given the number of people Malkus killed during his reign, the paltry few who died on Alpha Proxima II, Bajor's moon, Nramia, and Slaybis IV were minor.

Still, the most dangerous Instrument was still out there. Somewhere. And Aidulac was quite sure that the last would prove to be by far the most dangerous.

Especially if her suspicions were true.

The one thing that was different this time was that the Instrument had been moved from where it was found.

She had never been able to examine the sites on Proxima or the Bajoran moon.

But she was able to backtrack to where, precisely, the Maquis had found the third Instrument—a moon surrounding a gas giant in the Grovran system.

The *Sun* pulled into orbit around the moon. Her scanners showed her a most uninteresting world: rocks, vegetation, more rocks. A pang hit her as she realized that it was much like the planetoid where she had lived before Malkus took her away to have her supervise the creation of the Instruments. Like that long-dead planetoid, this moon was of no interest or consequence to anyone. That was why she had chosen the planetoid then, and also no doubt why the rebels chose this moon as a place to dispose of the Instrument.

The only thing to mar the landscape was the wreckage of a shuttlecraft.

She landed the *Sun* near that wreckage. A fierce wind blew through Aidulac's hair as she stepped out, but she paid it no heed. Instead, she checked the scanner she had built into her forearm, and found an area of ground that had a higher heat index than it should.

Approaching it, she found that the area had been fired upon by some kind of directed energy weapon. It was also the spot to which the trail of the Instrument led.

Her scanner found something else, as well. It was buried beneath the rock, and Aidulac needed to use her own weapon—a laser she had convinced a friend to give her years ago—to cut through the rock to get to it.

The component was small—probably too small for most eyes to see—and green and it glowed slightly. Aidulac recognized it as easily as she would have recognized a piece of her own flesh.

A segment from the weather controller.

Even her own work was subject to the ravages of entropy, it seemed. The component was a minor one, but it probably affected the Instruments' ability to interconnect.

For the first time in ninety thousand years, Aidulac smiled.

She placed the component in a pocket of her jumpsuit and walked back to the *Sun*. For the first time, she retrieved a part of her legacy. Now it was just a matter of waiting for the final act to start.

The third planet in the Narendra system had been part of the Zalkat Union once. It was called Horbin then, and it had been used as parkland. Few visited the world, and the parkland fell into disuse. It was an inconsequential part of the Union—which was why, when the rebels overthrew Malkus the Mighty, they chose this as one of the places to hide one of the Instruments of his rule. After all, why would anyone wish to come to this place?

After the fall of the Union, it lay unoccupied for many millennia. Until the Klingons came and put a base there.

Decades passed. The planet that one government had made into an uninteresting parkland had been transformed by another into a thriving colony. Dozens of cities had been built, many thousands of Klingons lived long and fruitful lives on the world, and it had become a prosperous part of the Klingon Empire.

Yet, in the ground beneath the smallest of Narendra III's twelve continents, the fourth and final Instrument of Malkus the Mighty's rule lay undisturbed. The only clue to its existence was a mild green glow and the endless yet silent scream of the mind that occupied it.

Or, rather, one of the minds. The psionic impressions of seven others had been made on the Instrument, simply waiting for the time when it was unearthed.

Then four more were added.

This surprised the screaming mind. He had not realized that the third Instrument had been found. But apparently it had.

Still, if more minds had been imprinted, then whoever possessed the third Instrument had failed just like the first two.

And so the screaming continued. . . .

THIRD INTERLUDE

"CAPTAIN'S PERSONAL LOG, *U.S.S. Voyager,* Captain Kathryn Janeway, Stardate 48391.7.

"While our mission to capture Captain Chakotay's Maquis cell and retrieve Lieutenant Tuvok from his undercover operation has technically been a success, everything else has gone to hell in a handbasket. *Voyager* is trapped in the Delta Quadrant, Chakotay's ship has been destroyed, and several of my crew were killed when the Caretaker violently took us seventy thousand years across the galaxy to the Ocampa homeworld. We have now begun our long journey home, with members of Chakotay's Maquis cell replacing the *Voyager* crew that was lost. Chakotay will replace Aaron Cavit, who was killed, as my first officer and serve as liaison between the Starfleet and Maquis crew members. I don't know if terrorists and officers will be able to work together, but I have to give it a try if we're to have any hope of getting home.

"The details of our enforced exile are in my official

log, but I would like to take this opportunity to note those under my command who lost their lives needlessly. Cavit was due to be reunited with an old friend when this mission was complete. My conn officer, Stadi, had family on Betazed. Chief Engineer Honigsberg had been chomping at the bit for months to take *Voyager* out into space. The entire medical staff . . .

"Computer, pause.

"Dammit.

"Computer, resume.

"I will get the rest of us home, one way or another."

Part 4: The Final Artifact

2376

This portion of the story takes place two years prior to
Star Trek: Nemesis; it also takes place shortly after
the *Star Trek: Gateways* book series, and a couple of
months after the *Star Trek: The Next Generation* novel
Diplomatic Implausibility.

Chapter Ten

J'LANG WISHED HE COULD REACH THROUGH the viewscreen and rip the Ferengi's ears off.

"The marble *still* hasn't arrived, Quark. We're breaking ground on the memorial today, and I don't have my marble. Why is that?"

"Captain Butterworth's freighter left Deep Space 9 yesterday," Quark said. *"They had a couple of delays—"*

J'lang growled. "I'm a sculptor, not a navigator, but even *I* know that your space station is *not* on a direct course from the Sol system to the Narendra system."

The Ferengi seemed unimpressed. *"And if the freighter was only carrying your marble, that would be an issue, but they also supply me with various other items from Earth. There's a good number of humans on this station, and I like to give them a taste of home. That's how I know Captain Butterworth in the first place, and how I was able to get you your precious mar-*

ble. In any case, he'll be in orbit of Narendra III first thing tomorrow morning, guaranteed."

"Quark, throughout this business association, every time you have ended a sentence with the word 'guaranteed,' it has been preceded by words describing events that have *never* happened as you described."

"Well, that won't be the case this time," Quark said primly.

J'lang scowled. "I was given this commission by Chancellor Martok himself, Quark. Do you know what that *means?"* The Ferengi opened his mouth to reply, but J'lang didn't give him the chance. "It means that this could be the opportunity of a lifetime. If the chancellor likes my war memorial, then it's only a short step to doing something for the Hall of Warriors! Artists *kill* for chances like this," he said, leaning forward, hoping that the Ferengi understood that he spoke literally, "and I'm not going to let it be destroyed because a Ferengi *petaQ* was too inefficient to get me my marble on time!"

Now, finally, Quark looked concerned. In fact, he seemed to be quivering. *"Look, I want this deal to go through as much as you—I just had a big land deal get yanked out from under me and honestly, I could use the latinum. Trust me, you'll have your marble."*

"I'd better. Because do you know what will happen if I don't?"

"I don't get my commission," Quark said matter-of-factly.

This time J'lang smiled. "Besides that. Are you familiar with Lieutenant Koth of the *Tcha'voth?"*

"Sure." The *Tcha'voth* was the Klingon Defense Force ship assigned to the Bajoran sector. *"He spends an hour a day in the holosuite killing things after he gets*

off-shift, and then drinks two mugs of that chech'tluth *stuff before heading back to the ship."*

J'lang's smile spread into a grin. That certainly sounded like Koth; you didn't need chronometers on ships he served on, you just had to follow his routine, and you'd know what the time of day was. "He's also my cousin—a member of my House, and quite happy to rip off your head and spit down your neck if I ask him to do so. Do I make myself perfectly clear, Quark?"

"Oh, quite clear, yes," Quark said, nodding quickly and swallowing nervously. *"Well, if you'll excuse me . . ."* The Ferengi cut off the connection.

Of course, the truth was that J'lang and Koth hadn't spoken in years. They were only distant cousins, and the sculptor seriously doubted that he could prevail upon the lieutenant to kill a Ferengi on his behalf. *But,* he thought happily, *Quark doesn't need to know that.*

J'lang turned off his screen and turned to look outside the window of the small, cluttered office. It was part of a prefabricated structure built on this, the smallest continent on Narendra III, meant to be here only as long as it took J'lang's apprentices to construct the Dominion War Memorial and the workers to put together the other buildings that would accompany it—a restaurant, a museum, and some other things that were of no concern to J'lang.

The idea had been to honor those who died in battle defending the empire. But what Chancellor Martok had specifically requested was that it honor not just the Klingon dead, but *all* those who died in service of the fight against the oppressors from the Gamma Quadrant. So J'lang was instructed to build something that would honor not only the Klingon Defense Force, but Starfleet and even the Romulan military.

J'lang had taken the idea one step further. The memorial would consist of representations of ship captains from each of the three forces—but each would be constructed in a stone from the capital planet of each government.

The human element was proving to be most problematic. He still hadn't figured out what pose to put the Starfleet captain in. For the Klingon, he'd chosen a classic pose of standing upright and hoisting a *bat'leth* over his head. The Romulan would stand in a slight crouch and aim her disruptor forward (and if that made the Romulan stand a bit shorter than the Klingon or the human, J'lang had no real problem with that, and he doubted the chancellor would either). But what to do with the human? *Perhaps just standing there with his arms on his hips. Standing around looking foolish is what humans do best, after all. . . .*

Out the window, J'lang could see several Klingons— some civilians, some volunteers from the Defense Force who wanted to aid in the construction of this dedication to their fallen comrades—laying the triceron explosives that would be used to carve out the space for the statues. J'lang had chosen the top of the largest hill on the continent for the memorial's site. Since the statues would be west-facing, the sun would rise every morning behind the statues, illuminating the figures majestically from behind.

J'lang smiled. *It will be glorious. After this, they'll be begging me to work on the next statue for the Hall of Warriors. The inductions into the Order of the* Bat'leth *are soon, and I know they haven't chosen the sculptor for that yet. If I can pull this off . . .*

The visions of artistic glory that danced in J'lang's head were suppressed by the site of the various Klingons moving away from the blast site. Just as they did, his intercom beeped.

"J'lang," said the voice of his assistant, Perrih, *"we're about to start the blasting. Do you want to come down to the observation room?"*

"I can see it fine from here, Perrih. Tell Dargh he can blow up the hill whenever he wants." Dargh was the engineer the local government on Narendra had sent to oversee the mechanical aspects of the memorial. J'lang had found him to be prickly and irritating, with beady little eyes that never looked at the same thing for more than half a second. He seemed to have an endless supply of questions about inconsequential minutae that were not J'lang's concern as an artist. So he left Perrih to deal with him. That was an assistant's purpose, after all.

The alternative was to deal with him directly, which would almost certainly lead to J'lang having to kill Dargh, and the project was *already* behind schedule as it was. . . .

Within a few minutes, a most satisfying explosion erupted from the hill as the triceron ripped through the dirt and grass and rock, pulverizing them to their component atoms and spreading them to the wind.

J'lang had never cared much for explosions—they usually resulted in damaged artwork—but he had to admit to admiring this one. And damn his beady little eyes, but Dargh had done his job superlatively well. When the dust and smoke cleared, J'lang saw a near-perfect L-shaped hole in the hill of just the right size. Oh, the edges would need smoothing, and the surface needed to be flattened and paved, but it was exactly what J'lang needed to start with.

The other thing he noticed as the smoke cleared was the small black box.

Then, suddenly, a sharp pain sliced through J'lang's skull.

Once, when he was a boy, serving as one of many apprentices to the great sculptor Dolmorr, J'lang had accidentally turned on a welder while it was facing his arm. The white-hot agony that shot through his forearm and wrist was greater than any pain J'lang had thought it was possible to feel. Decades later, he still sometimes felt phantoms of that pain when he closed his eyes.

The agony he felt now was a thousand times worse than that.

I AM FREE! AT LAST, AFTER AN ETERNITY OF TORMENT, I AM FREE!

The voice came from everywhere and nowhere. It only increased the pain in J'lang's skull.

Suddenly, the pain vanished. And with it, most of his other senses. He could no longer feel his body around him, no longer hear the hum of the generator that kept power in the prefabricated structure, no longer smell the plate of *racht* and bowl of *grapok* sauce that he'd abandoned an hour ago but never disposed of.

He could still see, however. And what he saw was the black box. He could not control his movements, so he could not take his eyes off it.

Then, minutes later, he saw several Klingons moving as one—indeed, moving in more perfect formation than any soldiers J'lang had ever seen—toward that black box.

And all J'lang could think was that the project was about to fall considerably further behind. . . .

Patience. That had always been Malkus's watchword. He knew that all he needed to do was not rush anything, and it would come to him. Pressure brought sloppiness. When rebels started agitating on Alphramick, he simply waited for them to make a mistake. True, there was a cost in the lives of his soldiers, but they had already pledged their lives to Malkus, and he could always get new ones. But, by waiting, the rebels exposed themselves for the disorganized fools they were, and Malkus was able to crush them far more spectacularly than he would have had he rushed things.

When he had Aidulac supervise the creation of his Instruments, he did not give her any kind of deadline. He knew that in order for her to truly accomplish what he wanted, he needed to give her all the time and all the resources she needed.

He ruled the universe. He could afford to wait.

Aidulac had outperformed even Malkus's expectations. Using his Instruments, and her team's other gift of immortality, he had ruled for many ages.

Until he was at last overthrown.

Even then, those who opposed him made one fatal mistake. They had been able to destroy his body, true—though Aidulac had given him the means by which to stave off entropy, he was by no means invulnerable—but first they placed his consciousness within one of the Instruments.

They had thought this would be the worst kind of torture.

They were wrong.

Oh, it *was* torture, true. To live for so long as nothing but thought was a hellish existence.

But it was still existence. And as long as Malkus lived in some form, he knew he would eventually triumph.

He just needed to wait.

First, he needed someone to colonize the world, as these Klingons finally did. Then they had to unearth the Instrument.

As soon as they did, Malkus was able to reach out to their minds, just as the other shards of his consciousness had done with Tomasina Laubenthal, Orta, and the third being who had been enslaved without Malkus realizing it. But where the mental shadows of Malkus that inhabited the other Instruments were limited in scope, Malkus was whole in this Instrument, and his powers were manifold.

Once he took command of all the minds currently inhabiting the world now called Narendra III, Malkus went further. Eleven minds had been imprinted on Malkus when the other three Instruments shut down. He now reached out to trace those minds. . . .

The first three were Guillermo Masada, Spock of Vulcan, and Leonard McCoy. Masada's mental trail ended shortly after being imprinted, which meant that he had died in the interim. Malkus was disappointed, but such were the risks. Spock's seemed to end and then start again, which confused Malkus, but his mental impression was still strong. McCoy's was also thriving.

Next were Declan Keogh, Joseph Shabalala, Benjamin Sisko, and Kira Nerys. Keogh's and Shabalala's trails also ended shortly after imprinting, and Malkus found that Sisko's trail led to a place he could not go. It was not death—but Sisko's mind was no longer within Malkus's purview. However, Kira's impression was quite strong, and she was as easily enslaved as McCoy and Spock.

The final four were Robert DeSoto, Liliane Weiss, Ellen Hayat, and Dina Voyskunsky—but of them, only DeSoto's trail did not end. His mind, too, now belonged to Malkus.

Four slaves where once there were eleven. Pity that mortals' lives are so brief.

But it did not matter. Soon, he would once again rule everything.

He gave instructions to his four new slaves. . . .

* * *

The bar on Starbase 24 didn't have any prune juice. It was the perfect ending to what had been a most wretched day for Worf, son of Mogh, former Starfleet lieutenant commander, and current Federation Ambassador to the Klingon Empire.

He dolefully sipped the weak *raktajino* and looked over the screen of his padd, but the words were starting to blur. He hadn't slept in almost forty hours. While Klingons did not share the human need for obscene amounts of sleep, he did need to rest eventually. Sadly, he was unlikely to get much chance to do so before the conference on Khitomer started.

In the months since the end of the Dominion War, the three major Alpha Quadrant powers, the United Federation of Planets, the Romulan Star Empire, and the Klingon Empire, had mostly settled down. A few crises had threatened to break the fragile peace, but each had been solved without plunging the quadrant again into war—or out-and-out destruction—and now the three powers felt the need to sit down and determine just what the future of the quadrant would be. So ambassadors from all three governments were going to assemble at Khitomer, a Klingon planet near the borders of the other two powers, in order to try to settle the inevitable differences that had come up: protectorate worlds, former Cardassian planets that were now up for grabs, relief efforts throughout the quadrant, exacting reparations from the Breen, and a great deal more.

Worf, as the ambassador to Qo'noS and a Klingon who had lived most of his life within the Federation, had been one of many diplomats invited to attend, given his unique perspective on both governments.

Before he left Qo'noS, though, several matters had demanded his immediate attention. He had to sign off on the latest reports from Emperor Vall on taD, look over the fifth draft of the resolution between the Klingon Empire and the Tholian Assembly regarding the incident on Traelus II, approve half a dozen visas, read over an application from a Bolian opera company to tour the Empire, and several other niggling matters that had all started to blend in Worf's head.

Then he was informed that the Defense Force vessel that was supposed to convey him to the conference had been detained by an emergency. Worf's aide, Giancarlo Wu, had managed to get a Starfleet vessel to divert to the Klingon Homeworld. It couldn't go to Khitomer, but could at least drop him off at Starbase 24, which was only a few hours away by shuttle. Given that it was the nearest Federation base to Khitomer, Worf was sure he'd be able to get a ride from there.

Then another crisis reared its head, involving some Tellarites who had managed to get themselves arrested on Mempa V. It was the sort of trivial stupidity that Worf was usually happy to fob off on Wu, and indeed he did so this time as well—but it meant that Wu would not be able to accompany him to Khitomer. Worf had been ambassador for four months, and he was quite sure that he would have committed several dozen homicides by now if it hadn't been for Wu's organizational skills, cool head, and ability to deal with irritating minutiae.

So Wu went off to Mempa and Worf boarded the *U.S.S. Musgrave,* a *Saber*-class ship that was rather small and had no guest quarters. For an eighteen-hour trip that was going through the ship's alpha and beta shifts, this probably didn't seem an issue to the *Musgrave*'s captain—a polite, if terse, human named Manolet Dayrit—but Worf had been hoping to take advantage of the opportunity to catch up on sleep. Instead,

Captain Dayrit installed him in the conference lounge, and he spent the time catching up on paperwork.

On arrival at Starbase 24, Dayrit informed him that a runabout, the *St. Lawrence,* was already scheduled to take one ambassador to Khitomer, and they could take Worf as well. He still had an hour, so he headed for the bar hoping for a prune juice to settle him down.

Then again, his last trip to Khitomer had not gone as planned, either.

"Attention, Ambassador Worf. Please report to Landing Pad F. Ambassador Worf to Landing Pad F, please."

Finally, he thought. He drained the rest of his *raktajino,* placed the padd in his jacket pocket, and strode out of the bar.

As he walked purposefully down the corridor toward the landing pad, a voice sounded out from behind him. "My goodness, if it isn't Mr. Woof!"

Worf felt a knot tie in his left stomach. *Not her,* he thought. *Please let that have been my imagination.*

No such luck. Worf stopped walking and turned around to see Lwaxana Troi, daughter of the Fifth House, Holder of the Sacred Chalice of Rixx, Heir to the Holy Rings of Betazed, and general bane of Worf's existence. For a time, Worf had pursued a relationship with Deanna Troi, one of his crewmates on the *U.S.S. Enterprise* and Lwaxana's daughter. That relationship had eventually ended, and one of the many benefits to that was that there was no danger of this woman becoming Worf's mother-in-law.

As always, Lwaxana was overdressed. Worf wore a simple brown tunic, black pants and boots, and a thick, ankle-length black leather coat decorated with both the Klingon and Federation insignias, in which he hid several weapons. Lwaxana, on the other hand, wore an elaborate fuchsia dress with numerous buttons and fastenings that probably took her hours to get into. The dress was decorated with a blue flower pattern—it gave Worf a headache just to look at it. Her hair was equally elaborate, held in an unnatural pattern with a variety of pins. The grooming rituals of most Federation races had always been incomprehensible to Worf, but he found ones involving hair to be especially ludicrous. Tying his own hair into a ponytail was as far as he was willing to go to accede to that custom. Lwaxana, of course, as with everything else, took it to an absurd extreme.

Bowing to the inevitable, Worf allowed Lwaxana to catch up. *I might as well get this over with,* he thought glumly. Like most Betazoids, Lwaxana was a telepath, so she probably picked up that thought, but Worf found himself unable to be too concerned with that. His negative thoughts had never even slowed her down in the past.

"What a pleasant surprise to see you here." Lwaxana hooked her arm into Worf's and led him onward down the corridor.

"Thank you," Worf said, not meaning it, and looking at the arm as if it were a poisonous snake.

"So, Woof, you're an ambassador now. I guess we'll be seeing a lot more of each other at diplomatic functions like this conference on Khitomer."

"It would appear so," Worf said neutrally, long since having given up correcting Lwaxana's perpetual mispronunciation of his name. For lack of anything better to say, he asked, "How is your son?"

"Doing as well as possible, under the circumstances," Lwaxana said, with a notable dimming of enthusiasm. Betazed had been conquered by the Dominion during the war. In fact, both Lwaxana and Worf had both been involved in the planet's liberation a little over a year ago—Worf had commanded the *U.S.S. Defiant,* one of the Starfleet ships involved in the mission, and Lwaxana had led the Betazoid resistance movement—though they did not encounter each other then.

"How is the rebuilding progressing?" he asked.

"Slowly. I just came from Earth, actually, and had a talk with the Federation Council about it. I spent two days wrangling with Minister al-Rashan and a tiresome little Cardassian who's trying to get the Federation to commit more resources to Cardassia than to Betazed! Can you believe it?"

"No," Worf said truthfully. Cardassia was the enemy. Betazed was part of the Federation, and deserved consideration before a foe.

"Neither did I. But this Eli Gark person, or whatever his name is, he's a sneaky one," Lwaxana said, not concealing her annoyance.

Worf started. "You mean Elim Garak?"

"Don't tell me you know the little toad?"

Hiding a small smile, Worf said, "Oh yes." *And,* he thought, *if ever two people deserved each other, it is Garak and Lwaxana.*

"I'll pretend I didn't hear that, Mr. Woof," Lwaxana said testily.

Worf suppressed a growl.

There was an uncomfortable silence as they continued down the corridor. Worf was not looking forward to the next few hours. He doubted he would be able to contrive an excuse to use the *St. Lawrence*'s aft compartment to grab a quick nap—not with Lwaxana accompanying him.

"Worf—" Lwaxana started.

This got Worf's attention, both because she pronounced his name properly and because she was hesitant. He had known Lwaxana Troi for twelve years, and he would never have used that word to describe her before.

Against his better judgment, Worf prompted, "Yes?"

"You saw Odo before he—before he went home?"

Suddenly, Worf understood. Odo was the security chief on Deep Space 9; both he and Worf had ended their tenures serving there at the same time. For reasons Worf could never comprehend, the changeling and Lwaxana had formed a close friendship. In fact, they had even temporarily married—something involving the custody of her then-unborn son.

"Yes," Worf said simply.

"I know what happened. He wrote me a very nice letter before he left explaining that he was returning to the Founders' homeworld to be with his people. I know that that's what he always wanted, but I need to know from someone who saw him. Was he—was he happy?"

Worf would no sooner have used *happy* to describe Odo than he would have used *hesitant* to describe Lwaxana. But Worf had come to respect Odo during their time serving together, and while they were hardly friends, Worf felt he knew the changeling fairly well.

Choosing his words carefully, Worf said, "He was—content. He had found a mission, a—purpose. It gave him strength."

They arrived at the landing pad. Lwaxana smiled and patted Worf on the biceps. "Thank you, Worf. I needed to hear that." She extricated her arm. "I need to get back to my room and meditate before my ship leaves tonight."

"Tonight?" Worf's heart almost sang. *She's not coming with me?*

"No, I'm not coming with you. I'm just waiting for these idiot engineers to finish repairing the matter inter-flux broomihator or some other such thing on my personal transport. Then I can go on to Khitomer. I'd offer you a ride, but I suspect you'll find your companion on the *St. Lawrence* more—entertaining." She smiled enigmatically. "I look forward to seeing you at the reception, Ambassador. And good luck to you. I'm sure you'll continue to serve the Federation with honor."

Worf blinked. It was the nicest thing Lwaxana had ever said to him. In fact, it might have been the nicest thing Lwaxana had ever said in his hearing. "To you as well, Ambassador Troi. Betazed could have no better advocate."

Lwaxana's smile widened. "See, Woof, you just proved my point. You lie like a diplomat. You'll do quite well."

And with that, she turned and continued down the corridor, laughing.

Which raised the question of who it was that Worf was sharing the runabout with.

The landing-pad door slid open to reveal the inside of a standard Starfleet runabout. Two humans in Starfleet uniforms sat at the fore of the vessel, going through the preflight checklist. One turned around and said, "Ah, Ambassador Worf, good to have you aboard. I'm Lieutenant Matthew Falce, and this," he indicated the person to his right, "is Ensign Hilary McKenna." He indicated one of the side chairs. "Have a seat—we'll be taking off within five minutes or so."

Worf was about to ask if the other ambassador had reported or not when a surprisingly familiar voice came from the entryway to the aft compartment. "Welcome aboard, Mr. Ambassador."

The last time Worf had heard that voice, it was in a corridor on Deep Space Station K-7 a hundred years ago. The *Defiant* had gone after an elderly Klingon spy who had traveled back in time to assassinate Captain

James T. Kirk and restore his own lost honor. They had succeeded in stopping the spy without altering the time lines—which meant, among other things, that the person in the *St. Lawrence* had not known of Worf's clandestine trip to the past.

They had encountered each other on several occasions besides that, of course, but this was their first meeting as colleagues.

Inclining his head respectfully, Worf said, "Ambassador Spock. It is an honor, sir."

And he meant it. Like Worf, Spock had become an ambassador after serving in Starfleet, but both his military and diplomatic service were the stuff of legends—admittedly, as much due to the sheer volume of them by comparison to Worf's own much shorter career in both fields.

Indeed, the man standing before him seemed to carry the weight of his years. He was dressed in an austere black robe that covered him from neck to foot; his face—the features of which displayed only his Vulcan heritage—was heavily lined, his black hair thinner than Worf remembered it being in the long-ago corridors of K-7.

Then he spoke, and his lips rose in the tiniest of smiles—the first betrayal of the human half of his lineage. "The honor is mine, Ambassador Worf. Your accomplishments have been quite noteworthy."

"You flatter me."

"Not at all. You have had perhaps more impact on Klingon politics over the past decade than any other individual. And I speak as one who has some passing familiarity with the vicissitudes of Klingon politics."

Worf took a seat on one of the rear chairs of the runabout. "That is something of an overstatement of my accomplishments, Mr. Ambassador."

One of Spock's eyebrows climbed up his forehead as

he took the seat opposite Worf. "Indeed? Given that your actions were directly responsible for the ascents of the last two chancellors, not to mention the installation of Emperor Kahless and the fall of the House of Duras, it is, if anything, an understatement."

"I simply have done my duty."

"As have I."

Falce and McKenna communicated with Starbase Operations to receive clearance to disembark. As they did so, Worf said, "An intereresting statement, Mr. Ambassador, given that you have spent the last several years attempting to reunify Romulus and Vulcan. Some might argue that such an act was contrary to your duty as a Federation ambassador."

"And would you be among those?"

"My—experience tells me that any attempt to deal with the Romulans is one fraught with peril. I have witnessed Romulan treachery firsthand on far too many occasions—starting on the very planet we are heading toward."

Spock nodded. "Ah, yes, the so-called Khitomer massacre."

Worf tensed. " 'So-called'?"

"My apologies—I did not mean to belittle your tragedy, Ambassador."

The words were a poor attempt at soothing Worf, and he was having none of it. When he was six, he had accompanied his mother, father, and nurse to Khitomer for an extended stay. That stay had been cut short by a cowardly Romulan attack on the planet, one that wiped out thousands of Klingon lives. Worf and his nurse were the only ones who were not killed or taken prisoner. While his nurse returned to Qo'noS, Worf was raised by a Starfleet chief petty officer and his wife on Gault and Earth.

"Still," Spock continued, "the symbolism of this particular planet is potent, wouldn't you agree? The site of the first significant peace talks between the Federation and the Klingon Empire took place at Khitomer after Praxis's destruct—"

"I'm aware of the planet's history, Ambassador," Worf said testily, "as well as your own role in the Khitomer Accords. What I have to wonder is if you truly intend to represent the Federation at this conference—or the Romulans."

The runabout cleared the station and went into warp. As it did so, Spock's head tilted. "An odd accusation, given that my presence at the conference is over the objections of the Romulan senate. They still view me as a criminal. In any event, the Romulans did ally with the Federation and the Klingon Empire during the war."

"Eventually, and only when confronted with evidence of the Dominion's treachery—treachery that *we* had to bring to their attention." Worf leaned forward, aware that his voice was rising, but too tired to really care at this point. "And even so, they are demanding equal reparations from the Breen even though their losses were a fraction of those suffered by the Empire *or* the Federation."

His calm in direct contrast to Worf's rising anger—which served only to make it rise further—Spock said, "The Empire's losses were as much due to the irresponsible troop allocations of Chancellor Gowron as anything. Given that you challenged him on that very basis, I should think you'd be aware of it. The Romulans should not be penalized for that." Before Worf could respond to that, Spock held up a hand. "I do not dispute your points, Mr. Ambassador. May I humbly suggest that we table our debate until we reach the proper forum for it?"

Worf bit back an instinctive reply. *Why am I having this argument?* he asked himself. He had had no intention of engaging Spock this way—indeed, he had nothing but respect for the man, even if he personally found his mission of reuniting Romulus and Vulcan to be a useless cause that would probably do more harm to Vulcan than good.

Instead, he leaned back, again inclined his head, and said, "Agreed."

"Good. I—" The ambassador cut himself off and put his hand to his forehead, closing his eyes.

Worf frowned. "Is something wrong?"

"Just an odd—" Again, he cut himself off, this time opening his eyes and letting his arms drop to his sides.

Almost robotically, Spock rose from his chair, turned, and walked toward the aft compartment.

"Ambassador?" Worf got up and went after him. Spock had a reputation for many things, but wandering off in the middle of a conversation—the middle of a *sentence*—was not one of them. And Worf had spent far too much time serving in Starfleet to be anything but completely on his guard when witnessing such behavior.

Worf followed Spock aft to find him opening the runabout's weapons locker. Taking a tiny palm-sized phaser out of a small pocket inside his jacket, Worf said, "Move away from there, *now.*"

Moving with surprising speed for someone of his age and encumbered by so large a cloak, Spock whirled and fired a hand phaser at Worf, who ducked out of the way and fired his own phaser. It glanced off the ambassador's shoulder, but he barely seemed to notice. The hit should have stunned him—or at least slowed him down.

It did neither. Spock dove for Worf, his free hand reaching for Worf's shoulder. The Klingon tried to twist out of the way, knowing full well what Spock intended, but the crowded confines of the runabout gave him little room to maneuver, and Spock was able to grasp at the nerve cluster in Worf's shoulder even through the thick leather of his jacket.

Worf's thumb spasmed on his phaser as he passed out.

"You call this a *bed?*"

Dr. B'Oraq smiled at the wizened old human who stared incredulously at the metal slab in the rear compartment of the shuttlecraft.

"Actually," she said, "I call it a *QongDaq,* and it's good for your back."

"Good for *your* back, maybe. Me, I'll take a feather bed any day of the week and twice on Sunday."

"Most humans with spinal difficulties have them because they sleep on surfaces that are too conforming. It encourages misalignment of the vertebrae."

"Look, little lady, you rationalize your Klingon excuses for hurting yourselves in the name of honor all you want, but what it comes down to is you folks just like pain too damn much. When you get to be my age, you start to appreciate comfort."

"Most Klingons don't get to be your age." B'Oraq tugged on the braid that extended down past her right shoulder. The hairs in that braid, which was secured at the end with a pin in the shape of her House's emblem, were the only ones of that length. The rest of her auburn tresses were kept at neck level.

"Good point." The human actually let out a smile at that one, which B'Oraq took as an encouraging sign. "Still, that'd go a long way toward explainin' why the state of your medicine's still so blasted appalling."

Smiling, B'Oraq said, "That's what I'm hoping to change, Admiral."

Leonard H. McCoy let out a noise that sounded like a bursting pipe. "Don't you start with that 'admiral' nonsense. I'm just an old country doctor tryin' to find reasons to keep on goin'. The name's Leonard."

Again tugging on her braid, B'Oraq said, "I could not be so—so *familiar,* sir."

"Poppycock. We're colleagues."

B'Oraq's eyes widened. "Hardly. You are—the same as a *Dahar* master, only in medicine. I am just a humble physician attempting to live up to your ideals. To call us colleagues would be like saying a third son of a low-level House is the same as a member of the High Council."

"Don't sell yourself short, B'Oraq," McCoy said, taking a seat in a metal chair next to the bunk. "You're doing some damn fine work."

The shuttle was the captain's personal transport from the *I.K.S. Gorkon,* B'Oraq's posting. Captain Klag had generously allowed his ship's physician to make use of it to escort McCoy to his speaking engagement on Qo'noS. The shuttle's aft compartment would normally serve as the captain's cabin, with the pilot, copilot, and up to four passengers using bunks lining the walls of the hallway between the cockpit and the rear.

Sitting on the edge of the *QongDaq,* B'Oraq said, "Perhaps. And perhaps one day, I will be able to call myself a 'colleague' of Leonard McCoy." She smiled. "After all, even the third son of a low-level House may get a seat on the Council—one day. But that day is *not* today."

He chuckled, a papery sound. B'Oraq was glad the elderly human was able to travel. He seemed fragile physically, even by the low standards of humans, but his mental acuity hadn't dimmed with age. When she had asked him to give a talk on improving medical practices within the Empire to the High Council, he had happily accepted.

"May I offer you a drink, Admiral?"

"If you're gonna insist on titles, stick with 'Doctor.' Just 'cause Starfleet promoted me out of lack of any better use to put me to doesn't mean I have to like it. As for a drink, no thanks. I don't think these old bones could handle your Klingon hooch—not to mention this old cardiovascular system."

"Actually, I had something else in mind." She turned to the replicator next to the *QongDaq* and said, "Bourbon."

McCoy's eyes went quite wide at that. Smugly, B'Oraq handed one of the mugs that materialized at her instruction to the human.

The old doctor took the mug and then gingerly sniffed its contents. He looked quizzically at B'Oraq. "Sour mash?"

She nodded. "One of the benefits of studying medicine at your Starfleet Academy. An old medical-school friend gave me the replicator pattern when I saw him last."

"Good ol' Southern boy, huh?" McCoy asked with a grin.

"Actually, he's a Trill, but he acquired a taste for the stuff during one of our post-finals pub crawls third year."

Another papery chuckle. "Yeah, I remember several pub crawls like that during *my* med school days, back in the mists of prehistory." He gave the mug a look, then raised it toward B'Oraq. "Mud in your eye."

B'Oraq watched as McCoy took a sip, rolled it around in his mouth, then swallowed. He closed his eyes tightly, opened them, shook his head from side to side twice, then let out a long breath. His voice cracking, he said, "Smooth." He coughed once. "Not bad, as replicated mash goes. Course, back in my day, we made this stuff ourselves."

"Unfortunately, the ingredients are hard to come by, and I didn't have the time to acquire them and brew them before you arrived, otherwise I would, of course, have provided that."

McCoy grinned. "Don't worry about it, B'Oraq. This is as fine a gift as you can give me. 'Sides, given what I'm about to face, I might be better off with a few of these in me."

"Don't be so sure. I had expected more resistance from the High Council when I first proposed this, but they were surprisingly receptive." She tilted her head. "Then again, Chancellor Martok spent many years stationed at Deep Space 9 with access to Federation medicine. That may have colored his perceptions. Besides, the Empire has become more receptive to advanced medical treatment over the past few years, especially thanks to the war."

"Really?" McCoy asked, then took another sip. B'Oraq noted that the second swallow was less of a struggle than the first.

"It's much easier to insist that you can survive with an injury and that having it treated shows weakness when you are just fighting alongside other Klingons. But when your Federation and Romulan allies are fully recovered from more devastating injuries in less than a day, you start to learn the value of being able to return whole warriors to the field of battle."

McCoy held up his mug again. "I'll drink to that."

"After the talk, I will take you back to the *Gorkon*— you'll be able to see in person the new medical ward I designed. It's not up to Starfleet standards, of course, but we're getting there."

"That mean I'll get to meet your patient?"

B'Oraq tugged on her braid. "I'm not sure who you mean."

"Klag. I read up on that transplant procedure on your captain after you invited me to hold this little kaffeeklatsch. I'm not sure whether to be impressed or appalled."

Chuckling, B'Oraq said, "Either will do. It took me a month to convince him to even replace his arm at all. He'd lost it while winning a heroic battle at Marcan V, and you *know* how my people love their heroic battles." That elicited a like chuckle from the human. She continued. "However, I did talk him into it—but he absolutely refused a prosthesis." In a passable impersonation of Klag's deep voice, B'Oraq said, " 'It must be the arm of a warrior or no arm at all!' " Back in her own voice: "I thought I would go mad. Finding a donor that met both the necessary biological qualifications *and* his parameters for what constituted 'the arm of a warrior' was nigh impossible."

"So what happened?"

"An odd bit of luck—if you can call it that. Klag's father died. I was able to have the body preserved in stasis until the *Gorkon* could return to Qo'noS. Then I performed the procedure."

McCoy shook his head. "A transplant. What'd you do, sew it on with needle and thread?"

B'Oraq laughed. "The captain might've preferred that—without anesthetic, of course. But no, the ancient nature of the procedure notwithstanding, it *was* done with proper modern technique—and in the *Gorkon*'s state-of-the-art medical ward, not some chamber of horrors on the Homeworld. I'm hoping that each new class of ship that the Defense Force constructs will improve on my designs."

Snorting, McCoy said, "So what the hell you need *me* for?"

"Because hope isn't always enough. You are a revered figure in Federation medicine."

"Yeah, but my history with Klingon medicine isn't exactly what you'd call stellar. My most famous operation was when I failed to save the life of the chancellor that your ship's named after."

B'Oraq sighed. "Perhaps, but that was hardly your fault, and I think people know the true political motivations behind your subsequent imprisonment."

"Don't remind me," McCoy said, taking another sip of his bourbon and not even seeming to notice this time. "Took me months to stop shivering after they rescued us from Rura Penthe." The ice planet where the empire sent their worst criminals had a deserved reputation as a hellhole. Worse, he and Captain James Kirk had been sent to Rura Penthe not due to any crime they had committed, but as part of an elaborate frameup designed to prevent a Klingon-Federation alliance.

"Still," B'Oraq said, "I've seen the footage of your attempts to revive Chancellor Gorkon after he was shot. I can assure you that your efforts were more successful than any contemporary Klingon doctor's would have been. In fact, your efforts then were probably more than most Empire physicians would have done now, eighty years later."

After draining his mug, McCoy said, "Maybe. In any case, B'Oraq, I hope you succeed. And I'm—well, honored to be part of your efforts."

"The honor is mine, Doctor." She frowned. "Doctor?"

The human seemed to fall into a daze for a moment, then blinked twice. "Just gettin' old, B'Oraq. I think I'd better see just how good that *QongDaq* is on my sacroiliac."

Wincing at his pronunciation, B'Oraq said, "I think it would be best if you just called it a bed, Doctor."

"Put a feather mattress and some cushions on it, and I'll call it a bed. Not befo—"

He seemed to fall into a daze again.

"Doctor?" Now B'Oraq got up from the *QongDaq* and went over to McCoy. "Are you all right?"

McCoy made a grunting noise, but said nothing. Then he got up, went over to his luggage, and started going through it.

"Dr. McCoy, what is wrong? Can I help you with something?" He hadn't mentioned any specific illnesses or other difficulties that he might need aid for. Then again, that didn't preclude the possibility that he had them. Physicians, after all, were notoriously awful patients, and he doubted that the elderly human would trust a Klingon doctor—even B'Oraq—with any kind of detailed information about any condition he might be suffering from.

Still, this sudden total silence from him as he rummaged through his bags was bizarre—and out of character.

She walked up to him and put a hand on his shoulder. "Doctor, are you—"

Before she could complete the sentence, McCoy whirled around with a speed she never would have expected from even a Klingon of his age, much less a human, and injected her arm with a hypospray. "What are you—?"

The depressant took hold in her bloodstream almost instantly. She tried to activate the communicator on her wrist, but her arms felt like dead weight. Her vision clouded over, and she managed to somehow ask "Why?" before unconsciousness overtook her.

Chapter Eleven

"SIR, WE ARE RECEIVING A PRIORITY CALL from General Talak," Lieutenant Toq said from the operations console on the bridge of the *I.K.S. Gorkon.*

Finally, Captain Klag thought.

"He wishes the communication to be private," Toq added.

Klag couldn't imagine why that was necessary, but he was hardly about to question a general. Not even this one. "I will take it in my office."

Then he had to get up.

Not, on the face of it, a difficult chore, but one that had presented more of a challenge these last few months.

It was a simple maneuver, one that Klag had performed without a conscious thought for most of his life: brace himself on the arms of the chair with his hands and push upward into a standing position. Then came Marcan V and the crash of the *I.K.S. Pagh* that had severed his right arm at the shoulder. He'd spent several months getting used to doing things with just the one arm—and eventually coming to the conclusion that he was a lesser warrior with only one good limb.

Then M'Raq, Klag's father, died.

It had taken him just a few weeks to adjust to having only one arm after Marcan V, but it had been months since Dr. B'Oraq had grafted M'Raq's right arm onto Klag's shoulder, and still he was not accustomed to the new limb. For one thing, M'Raq was built differently from his son: shorter, squatter, and with a right arm that was three centimeters shorter than Klag's left.

So now getting up from a chair became a major production. His left elbow bent more than his right elbow in order to brace himself. And no matter how many times he got up, he always listed to the right when he rose upward. Of course, he was conscious of this, tried to avoid it, failed, and listed even more to the right when he did so.

All this was magnified tenfold when he was on the bridge. He was the commander of a ship full of warriors. He had not had a say in his command crew when he was given the *Gorkon*, and they left much to be desired—at first. But over the months he had been their leader, they had turned into a crew that Klag would match against any in the Defense Force.

They deserved better than a captain who got out of his chair like an old woman.

Sure enough, he pushed himself upward and listed to the right. He did not, at least, stumble. Taking advantage of this, he quickened his gait toward the door to his office, keeping most of his dignity intact.

I will conquer this, he thought with anger. He had considered simply remaining standing when on the bridge, but that would be akin to admitting defeat. He had not admitted defeat when facing a Jem'Hadar squadron without benefit of a right arm on Marcan V; he was damned if he was going to do it now for so simple a thing as getting up from his chair.

"Commander Tereth, you have the bridge," he said.

The crew said nothing, of course. One of the *bekk*s at the sciences station to Klag's extreme left had snickered the first time he'd been on duty when Klag rose from his chair. Klag had not seen the *bekk* since.

He had Tereth to thank for that.

There were many reasons the *Gorkon* crew had come together over the past few months, but Klag gave Tereth most of the credit. With the welcome departure of Drex—the son of Chancellor Martok, and who had inherited none of his father's honor—from the first officer's post, and with his second officer, Toq, still too new to the position to be considered for promotion, Command sent Tereth, daughter of Rokis, to be his new second-in-command.

Klag entered his office and sat in the chair behind his desk—a much less onerous task, since the ship's artificial gravity was on his side and he could simply fall into the seat without the use of his uncooperative limbs.

Putting it out of his mind, he activated the small viewscreen on his desk. The face of General Talak appeared on it. Klag controlled his reaction. Talak was of the House of K'Tal, the same House that produced Captain Kargan—*may he suffer in* Gre'thor *for all eternity,* Klag thought—the captain's hated former commanding officer. The general had the same crest as Kargan, and the same perpetual scowl, though not nearly so fat a face.

"Captain Klag. Your request to search for your private craft has been granted—after a fashion."

Klag frowned. That was unusually vague. "What do you mean?"

"The disappearance of your craft would normally not

be worth taking you off your current assignment, but it is part of a larger problem."

"It is not the loss of my craft that concerns me, General, but the loss of my chief physician, not to mention a Federation dignitary." Klag did not mention the fact that their current assignment was hardly a priority. Kinshayan pirates had been raiding the border for centuries, and Defense Force ships had been putting them down for just as long. It mattered little whether the *Gorkon* or some other ship performed this duty.

"Ah yes," Talak said with a snort, *"your 'surgeon.' The one who put that—that thing on your right shoulder."*

Talak paused, perhaps hoping Klag would rise to the bait, but there was nothing to be gained by antagonizing the general, and quite a bit to lose.

Realizing that his gambit was fruitless, Talak went on. *"As I said, there is more to this. For one, that Federation dignitary."*

Klag smiled. "I imagine Ambassador Worf has expressed his concerns with the disappearance of a Starfleet admiral?" Klag would have expected no less from Worf. The *Gorkon* had escorted the Federation ambassador to his first mission, on the planet taD, and the ambassador had earned Klag's respect during that mission—a coin Klag did not part with easily.

To Klag's surprise, Talak said, *"No, he hasn't—because he has disappeared as well. He was on his way to that summit meeting on Khitomer along with Ambassador Spock. Their runabout has also disappeared—at approximately the same time as your shuttle, from what we can tell."*

Klag leaned back in his chair and rubbed his bearded chin with his left hand. Spock was a legend, of course, for his pivotal roles in both the Organian Peace Treaty and the Khitomer Accords, though the rumors about the Vulcan's undercover work on Romulus led Klag to think the old ambassador had lost his sanity.

"There is more," Talak said. *"A Bajoran colonel named Kira Nerys and a Starfleet captain named Robert DeSoto have also disappeared—as have a trio of artifacts from the human homeworld. These are powerful devices from the Zalkat Union—and Ambassador Spock, Colonel Kira, Admiral McCoy, and Captain DeSoto all have had interaction with these artifacts."*

Though he'd heard of the Zalkat Union, he knew nothing of the artifacts Talak spoke of. "What are my orders?"

"It has been decided," and Talak's phrasing made it sound as if the decision was made over the general's head and against the general's better judgment, which pleased Klag no end, *"to cooperate with the Federation on this matter. Therefore you are to rendezvous with a Starfleet ship and begin an investigation. The High Council will not lament the loss of a tedious lecture on pointless medical procedures, but it says little for the Empire if we cannot guarantee the safety of three dignitaries of an allied power within our borders. This entire business has also thrown the Khitomer conference into disarray."*

"I'm surprised the Romulans haven't insisted on sending a ship of their own."

"The Romulans are just as happy to be rid of the Vulcan and your friend Worf," Talak snapped. *"They have no interest in pursuing this."*

Klag thought it interesting that Talak referred to Worf—a member of the House of Martok, after all—in such a way. Martok was a very popular chancellor. To go against him at this stage was tantamount to suicide, and disparaging Worf publicly was an invitation to incur the chancellor's wrath.

"The coordinates of the rendezvous and all the details about these missing artifacts are being transferred to you now. Command out."

Talak's face faded from the screen. Klag leaned forward and activated the intercom. "Bridge."

"Tereth."

"Commander, we should be receiving information on our new assignment, as well as coordinates for a rendezvous with Starfleet."

"Coming in now, sir." A pause. *"We're to meet with the* Enterprise *at Terra Galan in three hours."*

Klag blinked. He had expected the rendezvous to be somewhere closer. Terra Galan was a useless lump of rock, with no real significance beyond its proximity to the Federation/Klingon border. Neither government had even bothered to claim it. In any event, the *Gorkon* would barely make it at maximum warp. "Best speed to Terra Galan, then, Commander."

"Yes, sir."

"Out."

He closed the connection, then once again leaned back. *The* Enterprise, he thought happily. *It will be good to see Riker again.* Over a decade earlier, Klag had served with Riker on the *Pagh,* as second officer to the human's first officer as part of an exchange program. They had formed a bond during the human's brief tour, and Klag considered Riker a true comrade-in-arms. *Perhaps at last we will get to die together.*

Klag read over the records that had been sent. The Malkus Artifacts were impressive devices. They had been found within Federation and Bajoran borders, as well as in the Demilitarized Zone between the Federation and Cardassia.

The assignment of the *Enterprise* made a certain

amount of sense. They were still the cream of Starfleet's crop, and Riker's previous post to the *Enterprise* was under DeSoto on the *Hood*. Plus, of course, both ambassadors and Admiral McCoy had served on previous ships called *Enterprise*.

Klag did not know DeSoto, but he had met Kira Nerys at her command on Deep Space 9—and both of them were heroes of the Dominion War. Klag particularly remembered the *Hood*'s heroic efforts at Chin'toka. Both of them had been alone when they disappeared, the captain never returning to the *Hood* from a vacation on Earth, the colonel never returning to her station from a meeting on Bajor.

And then there was B'Oraq, his revolutionary physician. The woman who had convinced him to restore his two-limbed status, and also allowed him to try to regain his father's lost honor.

Klag, son of M'Raq, vowed that he would do whatever it took to find them.

When the *Gorkon*'s beams deposited him, Captain Klag, and Commander Tereth in the transporter room of the *U.S.S. Enterprise*, NCC-1701-E, it was only the second time that Toq had ever set foot on a Starfleet vessel. And ironically, the last one was also called *Enterprise*.

Toq was born on Carraya on a secret prison planet run by a Romulan and populated by the survivors of the Khitomer massacre and assorted Romulan guards. The two species managed to live in peace for two decades, some even having children—Toq was one such. It was not until the arrival of Worf, son of Mogh—then a Starfleet lieutenant—that Toq and the other children even knew what being a Klingon truly *meant*.

The prison planet was, as far as Toq knew, still there.

He, Worf, and the others had sworn to keep Carraya's secret, which Toq was happy to do. He was eager to forget the place ever existed. He had been content on Carraya, but he had thrived once he came to live in the Empire. The House of Lorgh had taken him in—Lorgh himself had even made *R'uustai* with Toq, bonding the young man to the House. With the onset of the Dominion War, Toq had joined the Defense Force, and his position as a member of Lorgh's House enabled him to study to be an officer.

He had risen quickly in a short time, culminating in becoming second officer on the *Gorkon* after he slew Lieutenant Kegren when the latter's incompetence endangered the ship.

Until now, though, even with the war, he hadn't set foot on a Federation starship since that day Worf brought him on board the previous *Enterprise.*

That occasion had been Toq's first encounter with humans, and he hadn't been impressed. Humans seemed—unfinished, somehow. As if the designers of their bodies couldn't be bothered to give them any actual distinguishing features. Round tiny ears, smooth foreheads, uninteresting hair, skinny bodies—and they all looked the same.

Now three of them sat around a table, and the only way Toq could tell them apart was that one of them had no hair. That had to be the famed Jean-Luc Picard. The other two were the captain's old friend Riker and the android Data, but Toq wasn't sure which was which. Supposedly the android was the paler one, but they were *all* so pale it was not really possible to distinguish.

Picard stood. "Captain Klag, it's good to see you again—I'm sorry it isn't under more pleasant circumstances."

"Such circumstances are difficult to come by, Captain," Klag said.

Gravely, Picard said, "Indeed." He indicated one of the other humans with his hand. "Of course, you know Commander Riker, and this is my second officer, Commander Data."

Good, Toq thought with relief. *Data is the one with the yellow collar.*

"Commander Tereth, my first, and Lieutenant Toq, my second," Klag said.

Picard nodded to Tereth. "Commander." Then he turned to Toq. "It's good to see you again, Lieutenant. I'm glad to see you're doing well."

"Thank you, Captain." Toq was surprised that Picard remembered him. It had been many years, and Toq had been but a beardless youth then.

As everyone took their seats, Klag asked, "Is there any new information you have?" Klag sat at the opposite end from Picard, with Tereth on his right and Toq on his left. That put Klag in an equivalent position at the table to Picard, which was only fitting.

The android replied. "Starfleet Command has conducted an investigation of both the Rector Institute and the *Hood* shuttlecraft's last known position. The evidence points to Captain DeSoto being responsible for the removal of the Malkus Artifacts from the institute."

Tereth bared her teeth. "So the captain has gone rogue."

"No," Riker said with conviction. "Captain DeSoto's one of the most stable people I've ever known. He'd never do something like this willingly."

"You served with DeSoto, didn't you, Commander?" Tereth asked.

"Yes."

"Over a decade and a half ago? And have you seen him since the war?"

"What's your point, Commander?" Riker asked, folding his arms.

"My point," Tereth said, leaning forward, "is that humans are particularly susceptible to mental trauma following war. It is one of your species' unfortunate weaknesses. It is quite possible that he went mad."

Picard spoke before Riker could say anything. "The Dominion War was hardly the captain's first military engagement, Commander Tereth. And I don't see what is to be gained by assassinating the man's character. We're here to determine *what* happened, not why."

"I agree," Klag said, which earned him a look from Tereth. Turning to her, Klag continued: "Picard and Riker know DeSoto—I know them. Their word is enough for me."

Tereth smoldered, but said nothing.

A brief awkward silence was broken by the android. "There is a much more likely scenario, which relates to the Malkus Artifacts themselves. There is a fourth artifact still undiscovered: the one that can be used to control people's minds. The range of the device is unknown, but it is not beyond the realm of possibility that exposure to the other artifacts made both Captain DeSoto and Colonel Kira—not to mention Admiral McCoy and Ambassador Spock—susceptible to it."

Toq spoke up. "In the records Command forwarded to us, there was mention of a Zalkatian archaeological dig begun a year ago on Beta Lankal. One of the records there indicated that, when combined, the Malkus Artifacts become much more powerful. If someone *has* uncovered the fourth artifact, they may be using these thralls to bring them together."

Data nodded. "That would fit the pattern, Lieutenant. May we see those records?"

Rather than answer, Toq turned to look at Klag—it was his decision, after all. Klag nodded. "We will, of course, share all data."

"Of course," Picard said. "In addition to Starfleet Command's scans on Earth and near Starbase 24, we're awaiting a call from Deep Space 9 regarding their investigation into Colonel Kira's disappearance. All that information will be sent over as soon as this meeting is finished."

"Sir, if I may," Data said. "There was a discrepant sensor reading in the data from Starfleet Command."

Picard frowned. "Discrepant in what way?"

"I cannot say without further investigation."

Tereth turned to Toq. "You shall also investigate this discrepancy, Lieutenant."

Smiling, Klag said, "What is that human saying? 'Two heads are superior to one'?"

Riker returned the smile. "Something like that." Then he grew more serious. "I suggest we split up and do our own scans where the *St. Lawrence* and the shuttle carrying Admiral McCoy were last seen."

"We should also officially declare the four vessels missing," Tereth said, "if they haven't been already. Even to civilian ships. Someone may come across them."

Klag said, "I will also alert all Defense Force ships to search for these Malkus Artifacts. I understand they give off a particular emission?"

"Yes," Data said. "Starfleet ships are under general orders to confiscate a Malkus Artifact should they detect that emission."

Riker rubbed his chin. "I think we might be better off making that a more active scan. General Order 16 says that if anyone *happens* to find it, they should confiscate it. Until we find out what happened yesterday, *all* Starfleet *and* Defense Force ships should be on the lookout for those emissions."

Picard put his hand on Riker's arm, a familiar gesture that Toq thought to be horribly inappropriate. "Good idea, Number One. Captain?" he added with a look to Klag.

"Agreed."

Toq was about to speak with a thought of his own, but before he could, a female voice sounded from the intercom. *"Vale to Picard."*

Picard tapped the communications device on the emblem attached to his chest. "Go ahead."

"Incoming call from Commander Vaughn on Deep Space 9, sir."

Turning his chair to face the viewer behind him, Picard said, "Put him through, Lieutenant."

The viewer flickered, changing from a simple display to that of a human face. He looked just like all the others to Toq, though this one had a beard.

"Jean-Luc, we simply have to stop meeting like this," the human said with a smile.

Toq shook his head. *What is it about humans?* Toq wouldn't have minded their obsession with humor at odd times, if the attempts were actually funny.

"Such is the nature of our business, Elias, sad to say," Picard said. "I believe you know Captain Klag?"

"Of course," the human said with a simple nod to the captain, who returned the gesture.

"What news do you have for us?"

"Nothing good, I'm afraid. There's too much traffic between Bajor and the station to filter out the warp signature of the Rio Grande from all the other ships that went back and forth yesterday. We're questioning some of the ship captains and going over the sensor data.

That's being forwarded to you. Oh, and we found an odd sensor reading that we haven't been able to nail down."

Picard nodded. "Starfleet Command found something similar on Earth."

"In the meantime, I'm going to take the Defiant *out to search the area, try to find the runabout's warp signature. We'll keep you posted."*

"Excellent. Picard out."

At almost the precise moment that the screen went blank, the Vale woman's voice came over the intercom again. *"Bridge to Picard. Sir, we've got another transmission, this time from Commander Buonfiglio on the* Hood."

"Put it through," Picard said.

Yet another indistinguishable human face appeared on the viewer.

"Captain Picard, I'm contacting you to let you know that the Hood *is at your disposal."*

Frowning, Picard said, "I was told that the *Hood* was assigned to Sector 817."

"We were, but I managed to talk Admiral Koike into cutting that assignment short. He then told us to contact you—said you were handling the investigation." The human's eyes seemed to blaze with an almost Klingon-like fury that Toq admired. *"That's our captain who's gone missing, sir. We're not about to sit around mapping quasars. We want to help."*

Toq saw this as the perfect opening for what he had been about to say when Commander Vaughn called. "Sir, there is, perhaps, something the *Hood* might be able to accomplish."

All eyes at the table turned to Toq—even that of the human on the viewer. Toq turned to Klag, who nodded his approval for Klag to continue.

"It is possible that the location of the fourth artifact

can be determined using the locations of the three previous artifacts as a base."

The android pursed his lips. "All indications are that the artifacts were hidden at random points on the outskirts of what was then Zalkatian territory, Lieutenant."

"There still could have been a pattern—even an unconscious one," Toq said stubbornly.

"It is worth looking into," Tereth said, and Toq was grateful for the implied approval.

Picard nodded. "The location of the fourth artifact is a likely place for the missing people to have gone. Very well. Commander Buonfiglio, your assignment is to try to locate the fourth artifact."

Data added, "You will need to compensate for stellar drift. The calculations will be imprecise, as we do not know the exact date when the artifacts were hidden."

Buonfiglio smiled. *"We'll figure it out, Commander. And thank you, Captain. We lost a lot of good people during the war—including my predecessor as first officer. We're damn well not going to let them take our captain from us, too. Hood out."*

Again, the screen went blank. Tereth gave Toq an approving look, which Toq basked in.

Passing an intense gaze around the table, Picard asked, "If there is nothing else?" No replies were forthcoming. "Very well, then, let us make it so."

It was even harder to get out of the irritatingly soft and decadent Starfleet chair than it was any of the chairs on the *Gorkon*. But somehow Klag managed it. And he didn't even stumble.

To Tereth, he said, "Wait for me. I will be along shortly."

Tereth's eyes widened, but she said nothing and simply left with Toq.

As the three humans moved toward the other door, Klag said, "Riker. I would speak with you."

Riker looked to Picard, who gave a brief nod. Picard and Data then exited, leaving Klag and Riker in the room together.

Smiling, Riker said, "Seems every time I see you, Klag, you've got a different number of arms."

Klag returned the smile. "It is good to see you again, Riker—even if you insist on remaining beardless."

"Same here, Klag." Riker rubbed his smooth chin. "As for the beard—for the time being, at least, it's still a thing of the past."

Throwing his head back, Klag laughed. "I will take that as an encouraging sign."

"So where'd the arm come from?"

"I do promise, my friend, that when this is all over, I will tell you the full story over a case of bloodwine, but for now— Do you remember what I told you all those years ago on the *Pagh* about my father?"

Nodding, Riker said, "You said he was on Qo'noS. 'Waiting for death.' "

"His wait is now over." He held up his right arm. "This is all that remains."

Riker started. "You mean—that's—" He shook his head. "I have to admit, Klag, I'm confused. That's not biosynthetic?"

Klag didn't even try to hide his distaste at the very thought. "Of course not. I would never attach a machine to my shoulder and call it my arm. No, I have decided to restore my father's honor in a way that he refused to: by living on in his son."

"An interesting solution," Riker said slowly. "How long have you had it?"

"Dr. B'Oraq performed the procedure approximately three weeks after the last time we saw each other." Klag placed his right hand on Riker's left shoulder. "As I said, it is a long story—and if we survive this mission, I shall tell it." Then he smiled. "And if we do not, we will at last have the chance to die together."

Riker's face split into one of those foolish human grins of his. "I look forward to either one, Captain."

"As do I, my friend—as do I." He let out a quick breath. "And now I must go. We have people to find—or perhaps their deaths to avenge. Either way, we go to glory. *Qapla'*, Riker."

Riker nodded. *"Qapla'*, Klag."

Klag left the observation lounge then, content. Riker was one of the few people who knew the whole story about M'Raq, and he deserved to know the details regarding his new right arm now.

He arrived at the transporter room to find Tereth and Toq waiting for him, along with the *Enterprise*'s transporter operator and a security guard.

"Your business is concluded, Captain?" Tereth asked.

Klag simply nodded and stepped onto the platform. His first and second officer did likewise. To the operator, he said, "Energize."

Chapter Twelve

THE LAST OF MALKUS'S SLAVES FINALLY ARRIVED.

Robert DeSoto had had the farthest to come, and the most to do before his arrival. His was by far the most important task: he had to bring the other Instruments.

Now he was here.

Now all the pieces would come together.

Now the campaign could truly begin.

Even Malkus's great power was limited, after all. He was able to control the entire population of Narendra III, but not the occupants of the ships in orbit as well. So he had several hundred Narendrans place themselves into confinement—an enclosed sporting arena on the planet's largest continent served the function; the thralls created a forcefield to keep everyone in—and then he loosed control of their minds.

Then he took command of the four Klingon Defense Force ships in orbit, as well as a human freighter that was bringing supplies of some kind.

Soon thereafter, Leonard McCoy and Spock of Vulcan arrived. They had had company in their conveyances—three drugged Klingons with McCoy and a Klingon and two humans, all victims of some kind of nerve damage, with Spock—and Malkus had them imprisoned in McCoy's conveyance, after having all the ship's power neutralized and a forcefield placed around it.

Kira Nerys arrived alone, and then, finally, DeSoto came with the other Instruments.

Malkus knew that the wind was blowing through this piece of a hill that had been excavated by the Klingons only because he could feel the wind blow through the hair of his four thralls, but he could not feel it himself. If his thralls were cold, Malkus did not permit them to show it. They simply stood obediently, awaiting instruction, hands at their sides. In front of DeSoto was a sack containing the other three Instruments.

Bring them to me.

DeSoto picked up the sack and walked over to where his Instrument sat on the cold ground of Narendra III.

Put the Instruments together. Then my power truly shall be an awesome thing to behold.

Kneeling down, DeSoto fit one Instrument next to Malkus's. The two sides of the Instruments came together as if magnetized.

Malkus felt the power surge through him.

Then DeSoto fit another onto the side perpendicular to the one Malkus's Instrument was attached to. Again, they came together, and again, Malkus felt the power sing within him. Aidulac and her team had done their job *so* well. Soon, his power would be all-encompassing. No one would be able to resist him—none could escape his mental domination; he could infect an entire world with the adrenal virus, not just a few hundred; and he could destroy suns with the beam of force.

The unthinkable happened when DeSoto moved to attach the final Instrument into the corner that would fill out the Great Rectangle. A much less pleasant surge went through Malkus—feedback on an incredible scale. If the other two attachments were like magnets coming together, the final Instrument repelled the other like magnets of the same pole.

Malkus had thought himself beyond feeling pain, but he was wrong.

That pain was transmitted to his thralls, as all across the planet and in orbit, thousands of beings screamed in agony.

The moment passed, then, and Malkus surveyed the ground before him. The four thralls had collapsed to the ground in great pain. One of them—McCoy—was frail and had difficulty getting back up, but the others rose to their feet with little difficulty.

Three-quarters of the Great Rectangle was assembled, at least. His powers *had* been boosted—his control was even greater. To test it, he infected all those imprisoned in the sports arena on the largest continent with the adrenal virus. They would die before long. In fact, knowing this species, they would probably react to the heightened adrenaline levels by massacring each other long before the virus did its work.

But something was wrong with the last Instrument. And he could not inspect it for himself.

Of his four thralls, only Spock had had any opportunity to study the Instruments, so Malkus instructed him to examine it. Malkus suspected that there was a flaw in it, since he had not been able to feel when that particular Instrument had been uncovered. According to DeSoto's memories, an Andorian named Tharia ch'Ren had used it to sow chaos in a then-disputed region of space. Malkus wished he had been able to see the destruction that had been wrought in his name.

Spock hesitated. *Examine the Instrument!* Malkus mentally bellowed, and this time the thrall obeyed.

It was odd that the half-breed had been able to hesitate so. Malkus's control should have been complete. Perhaps that feedback was worse than he thought. . . .

"There is a flaw," Spock said, and with the half-breed's eyes, Malkus saw that he was correct. There was a small opening in one of the corners of the Instrument, virtually undetectable unless one was actively seeking it out—he was glad he had chosen the half-breed Vulcan, as his eyesight was superior to that of the two humans or the Bajoran.

Kira had a scanning device in her possession, and Malkus instructed her to use it on the Instrument.

As he had surmised, there was a component missing.

Unfortunately, a scan of DeSoto's memories showed that the human captain did not know precisely where the Instrument had been found. The best it could be narrowed down to was a particular area of space.

Worse, it was an area of space that was currently politically unstable: on the border between a once-great power that had recently lost a war and a still-great power that had won it.

He had to have the component.

Of the four thralls, Kira was by far the most skilled pilot, and she also knew the region of space well. He instructed her to take one of the conveyances—the one marked with the name *St. Lawrence*—and travel to that region of space to find the component.

A part of Malkus bridled under the delay, but it was a small part. Patience. That was, and always would be, his greatest asset. He had waited this long, after all. The time it would take Kira to find the last component and complete the Great Rectangle was infinitesimal by comparison.

Soon . . .

A confusing mass of light and sound assaulted B'Oraq as she regained consciousness. Half-formed noises and blurred images started to slowly coalesce into something she could justifiably interpret as real or familiar— up to and including a dull ache in the top of her skull.

I truly hate being sedated, she thought. The curse of being a physician was that she knew precisely what the drugs did to her and what the potential long-term effects were, so she was hyperaware of the precise damage to her bloodstream—and, thanks to the headache, her cranium—caused by the sedative that Admiral McCoy had given her.

McCoy. It was absurd on the face of it. Why would a century-and-a-half-old human in the middle of a shuttle journey from the base on Tynrok to Qo'noS subdue the doctor who had invited him in the first place?

"Are you all right, Doctor?"

Finally, B'Oraq focused on what it was her eyes told her, especially since she recognized the voice—which matched the face that stood over her prone form, looking vaguely concerned.

"Am—Ambassador Worf?"

"Yes."

"What are you doing here? How did you get on board?" She sat up, which only made her headache worse. She had been lying on the very *QongDaq* that McCoy had been whining about.

"I do not know," Worf said. "I was in a runabout en

route to Khitomer when Ambassador Spock subdued me with the Vulcan neck attack. I awoke on this shuttle."

"I need to check on the pilots—" She started to get up from the *QongDaq,* but Worf put a restraining hand on her shoulder.

"They are both fine—as are my pilots. They are attempting to dismantle the forcefield that surrounds the runabout."

She got up anyhow, despite the ambassador's hand. "Where are we?"

"The shuttle's systems are offline. However, according to the readings we have been able to obtain with hand scanners, we are on Narendra III."

B'Oraq shook her head in confusion. "Narendra III? Why would McCoy bring us here?"

"I do not know," Worf repeated.

"Didn't Spock and McCoy serve together in Starfleet?"

Worf nodded. "For many years on the *U.S.S. Enterprise.*"

A half-remembered history course came back to her. "And the *Enterprise* was destroyed at Narendra III. Perhaps this is connected?"

"Unlikely," Worf said. "The *Enterprise* that sacrificed itself on this world was not the same one that the ambassador and the admiral served on." He took a breath. "If you are all right, Doctor, I will continue to aid the others in attempting to bypass the forcefield."

"Of course. I'll—I'll help."

B'Oraq had expected some kind of objection, but the ambassador simply nodded, and they both exited the aft chamber of Klag's personal craft and went to the fore. She found herself admiring the ambassador. She had only met him once before, when the *Gorkon* brought him to his mission on taD, but she had had very little interaction with him then. *He's quite attractive,* she thought. *And if memory serves, his mate died during the war. Perhaps when this is over . . .*

She cut the thought off, filing it away for later use, assuming they got out of whatever mess McCoy had put her into.

She saw her two pilots—Davok and G'joth—and two humans in Starfleet uniforms all bent over a console.

Upon Worf and B'Oraq's entrance, the human male stood up. "The forcefield's definitely being powered from the outside, sir. And all this ship's systems are completely dead."

B'Oraq looked over at the viewport. She hadn't even realized that the only light source in the aft compartment had come from the viewport in there, and now she realized the same was true of the flight compartment up front. When night fell on Narendra III, they'd be plunged into darkness. *Although,* she thought, *there was light in the corridor, too.* She then inhaled; the air didn't seem to be stale. "Is life-support also cut off?"

G'joth said, "Yes, ma'am. However, the forcefield is air-permeable, and the rear hatch is still open."

That explained the light in the corridor—she had only to have looked behind her to have seen that.

"How soon until sunset?" Worf asked.

Davok answered. "Five hours."

Nodding, Worf said, "Then we have that long to come up with a way to overload the forcefield. I will need all the weapons on board this ship, and any handheld devices—scanners, communicators, anything with an independent power source."

"What are you planning?" B'Oraq asked.

Before Worf could answer, the human female said,

189

Keith R.A. DeCandido

"You want to try to create a pulse to knock out the force-field?"

"That is my intention, Ensign McKenna."

Making a snorting noise, Davok said, "That may work on Starfleet forcefields, but these are Klingon fields. They are made of sterner stuff."

"I would suggest, *bekk,* that you hope your assumption is incorrect if you wish to get out of here."

Davok snarled, but said nothing.

The five of them worked, cannibalizing anything they could lay their hands on—even some of the dead equipment from the shuttle itself. B'Oraq's medical equipment had been removed—along with the shuttle's armory stores, though Davok, G'joth, and Worf all carried weapons on their persons that had not been taken—so she felt particularly helpless. Her technical skills were nonexistent—that's what engineers were for. Her only use would be if someone was injured. *And then what? I can tell them to put pressure on their wound or watch helplessly if they need more than that. I have no bandages, no scanners, no alcohol—*

Suddenly, a thought occurred. She went back into the aft compartment, and found what she had hoped would be under the *QongDaq:* half a case of bloodwine.

Worf had followed her. "What did you find?"

"Bloodwine. I'm attempting to assemble what medical equipment I can, and this is the closest to a disinfectant we have."

The ambassador looked pensive. "We may be able to use that as well—for weaponry."

B'Oraq frowned. "You're going to drink your enemy to death?"

"No." Worf almost smiled.

He was remarkably taciturn for a Klingon. She won-

190

dered why that was. *A by-product of living among humans, no doubt,* she thought. Having lived among them herself during her time at Starfleet Medical, she knew how fragile they could be—most were physically incapable of handling Klingon passion.

He continued. "Have you ever heard of a human weapon called a Molotov cocktail?"

"Uh, no."

"It involves lighting a fire on a rag attached to the neck of a bottle of alcohol."

Understanding, B'Oraq nodded. "Of course. You get a fire grenade."

"Of sorts, yes. Since we have needed to use the weapons to power our—device."

Now B'Oraq smiled. " 'Device'?"

"We have yet to come up with a name for it," Worf said dryly. "Lieutenant Falce wishes to call it 'Fred.' "

"As good a name as any," B'Oraq said with a shrug.

"I prefer more—direct terms."

"Yes, but 'forcefield overloader' doesn't have much poetry to it."

"True. Shall we return to the fore?"

"I will be right there," she said. "I want to see if there is anything else I can use in case someone—"

A scream came from the fore compartment.

B'Oraq sighed. "Gets hurt."

Both doctor and ambassador ran back up front to find the human male—what was his name? Falce?—on the deck convulsing.

The woman—McKenna—said, "There was feedback—*somebody* didn't align the circuits properly." This last was said with a look at Davok.

Predictably, Davok responded by unsheathing his *d'k tahg.* "Are you accusing me of something, human?"

B'Oraq knelt down beside Falce. He was a young human of considerable height for his species—which made him average by Klingon standards—with close-cropped black hair. At present, all that hair was standing on end, thanks to the shock he'd received. B'Oraq felt naked without her scanner, but the galvanic response of Falce's skin was already lessening. She suspected this was an intense, but brief, surge of electricity through his system.

"What—what—what—what happened?" Falce managed to ask.

"This idiot didn't align the circuits the way he was supposed to," McKenna said.

"That is enough, woman!" Davok cried, and lunged at McKenna with his blade. G'joth made no move to stop him, but simply stood smiling.

Worf started to move to intercept the *bekk,* but before he could, McKenna herself deflected the attack and, in one smooth motion, relieved Davok of his *d'k tahg.* Then she twisted his arm around to his back, immobilizing him. It looked to B'Oraq like a poorly executed *mok'bara* maneuver—probably something from some human martial art.

Then she threw Davok to the floor. G'joth bent over, picked up Davok's *d'k tahg,* and handed it to his fellow *bekk* with a smile. "I think you dropped this, Davok."

Growling, Davok snatched the blade and started to get up, when a deep voice rang out in the shuttle.

"Enough!" It was Worf. "If you wish to squabble like children, do it another time! We have *work* to do!" In a quieter voice, he said to Davok, "If you wish to challenge Ensign McKenna, do so *after* the crisis has passed. But *not* now."

"When a woman spreads lies, there is *always* time for a challenge!"

192

Worf then grabbed Davok by his chestplate and pulled him close with one hand. With the other, he held the device that they had been working on. B'Oraq hadn't even noticed Worf picking it up.

"You were aligning these circuits when I went aft moments ago. They are now misaligned, and Lieutenant Falce is injured. Did she spread lies or simply state facts?"

Davok's face contorted, but he said nothing.

Worf let go of him and turned to B'Oraq. "How is he?"

"I think he'll be fine." B'Oraq hoped her voice carried more confidence than she felt. "He needs to take it easy for a bit—and stay away from any live current—but he should recover."

"Good." He turned to the others. "We will finish this so we can overload the forcefield and leave this shuttle. Then we will find who has done this to us and we will defeat them. Personal issues can wait. Am I understood?"

"Perfectly," G'joth said jovially and with a large grin.

"Understood, sir," McKenna said.

Davok said nothing. Worf turned to him. "Am I understood?"

"You don't have any authority over me, *petaQ*. You are a traitor to the empire twice over who gave up a life of glory to be an ambassador of fools. I will not follow your orders."

"Very well," Worf said.

Then he reached into an inner pocket of his jacket, took out a tiny hand phaser, and fired it on Davok, who collapsed to the deck.

B'Oraq dashed over to the fallen *bekk*. "It was on stun," Worf said. The doctor checked Davok over and saw that he showed all the outward symptoms of a phaser blast on the stun setting—which meant that he'd sleep not-very-peacefully and wake up at some point in an even worse mood.

But that was for later. "I take it," she said, "that you figured stunning him was better than his getting in the way?"

Worf nodded. "Something like that."

"Good plan," G'joth said. "Davok is not a true warrior. He is simply a boor. Shall we continue working? I believe we should start by realigning these circuits."

"I like that plan," Falce said, sitting up and moving over to the workstation they had set up. Looking at Worf, the lieutenant asked, "By the way, Mr. Ambassador—how many weapons you have on you?"

Again, the not-really-a-smile. "Enough."

While the quartet worked, B'Oraq picked Davok up—not making any effort to be gentle—and laid him down on the *QongDaq* in the rear. With the power out, she couldn't seal the room, but at least he'd be out of the way there.

"Doctor," McKenna said when she came back to the fore, "this thing is set to give off a level-four nelaron pulse. Will that have any negative impact on us?"

B'Oraq thought a moment. "For how long?"

Falce said, "As long as it takes to bring the forcefield down."

Closing her eyes, B'Oraq juggled figures in her head. Then she opened them. "At level four, we should be fine as long as you don't go over five minutes."

G'joth laughed a hearty laugh. "That is hardly an issue. This thing will burn out after three minutes."

"In that case, Ensign, I'd say no negative impact whatsoever." B'Oraq smiled.

A few minutes later, Worf announced that they were ready. B'Oraq noticed that the phaser Worf had used on Davok was now part of the device, as well.

McKenna placed the device—which looked like

nothing else to B'Oraq but a piece of surrealist sculpture she'd seen on Earth—next to one of the bulkheads. The forcefield went all around the ship, so the device could apparently be placed anywhere.

"Activating nelaron pulse—now."

On *now,* McKenna touched a control. A low-level hum started to build in intensity.

Forcefields were generally only visible when they were interfered with: when they turned on, when they were turned off, and when someone or something touched them. So when B'Oraq saw a flicker in the field, she felt a similar flicker of hope.

Then the forcefield crackled and went offline.

Half a second later, the device that they had constructed exploded in a shower of sparks and a small fire.

G'joth immediately reached for the fire extinguisher that sat under the copilot's seat and used it to put the small fire out. The chemicals probably weren't good for the device, but an explosion was far worse.

"Well, the good news," Falce said, "is that we got the field down. The bad news is that there's no way in hell we'll be able to reconstruct this thing—and we lost some of our most potentially useful equipment—including all our weapons."

B'Oraq smiled grimly. "Isn't there some kind of human expression about lemons and lemonade?"

"What is a lemon aid?" G'joth asked. "For that matter, what is a lemon?"

"A foul drink made from a foul fruit." With a more playful smile at McKenna and Falce, B'Oraq added, "No surprise from a race that can't even handle bloodwine."

"Hey, I like bloodwine just fine, thanks," Falce said,

returning the smile. "It makes a dandy lubricant when I have engine trouble."

"Enough," Worf said, though in a gentle voice. "Let us see what we can find outside." He turned to B'Oraq. "Doctor, it might be best if you remained behind."

"I can take care of myself, Ambassador. And I want to know what is going on here, and I can't very well learn that sitting here."

"You are just a doctor," G'joth said dismissively.

"I can use my *d'k tahg* just as well as you can, G'joth. Better, probably, since I'm trained in, shall we say, surgical strikes?"

McKenna snorted. Falce tried to hide a grin.

G'joth stared at her for a second, then burst into laughter. "Very well, Doctor. We shall face—whatever it is that has taken us together."

Nodding, Worf said, "Let us proceed."

B'Oraq was glad no one had argued. On top of everything else, she had no desire to be alone in the shuttle when Davok woke up.

Worf led them out through the open—and now usable—rear hatch. Behind him were Falce and McKenna, then B'Oraq, with G'joth bringing up the rear.

PAIN!

The moment they were all out of the shuttle, she felt intense pain in her skull that made her earlier headache seem meaningless.

As she fell unconscious for the second time in as many days, she decided that staying in the shuttle might not have been such a bad idea. . . .

Chapter Thirteen

COMMANDER TERETH GAZED OVER THE BRIDGE of the *Gorkon* and was content.

She had requested this posting the instant she knew that it was available. Tereth had gone far in her career because she had always had a good instinct for picking winners. It had been a necessary survival skill. The House of Kular was not an especially powerful one when Tereth was a girl, and she was the only child left. Her parents had hoped she would mate well and bring the House glory that way, but she had been mated twice to men who subsequently died before they had a chance to forge a path of honor that would bring Kular to greater glory.

But neither of those mates had made her crest ache. They were adequate *par'machkai,* but nothing spectacular.

So, though her doddering father was the ostensible House head, she took over running the House herself—behind the scenes, of course, since women were not permitted to be House heads without special dispensation from the High Council, which Kular was hardly in a position to get.

When Gowron—an outsider and political agitator—campaigned to be considered a worthy successor to the aging Chancellor K'mpec, Tereth had insisted that Kular back him, even though Duras—a councillor from a most influential House—seemed the favorite. Her parents had argued, but she insisted. Besides, their debts were huge, their prospects growing dimmer with each turn. They had very little to lose.

Sure enough, Gowron eventually became chancellor, Duras died in disgrace, and the House of Kular reaped the benefits. Gowron forgave many of Kular's debts, paved the way for others to be easily repaid, and also sponsored Tereth's application to become an officer in the Defense Force.

Since then, she had flourished. She had served with Captain Akhra when he took the Cardassian world of Hranish. Given the opportunity to serve directly under General Talak, she chose instead a less prestigious post with Captain Huss as part of the general's armada. Once again her instincts proved prophetic: Huss was soon inducted into the Order of the *Bat'leth*, then went on to win several major campaigns against the Dominion.

Her crest ached again when she encountered Klag on Qo'noS when the latter was recovering from Marcan V. She kept an eye on him, and he soon was given one of the mighty *Qang*-class ships. He, too, was destined to join the Order, and within a month of his shakedown cruise, he had an opening for a first officer and no viable candidates on-ship.

As with so many others Tereth had chosen as patrons,

Klag seemed odd on the face of it. He had served on the *Pagh* for an absurdly long time without promotion or attrition, and even though he was rewarded for his actions on Marcan V, he was also given no say in his own command crew. His exploits to date were satisfactory, but he had won no great victories, defeating only simple foes—Kreel, Kinshaya pirates, *jeghpu'wI'* rebels. Still, Tereth's instincts had not failed her yet.

The *Gorkon* pilot, a newly assigned youth named Vralk, recently promoted to lieutenant and still with a sad excuse for a beard dirtying his face, said, "We are at the last known position of the captain's shuttle, Commander."

"Full stop." Tereth strode to her position on the captain's right. To Toq, who stood at the operations console behind the captain's chair, she said, "Report."

"I am picking up the shuttle's warp signature, Commander," Toq said. "Its heading is 156 mark 7—right on course for Qo'noS. They were traveling somewhere between warp five and warp seven-point-five."

Tereth nodded and turned to Vralk. "Set course 156 mark 7, execute at warp five."

Vralk acknowledged the order and set a course.

"Toq, inform me if the warp signature changes."

Within a few minutes, Toq said, "Warp signature lost, Commander."

That was fast, Tereth thought. "Feed the coordinates where you lost it to Lieutenant Vralk. Bring us to that position and then full stop, Lieutenant."

Both Toq and Vralk acknowledged and carried out their orders.

At the coordinates, Vralk said, "All stop, Commander."

Tereth got up and walked over to the operations console. "Toq?"

"I have the signature, Commander." He looked up from his readings. "The heading is 211 mark 1."

Vralk turned around to look at Toq. "That brings them right to the Laktar system."

Tereth blinked. The Battle of Laktar was one of the more vicious skirmishes of the Dominion War. Captain Huss's fleet had arrived at the tail end of it, but the battle was over by then: it was a victory for the Empire, but the radiation that infused that system from the sheer volume of destroyed ships made any kind of sensor scan impossible.

Anticipating Tereth's question, Toq said, "The warp signature goes right through the radiation, Commander. We cannot track them any farther."

Tereth muttered a curse.

"Something else, Commander," Toq said. "The discrepant reading that was found on Earth and Bajor is also here. It was *not* present when we first encountered the shuttle's warp trail, but it is here now."

"Have you determined what that reading is?"

Abashedly, Toq said, "Not yet, Commander."

Tereth kept her smile to herself. Toq took great pride in his work, something Tereth had done her best to encourage. He had the makings of greatness in him. "The next time I ask that question, Lieutenant, I expect a different answer."

"Yes, sir!" Toq said.

Leaving Toq to his work, Tereth walked over to the helm control. "Vralk, project the shuttle's course ahead. I want to know all the possible places they could have gone."

Vralk punched up a display on his console. "I am afraid that list is very long, Commander." Tereth was pleased that Vralk had already projected the course, but had not been foolish enough to volunteer the information before Tereth was ready for it. "The course takes them directly through the Ch'grath Stellar Cluster."

Tereth growled low in her throat. Vralk said, "Commander, I—"

She waved him off. "It's not your fault, Vralk." She bared her teeth. "If my displeasure was with you, you would not be able to apologize."

"Yes, sir," Vralk said quickly. The boy had only been assigned to the *Gorkon* for a week. *He will learn the protocols soon enough,* she thought, *or he will be reassigned.* She smiled, remembering *Bekk* Kelad's thoughtless burst of laughter at Captain Klag's unfortunate—and temporary—difficulties adjusting to his new limb. Tereth had thought her captain to be courageous in putting his own ability to fight over outmoded medical practices and allowing Dr. B'Oraq to give him a new limb. An adjustment period was to be expected, and it hadn't affected his ability to lead them so far. If it did, Tereth would deal with it, as any first officer would—and as long as it didn't, any who dared to mock the captain would pay for it.

Kelad certainly had been paying. His assignment to waste extraction was not due to end for another two months.

Since Toq was occupied with his sensor sweeps, Tereth went directly to the ensign at the communications console to Toq's left. "Send to all ships, planets, and outposts in the Ch'grath cluster to be on the lookout for the captain's shuttle."

"Yes, sir," said the ensign.

Again, Tereth looked around the bridge. Vralk kept the ship in position for Toq to make his sensor sweeps. Next to Toq's operations station, Lieutenant Rodek stood impassively at the gunner's position, presumably ready to go into battle if needed. Behind the two of them, the four gunner positions sat empty for the moment. The other secondary stations remained staffed and occupied.

At this point, Tereth realized, she needed to inform Klag of their progress. Until Toq found something substantial—or something else happened—there was nothing more to be done without orders from her commander.

"You have the bridge, Toq. I will be with the captain."

Toq's head was pounding when Tereth walked up behind him.

"Lieutenant, why are you still here?"

Toq looked around the bridge. He was currently sitting at one of the two science consoles, taking advantage of its ability to do more in-depth study than the more general applications of his operations station. Ironically, it was the same post on the bridge that he had served at when he came on board the *Gorkon*—and from which he warned the second officer, Lieutenant Kegren, that there might be an explosive device in the debris of a Breen ship. Kegren ignored this warning, and the ship was almost destroyed by such an explosive. Toq challenged Kegren, with Klag's support, and defeated him; Klag rewarded him with the post of second officer.

As he looked around, he realized that none of the same people were on the bridge anymore—aside from himself and Tereth. He checked his chronometer and saw that his shift had ended almost half an hour earlier. Since he had been in charge of the bridge, he should have noticed that. And, for that matter, noticed Tereth returning from the captain's office . . .

"I have not yet determined what this sensor reading

is, Commander," Toq said in answer to the first officer's question.

"And you will not if you die of starvation. You have not eaten since you came on-shift, and you are of no use if you collapse from hunger. Go eat." Toq started to object, but Tereth didn't give him the chance to speak. "You have been staring at those waveform patterns for over an hour, Lieutenant. You need a distraction. This is *not* a request."

Tereth had an odd style of giving an order in such a way that it felt like she was doing you a service by giving it. Toq wasn't sure how she did it, but he found himself getting up from the science console and exiting the bridge via the turbolift.

He was late for the evening meal, but since tonight was B'Elath's turn to sing the traditional song before dinner, Toq didn't consider that a hardship. B'Elath always sang the dreadful "Campaign at Kol'Vat," and always sang it very badly.

She finished the song just as Toq walked in. She had ended on the tenth verse instead of singing all fifteen, which no doubt pleased all the inhabitants of the mess hall.

Toq grabbed a plate of *pipius* claw and *bregit* lung, then tossed some *gagh* into a bowl, grabbed a mug and poured it only half full of bloodwine—he was going right back on duty after dinner—and went to sit with Rodek and Vralk.

As he sat, Toq asked, "Why do we keep letting that woman massacre that awful song?"

"You mean she has done that before?" Vralk asked with revulsion.

Rodek nodded. "Many times."

"And she has not been killed to spare our ears the damage?"

Toq laughed at the young pilot. "Not yet, no."

"I do not know if you've noticed, Toq," Rodek said, "but every time she sings before dinner, the next day we are victorious in battle."

Frowning, Toq said, "That is ridiculous."

"It is the truth." Rodek ate a piece of skull stew, but kept talking as he chewed. "The first time she sang was the night before we arrived at taD and destroyed those rebel ships. The second time, we engaged those marauders on Galtra the following day. The third—"

"You are right," Toq said, as he thought back on their missions. Then he smiled. "No doubt it is better to die gloriously than to risk hearing her sing again." All three shared a laugh at that, though Toq noticed that Vralk's laugh was strained. "I suppose that bodes well for my abilities."

Swallowing his *bok-rat* liver, Vralk asked, "How?"

"I will soon determine who our foe is, and we shall defeat them tomorrow."

"So you haven't unlocked the secrets of the sensor reading?" Rodek asked before sipping his own mug of bloodwine.

"No," Toq said with annoyance. "Commander Tereth ordered me to get dinner."

Muttering into his liver, Vralk said, "That is all she does is give orders."

Rodek barked a laugh. "She is the first officer, fool. Giving orders is her duty."

"Her duty is to find a mate and provide him with sons."

Toq rolled his eyes. Vralk was the third pilot they'd had on the *Gorkon* since Lieutenant Leskit was rotated back to the *Rotarran,* and each one made Toq miss the old *toDSaH* even more. Leskit had been a fine dinner companion and a good comrade. Vralk was the latest in a series of idiots Command had sent to poorly fill his boots.

"Feel free," Toq said, "to challenge her authority, Vralk. I am sure she could use the *d'k tahg* practice on your hearts."

Rodek joined Toq in a laugh. Rodek, Toq noticed, had lightened up considerably these past few months. When Toq first signed on, he would happily have taken the humorless gunner's life as he had Kegren's, but Rodek had shown signs of acquiring both a sense of humor and a zest for life. He still performed his duties as gunner with all the passion of dead *racht,* but he did his job well.

Vralk, on the other hand, looked like someone had poisoned his *bok-rat* liver. "Laugh all you wish, but we could not possibly have a less worthy first officer than a woman."

"Spoken like someone who never served under Drex," Rodek said, wiping *grapok* sauce off his face with his sleeve.

At that name, Vralk's eyes grew as wide as saucers. "The son of Martok? You served with him?"

"He preceded Tereth as first officer," Toq said as he chewed on his *pipius* claw. "The captain had him transferred off the ship as fast as he could."

"Then the captain is a fool," Vralk said unhesitatingly.

Vralk had spoken just as Rodek was sipping his bloodwine, and the gunner gave out a bark of laughter that caused the wine to spill all over the table. Rodek set the mug down and said, "Perhaps you should challenge the captain, then, since you think him to be so—unworthy."

At that, Vralk squirmed. "Well, no, but—Drex is the son of the chancellor! He deserves respect!"

"Respect must be earned, boy," Rodek said.

"And your commanding officers deserve respect, as well," Toq added. "Klag and Tereth have led us well, and you will find no one on this ship to support your cause."

"Really?" Now Vralk sounded more sure of himself. "You mean to tell me that all twenty-seven hundred warriors on this ship support a captain who mutilates his body and a *female* first officer?"

Toq looked at Rodek. "He sounds like a Ferengi, doesn't he?"

"Laugh if you want," Vralk said. "But if I did challenge the authority of those in charge, do not be so sure that I would be acting alone."

With that, Vralk swallowed the last of his liver and got up and left.

Rodek laughed as heartily as he ever did. "Yet another fool pilots the ship. I never thought I would wish for Leskit's return."

Toq, however, did not return the laugh. "Is he truly a fool, Rodek?"

"Of course he is. Only a fool would challenge Klag—they'd be dead before they could get near him."

"On the bridge, perhaps. But what of the troops? The engineers? We do not know their thoughts."

Polishing off his bloodwine, Rodek said, "Troops are loyal to their commanders unless given good reason not to be. Has Klag given such a reason?"

"His arm."

Rodek snorted. "He has made himself a better warrior. Don't tell me you believe that stupidity about 'hiding the scars of battle.'"

"No," Toq said quickly, and he meant it. On Carraya, he had grown up with Romulan medicine. Indeed, the one aspect of life in the Empire that Toq did not appreciate was the appalling state of Klingon medicine. One of the many reasons for his contentment on the *Gorkon* was the fact that their physician studied in the Federation. "But if a young fool like Vralk believes it . . ."

Rodek looked sour—or, rather, more sour than usual. "I will speak with Lokor."

Lokor was the head of on-ship security, and generally knew everything that occurred on the *Gorkon*. Rumor had it that he was also with Imperial Intelligence, but Toq had always discounted those rumors. Surely there was an II operative or two on the ship, but Toq doubted that II would place someone in so obvious a position as security. Indeed, Toq suspected that Lokor himself spread those rumors for his own purposes.

"And what if Lokor *is* one of the people who is against the captain?"

"Then I will kill him," Rodek said simply. "And anyone else who is disloyal."

Toq dropped some *gagh* into his mouth. As they wriggled down his throat, he said in as grave a tone as he could muster, "And I will help you." He wanted Rodek to know he was serious. Toq felt more at home on this ship than he had anywhere else since he left Carraya, and he would not let a young *petaQ* like Vralk ruin it.

Klag was on the holodeck, about to commence his first *bat'leth* drill since getting his new arm, when the call from the bridge came.

"*We are receiving a hail from the* Enterprise, *Captain.*"

That was Toq, Klag noted, *still on duty.* The young second officer had taken a dinner break, but otherwise refused to rest until he determined what the odd reading was at the shuttle's divergent point. Every resource of the *Gorkon's* considerable sensor power had been trained at this region of space, thus far to no avail. But Klag had confidence in the young man.

"I will be right there. Summon Commander Tereth as well." A pause. "Progress, Lieutenant?"

"All I have been able to determine, sir, is that there are some superficial similarities between this energy reading and the one given off by the Malkus Artifacts."

"Which tells us nothing we do not already know," Klag said as he shut down the holodeck.

"No, sir."

"Continue scans. Out." He let out a breath. In a sense, he was grateful. He had been hoping that B'Oraq would be present for his first drill. If the call from the *Enterprise* was good news, perhaps they'd rescue her before he'd have the chance to engage in the drill, and she could indeed be there for it.

Klag didn't bother changing into uniform, since he didn't want to keep Picard and Riker waiting, so he went to the bridge dressed only in *mok'bara* clothes—a tight-fitting white cloth shirt and pants.

Ensign Morketh, currently staffing the gunner position, gave Klag an odd look as he entered. The look was mostly directed at the captain's shorter, lighter, squatter right arm, which was more visible in the *mok'bara* shirt than it was in his more elaborate uniform.

"Speak, Ensign Morketh," Klag said.

Morketh seemed surprised at the instruction. "I— have nothing to report, sir."

"Good. Mind your post, then."

"Yes, sir," he said quickly.

"Enterprise standing by," Toq said. Klag nodded in reply.

Tereth—in full uniform—entered the bridge a moment later. As she did, Klag sat in his chair—as usual, falling rather than sitting with his arms. "Screen on," Klag said to Toq.

The bridge of the *Enterprise* replaced the starfield on the main viewer. Picard and Riker were present, with Data and a Trill female visible in front of them, and a human female behind them.

"Progress, Captain Picard?"

"After a fashion, Captain Klag. We've picked up the St. Lawrence*'s warp signature, but it takes it to the Ch'grath Stellar Cluster. There are hundreds of possible destinations."*

Klag filled Picard in on their own discoveries. "It seems likely that both ships are going to the same place."

"The question being where."

"We have found the same peculiar reading that was at the other sites, as well. The reading does not appear until right before my shuttle changed course. Thus far, we have only been able to learn that it is similar to the Malkus Artifact energy."

"That was true of the St. Lawrence *as well, and Mr. Data's conclusions were similar."*

Klag wondered if Toq took any pride in the fact that his accomplishments were the same as those of Starfleet's legendary android officer.

Speaking of whom, Toq said, "Sir, we're receiving a message from the *U.S.S. Musgrave.*"

On the viewer, Riker frowned. *"If memory serves, the* Musgrave *was the ship that took Ambassador Worf from Qo'noS to Starbase 24."*

"Tie the communication in, Lieutenant," Klag said.

The viewer went to a split-screen image, with the much smaller bridge of the *Musgrave* now occupying the right-hand side, and the *Enterprise* bridge confined to a smaller space, focused on Picard, on the left-hand side.

The *Musgrave* captain, a round, blocky human with thick black hair and an indeterminate neck, said, *"This is Captain Dayrit of the* Musgrave. *I see I got both of you—good, saves me from having to call you both."*

"I am Klag of the *Gorkon*. You have something to report, Captain?"

"Yes—we're on our way to an emergency in the Trivas system, so we can't investigate this ourselves, but—we found the St. Lawrence *while en route to Trivas. It's headed toward the Dorvan system."*

Tereth started. "That's in the old Federation/Cardassian Demilitarized Zone."

"And, ironically, one of the subjects of discussion at the Khitomer conference," Picard said with a nod.

Riker added, *"It's also not especially close to the Ch'grath cluster."*

Dayrit let out a breath. *"As I said, we're answering an emergency call, or we'd investigate it ourselves."* He made some kind of odd human noise. *"Now I'm sorry I didn't take the time out to drop the ambassador off at Khitomer."*

"I doubt that would have made a difference, Captain. We'll investigate this further."

"Thanks, Captain. Captains," he amended with a nod to Klag. "Musgrave *out."*

The screen returned to just the image of the *Enterprise*.

Tereth walked over to the pilot's station. "Vralk, set course for the Dorvan system, maximum warp."

"Yes, sir," Vralk intoned.

"Ensign Perim," Riker said with a smile, *"do likewise, if you please."*

"Aye, sir," the Trill said.

"When will we arrive?" Klag asked.

"Six hours, ten minutes at warp nine," Vralk said.

Klag looked at his first officer. "Impress upon Commander Kurak the need for warp nine-point-eight. And have the cloaking device standing by."

Tereth smiled. "Of course, Captain."

As the first officer headed for engineering, Riker said, *"You're gonna beat us there by a couple of hours, Captain. More if your first officer is a good impresser."*

"She is," Klag said with a grin.

"Our chief engineer is something of a wiz himself, so it might be less. We'll see."

"We will," Klag said, trying not to smile at Riker's use of the word *wIj*. Somehow, he didn't think Riker meant to say that the *Enterprise* chief engineer was a farm. "But I'm sure our mighty vessel can handle one Starfleet runabout without your aid. We shall see you there."

"Indeed," Picard said. "Enterprise *out.*"

Chapter Fourteen

KIRA NERYS GATHERED EVERY BIT OF WILLPOWER she
possessed and instructed her right arm to touch the control on the runabout console before her that would bring
the *St. Lawrence* out of warp and discontinue its journey
to the former DMZ.

Her right arm remained where it was.

I will not succumb to this.

Once, two years earlier, Kira had willingly allowed
her body to be a vessel for the Prophets in order to aid
in the coming about of the Reckoning. But she had
spent her life in devotion to the Prophets and was
more than happy to give herself over in service to
them.

She was considerably less willing to do so for a
ninety-thousand-year-old tyrant.

It had started on the way back from a committee
meeting at the Chamber of Ministers. The *Defiant* had
returned from its mission to Trill, so Kira had left

Vaughn in charge while she went through her least favorite chore: chatting with politicians.

The meeting started an hour late, went on for two hours longer than it should have, and accomplished absolutely nothing of substance. Mentally exhausted and physically restless, Kira boarded the *Rio Grande,* looking forward to a very long bath.

So when she found herself changing the runabout's course toward Klingon space, she was rather surprised.

That surprise increased when she tried to stop herself, but her body no longer responded to any mental directives. As she got closer to her destination—Narendra III, based on the course she'd laid in—her control lessened. Even such simple functions as blinking and swallowing were out of her purview.

She remembered the Malkus Artifact that Orta had found six years ago, of course, and had heard that another one was found in the DMZ a few months later, though she had chosen not to dwell on it much in the ensuing years. Thinking of that just reminded her of the *Odyssey* and its crew, and of sitting helpless in the *Orinoco* while she watched a Jem'Hadar ship do a suicide run into the *Galaxy*-class vessel's deflector dish, annihilating both the ship and its crew.

Kira hated being helpless.

With every fiber of her being, she fought Malkus's influence.

With every fiber of her being, she failed.

Yet, she kept trying, even as Malkus had her get into the *St. Lawrence*—the runabout that had brought Ambassador Spock to Narendra—and take it to the former DMZ to try to locate the missing piece of the third artifact. Kira had no idea why she had been sent in this ship rather than the one she had arrived in—perhaps Malkus couldn't tell the difference between the two ships, which were, after all, virtually the same.

The runabout came out of warp in an area of interstellar space. It was here that the *Hood* and the *Voyager* had first detected the third Malkus Artifact on the Maquis ship *Geronimo,* and it seemed as good a place as any to start the search.

Except Kira didn't wish to search for the component. She wished to open a hailing frequency, to bring the *St. Lawrence* to DS9 and then take the *Defiant* to Narendra III, along with any other ship she could corral, and blow Malkus into his component atoms with the *Defiant's* considerable weaponry.

She gathered every bit of willpower she possessed and instructed her right arm to touch the control that would open a hailing frequency.

Her right arm moved toward the comm panel.

I've done it! Kira thought with surprise. She opened a channel.

Then she tried to talk, but found that she could not.

However, even opening the channel was a small victory. It would serve as an additional beacon to her location, and maybe—just maybe—someone would notice. Of course, given what this region of space was like these days, that "someone" could be anyone from a clapped-out Cardassian military ship limping on its last antimatter pods to Yridian privateers to Ferengi merchants to civilian supply ships. But getting in touch with *anyone* was a bonus at this point. Someone needed to be informed about what Malkus had done on Narendra.

Then a sensor alarm went off. She looked up to see a Klingon vessel decloaking.

No! They've found me! Malkus had apparently sent one of the Klingon ships in orbit around Narendra to tail her under cloak, and stop her if she threw off Malkus's control.

That doesn't make sense. Why not send them in the first place?

Look at them. That's one of those new Chancellor-class ships. That would draw a lot more attention than a little runabout. Malkus probably kept it around in case of emergencies.

Stop talking to yourself and do something!

Kira raised the shields and armed the phasers. *She* did that, not Malkus. Another victory. She also recognized the ship: the *I.K.S. Gorkon,* commanded by Captain Klag. She directed her hail to them—but she was still unable to make her voice work.

Well, the hell with it—it's not like I have anything to say to them anyhow.

She fired phasers.

Then the ship hailed her. *"Attention runabout. This is the* I.K.S. Gorkon. *If you do not lower your shields immediately, we will fire upon you."*

Gee, Klag, thanks for the warning.

Wait a minute. Why would they give a warning? That doesn't make sense.

She tried to lower the shields, but this time she couldn't. Malkus was attempting to reassert his control.

You've spent enough time in my head. Get out!

Then the *Gorkon* fired on her.

She had no idea if it was her will or Malkus's that made her take evasive action, and ultimately it didn't matter. The one goal she and Malkus shared was a desire to keep her body intact.

However, her maneuver came too late. The blast didn't penetrate the shields, but reduced them to a mere ten percent.

She continued the evasive maneuvers, laying down covering fire.

Covering fire, right. I'm about as overmatched here as our old Bajoran sub-impulse raiders were against Cardassian warships.

Then again, we beat them eventually.

After several decades.

I have got to stop talking to myself.

The *Gorkon* fired again, though this time with a beam at a much lower power level. It was just enough to wipe out the runabout's shields.

They want me alive.

Why do they want me alive?

She got up and went back to the aft compartment to get a phaser.

As she did, her mouth almost fell open from the shock. "How did I—?"

Then she grinned. She had control of her movements and her voice. She could still feel Malkus's presence in her mind, but it was not as strong. *Maybe he's got limits. Maybe I'm out of his range. Or maybe I'm just better than him.*

"Whatever," she said aloud, reveling in her ability to do so once again. "There's no way I'm letting him take me back."

The next step was expected. She felt a transporter beam start to envelop her. It was neither the raw pins-and-needles sensation of Deep Space 9's Cardassian transporter nor the gentle vibration of a Federation transporter. In fact, it didn't feel like much of anything.

A moment later, she was standing in a darkened room full of Klingons, all pointing weapons at her. She counted five aiming at her, with another one behind the transporter console. She didn't recognize any of them, but the one time the *Gorkon* had been to DS9, Kira had met only the ship's captain.

Kira pointed her own phaser at the tall one who moved toward her as she materialized. "You're not taking me back to Narendra."

This seemed to confuse the Klingon, whose hair was waist length and in a series of intricately tied braids. "You have been to Narendra recently?" The Klingon had a surprisingly pleasant voice.

This *did* confuse Kira. "You didn't follow me from there?"

"I've never even been there, Colonel. Now lower your weapon, or I will order my people to open fire on you. Disruptors do have a setting that leaves the victim alive, but it is not nearly as—bloodless as your Federation's 'stun' setting. I do not recommend it."

Kira hesitated. *It could be a trick,* she thought. But then, what possible reason would this Klingon have to trick her?

She lowered her weapon. "How did you find me?" she asked, noting that, though the lead Klingon did likewise, the other four did not.

"The captain can explain that." He touched the communicator on his wrist. "Lokor to bridge. We have the Bajoran."

"Bring her to the wardroom," came a deep male voice that Kira recognized as Klag's.

Lokor nodded to the quartet of warriors, who finally lowered their weapons. Then he turned to Kira. "Come with me."

Klag sat in the wardroom and listened to Kira Nerys's tale. With him were Tereth and Toq and, on the viewscreen, Picard, Riker, and Data. Upon learning that Kira had come from Narendra III, Klag had immediately had Vralk set a course for that planet. Once the *St. Lawrence* was taken on board and placed in the *Gorkon*'s shuttlebay, they proceeded at warp nine-point-eight, with instructions to Commander Kurak to attempt a greater speed.

The *Enterprise* was, of course, alerted, and they too had changed course. Indeed, they had only been twenty minutes away when Klag had contacted them. "Told you our chief engineer was a wiz," Riker had said with one of his human grins.

"One last thing," Kira said after telling her story. "Malkus couldn't control the entire planet, and the ships in orbit, so he had a large chunk of the population imprison themselves somewhere. Once Captain DeSoto started putting the artifacts together, Malkus gave the prisoners the disease that the first artifact gave off. If we don't get back to Narendra soon, those prisoners will die."

There was a pause. Finally, Picard said, *"You did well, Colonel."*

"Thank you, Captain, but it wasn't easy. If you don't mind my asking, how'd you find me?"

"The *St. Lawrence* was listed as officially missing," Tereth said. "You were sighted by a Starfleet ship that couldn't stop to investigate. When we arrived we found a Bajoran in a runabout last known to have a Klingon, two humans, and a Vulcan/human hybrid."

Riker smiled. *"Needless to say, that set an alarm bell or two off."*

"I can—" Kira hesitated, then shook her head. "Dammit. I think Malkus is starting to reassert himself."

Toq said, "The only tales of Malkus using this artifact involve him controlling people on a world where he was present. His range may not extend this far."

"Bajor is farther from Narendra III than the region where Colonel Kira was found," Data said.

"Yeah, but I wasn't fighting him tooth and claw on Bajor," Kira said grimly. "He caught me off guard. I may have just worn him down."

"Earth is even farther away, yet Captain DeSoto was sufficiently enthralled to steal the artifacts," Data added, sounding nonplussed. Klag had heard that the android was emotionless, so this almost petulant tone was something of a surprise.

Tereth bared her teeth. "While I am sure he is a fine leader, Captain DeSoto is not a warrior."

Klag nodded. Unlike Klag, Tereth had never met Kira, but they both knew her reputation.

"And for all we know," Picard said, *"DeSoto is fighting control just as hard."* Klag smiled at Picard's attempt to come to the defense of his friend. *"Such speculation, however, is irrelevant for the moment. Colonel, how many ships are defending Narendra III?"*

"I'm not sure. At least three were in orbit when I took the *St. Lawrence* out, but there could have been more. And there was a civilian ship. I wasn't exactly in a position to do a full scan. But all those ships were under Malkus's control."

"Understood. Captain, I suggest we rendezvous at the Narendra system's Oort cloud. We can survey the system from there, then plan our next move."

Tereth cast a disdainful glance at the viewer. "There is only one next move, Picard—to attack this Malkus and destroy him, so we can rescue those he has enslaved and cure those he has infected."

"Yes, but Picard is right," Klag said. "We need to reconnoiter before charging in."

"Of course," Tereth said, conceding the point.

"Have you made any progress regarding the sensor readings, Captain?" Klag asked.

"*No.*" Picard spoke with a certain amount of annoyance.

"Nor have we, though Lieutenant Toq has, at least, eliminated several possibilities. We will send you what we have done so far."

"*We will do likewise.*"

"Good." Klag stood up. "We are due to arrive at Narendra in seven hours. We shall speak again then. *Gorkon* out."

Kira stood up as the viewer went blank. "Captain, I think it might be best if I was sedated in your medical ward."

"You anticipate Malkus reasserting his control?" Tereth asked.

"He might. And if he does, he'll know everything I know. That's too much of a security risk, if we're going to catch him off guard."

Klag considered. "A wise move. My physician is, of course, not available," he said with a wry smile, "but I'm sure her nurse can handle so simple a task as administering a sedative." Klag opened the door to the wardroom and said to one of the guards posted outside, "Take the colonel to the medical ward and have Nurse Gaj attend to her."

The guard nodded and Kira headed toward the door.

As she reached the threshold, Tereth said, "Colonel?"

Kira turned around.

"Should we live through this, I would be honored if you would share a drink with us. There is a song you might wish to hear."

Kira frowned. "Really?"

"We do not often immortalize our defeats, but—after the war, a song was written called 'The Battle for Deep

Space 9.' It was about Gowron's failed attempt to take your station four years ago. The third verse is primarily about you and the way you slew ten warriors in your operations center while mortally wounded."

Kira gave her an odd look. "Actually it was only five, and the reason it wasn't more was because the fifth one stabbed me, but—" She broke into a smile. "Thank you, Commander. I look forward to hearing it."

Toq also stood up. "With your permission, Captain, I will transmit data to the *Enterprise* and see if theirs is of any use."

Klag dismissed him with a nod. Once he departed, Klag was left alone with Tereth. She had a look on her face that Klag had learned to recognize over the past few months. He was also quite sure that Tereth herself didn't realize that Klag could read her so easily. "You are concerned?"

Tereth looked up suddenly in surprise. Klag hid a smile.

"Picard is known for many things," she said after a moment's hesitation. "Warfare is not among them. In single engagements, he has performed well, but—I am not sure how useful an ally he will truly be if we have to go into battle against multiple Defense Force ships."

"I think," Klag said, "the person who twice drove back Borg invasions of the Alpha Quadrant and liberated Betazed from Dominion control is someone I am proud to have by my side."

"He turned back the Borg because he used their assimilation of him against them—that is not an advantage he will have today. He liberated Betazed with the aid of four other vessels, including that warship of theirs, the *Defiant*." Before Klag could respond to that, Tereth held up a hand. "I'm not saying he is not a *worthy* ally, Captain, but I *do* think that you should take the lead."

Klag stared at his first officer for several seconds. He wondered if she was attempting to curry favor with him or if she truly believed what she said. Or, perhaps, both. She had been a superlative first officer—though anyone would have been an improvement on Drex—but she also had far more ambition than Klag was always entirely comfortable with.

"Perhaps you are right," he finally said. "But Picard has been commanding starships since before either of us was born. I would no more presume to lead him into battle than I would Chancellor Martok. However," he added, standing up from his chair, "I will not defer to him, either. This mission has been a cooperative effort from the beginning. If we learned nothing else from the war, Commander, it is that a united front is strongest."

Tereth smiled. "Which applies to arms as well as battles, it would seem."

Frowning, Klag asked, "What do you mean?"

"You just rose from the chair without stumbling, Captain. Congratulations."

Klag turned around and stared at the chair. He hadn't even thought about it. He was too busy focusing on what he was saying to Tereth. . . .

He threw his head back and laughed. Then he turned to his second-in-command. "May it be the first victory of many this day."

The second time B'Oraq awoke from unconsciousness in Klag's shuttle was much worse than the first. For one thing, where McCoy had apparently gently laid her on the *QongDaq,* whoever their latest attacker was had simply tossed her unceremoniously onto the deck of the fore compartment. For another, this time the headache extended to her feet.

Once again, she awoke to Ambassador Worf's face, and once again he asked, "Are you all right, Doctor?"

"No. My head feels like a *targ*'s running loose in it. What happened?"

Worf helped her to her feet. B'Oraq noted that G'joth was still unconscious and propped up against one of the bulkheads, and McKenna and Falce were standing and rubbing their temples, looking like they were in considerable pain.

"We were victims of a telepathic attack," Worf said. "Our captor rendered us unconscious, placed us back inside the shuttle, and reactivated the forcefield."

B'Oraq tugged on her braid. "I assume that we won't be able to cobble together another miracle device to wipe out the forcefield?"

"No." Worf masked his anger well, but B'Oraq could feel the undercurrent in his voice. She found it oddly appealing.

"So what do we do now?"

Falce muttered, "Panicking might not be a bad idea."

"Oh, cut that out, Matt," McKenna said. "There's got to be a way out of this."

A voice came from the still-open rear hatch. "Perhaps there—there is."

B'Oraq turned to see a Vulcan male standing on the other side of the hatch. After a moment, she realized that it was Ambassador Spock. After another moment, she remembered what Worf had told her.

"Are you responsible for this?" she asked.

"Not—as such, no. I do not have much time. Malkus will reassert his control over me—soon."

Falce frowned. "Who's Malkus?"

"A—tyrant from many millennia ago. Are you familiar—with Starfleet General Order 16, Lieutenant?"

B'Oraq knew nothing of the regulation, of course, but Worf immediately said, "The fourth artifact?"

Spock nodded. "It was unearthed—here. Apparently, my exposure to—to one of the other artifacts made me—susceptible to Malkus's control. Three others—Dr. McCoy, Colonel Kira Nerys, and Captain Robert De-Soto—are also enthralled. And, Ambassador—I must apologize for my actions against you, Lieutenant Falce, and Ensign McKenna. I was—not in my right mind at the time."

"How are you able to resist now?" Worf asked.

"I am—not sure. Possibly because my brain chemistry has—changed since I encountered the first artifact—when I died and was reborn on the Genesis Planet."

"Of course," Worf said matter-of-factly, as if people talked about being resurrected every day. B'Oraq looked at both of them as if they were insane.

McKenna saw the look, and gave the doctor a smile. "Trust me, this sort of thing is normal for those two," she said in a whisper. "Read any six random captain's logs for any ship named *Enterprise*, and you'll see what I mean."

"Malkus sent me," Spock continued, "to place you back in the shuttle and—reactivate the forcefield. I must—return soon or he will notice—that I have taken too long—or that his control is not what it should be."

Falce started fidgeting. "So why don't you just deactivate the forcefield?"

"Great idea, Matt," McKenna said. "Then we can get zapped again."

"The ensign—is correct. I had hoped that another—possibility might present itself."

Spock, B'Oraq noticed, was giving Worf what seemed to be a very significant look. *Is this some kind of diplomat code or something?* she thought.

Then she recalled her studies of Vulcan anatomy—particularly as related to the Vulcan brain. "You're suggesting a mind-meld, aren't you?"

"*I* am—not, no," Spock said. "However, it would—be a useful tool for allowing two of us to resist—Malkus's control."

Worf stepped forward. "I will volunteer."

"I don't like this, Mr. Ambassador," Falce said. "I'm not so sure he should be trusted."

"Perhaps," Worf said. "But I would be the most—logical choice. I was the first to recover from the psionic attack earlier, and I have felt no ill effects from it. You are still obviously in pain, as are Dr. B'Oraq and Ensign McKenna—and G'joth is still unconscious."

B'Oraq hadn't realized that her headache was so bad that the ambassador could see it in her face. "I agree with Ambassador Worf," she said. "His quick recovery makes him the best choice. It means he's more likely to be able to retain his own self, and not be lost in the melding."

Spock regarded B'Oraq. "You are—familiar with the mind-meld?"

She smiled. "I studied medicine at Starfleet Academy. It included a primer on the medicinal applications of psionics, particularly as related to Vulcans, Betazoids, and other telepathic races."

"Indeed. We are—fortunate, then, that you are here to monitor."

"I'm not sure how much I can monitor without equipment," B'Oraq said ruefully, "but I will try my best."

The Vulcan ambassador removed a control from the folds of his robes and pressed a button on it. The forcefield fell and he stepped inside the shuttle. "We must—we must hurry. I can feel myself beginning to lose control once again. Malkus has—spread himself fairly thin, which has—aided in my ability to resist. But that ability—may weaken without the extra support—from Mr. Worf's mind."

Turning to Worf, B'Oraq put a hand on his arm. "Have you ever experienced a mind-meld before?"

"No."

"It can be a very—overwhelming experience. Try to focus on one particular thing—a favorite song, a face, an image, *anything*—before you start. Use that as a mental anchor."

Worf nodded. "I understand."

I hope so, she thought.

"Are you—are you ready?" Spock asked.

B'Oraq took a look at the older ambassador and thought that question applied more to him. He looked horrible; the strain of trying to resist this Malkus person's control was obviously wearing on him. She hoped that this worked, because if it didn't, Spock would be in Malkus's thrall again, and they'd be back stuck in the shuttle with no way out. *Or he might just decide we're better off dead. . . .*

In answer to Spock's query, Worf simply said, "Yes."

I don't like this, B'Oraq thought. *Usually the participants have some time to get ready—a half an hour at least, especially if Spock is going to attempt a meld as deep as I think he's going to.*

Spock stood face-to-face with Worf and placed his fingers on the areas of Worf's face that were closest to the neural pathways to the cerebellum.

"My mind—to your mind. My thoughts—to your thoughts. Our minds—become one . . ."

Chapter Fifteen

YOUNG WORF STOOD IN THE DOORWAY of his ancestral family home on Vulcan. His father, Sarek, demanded to know where he'd been.

"I have been in the mountains," Worf said.

"You are not to travel to the Llangon Mountains," Sarek said.

Confused, Worf started to say that Father had taken his brother Sybok to the Ural Mountains only last week.

"Come," Sarek said. "It is time."

Young Spock stood in the doorway of the Rozhenko home in Minsk. His adoptive father, Sergey, demanded to know where he'd been.

"I have been in the mountains," Spock said.

Father laughed. "We just went to the Ural Mountains with your brother Nikolai last week."

Confused, Spock started to say that Father had forbidden him travel to the Llangon Mountains.

"Come," Sergey said. *"It is time."*

(My mind . . .)

"Oh, look, it's the little human boy!"

"Stinking half-breed!"

"Why don't you go back to Earth?"

"You're not a *real* Vulcan!"

Young Worf was angered at the insults the other Vulcan children threw his way. He wanted to kill them all—it wasn't his fault that Mikel had died. He hadn't sufficiently restrained himself in the soccer game, but it wasn't his fault that their collision resulted in a broken neck!

"My God, he killed him!"

"Murderer!"

"Mikel's dead!"

"Klingon savage!"

Young Spock was confused at the epithets the human teenagers on Gault threw his way. He wanted to fight back—it wasn't his fault that his mother was human and that he couldn't be like the other, full-blooded Vulcans.

(. . . to your mind . . .)

"Why do you reject the ways of logic, brother?"

Sybok smiled indulgently at Worf's question. "I don't expect you to understand."

"Vulcan is your home, even more than it was ever mine!" Worf cried.

"You have made this your home," Sybok said, putting a hand on Worf's shoulder. "But I never truly belonged here."

With that, Worf's half-brother turned on his heel and

left the house at ShiKahr. Worf would not see him again
until many years later while serving on the *Enterprise*. . . .

"Why are you leaving Starfleet Academy, brother?"

*Nikolai smiled indulgently at Spock's question. "I
don't expect you to understand."*

*"You belong here, even more than I do," Spock said
calmly.*

"No, this is where you *were meant to be," Nikolai
said, putting a hand on Spock's shoulder. "But I never
truly belonged here."*

*With that, Spock's foster brother turned on his heel
and left the grounds of the Academy. Spock would not
see him again until many years later while serving on
the* Enterprise. . . .

(. . . my thoughts . . .)

Images of K'Ehleyr's broken, bloody form filled Worf's
head as he lunged at Jim Kirk. As they tumbled, Worf
wrapped the *ahn-woon* around his old friend's neck.

He had failed with the *lirpa*, but he would not fail
now. As he lifted Kirk off of him and all but dragged
him to the coal fire, his mind was ravaged with but one
thought: *K'Ehleyr will be mine forever!* The needs of the
Pon farr would be fulfilled.

Kirk made a last, desperate lunge, which saved him
from the heat of the coals, but Worf never lost his grip
on the *ahn-woon*. The light died in Jim Kirk's eyes.

Victory was his. . . .

*Images of T'Pring's serene face filled Spock's head as
he lunged at Duras. Spock deflected Duras's tik'leth
strike with his bat'leth.*

He had failed to save T'Pring from Duras, but he would not fail now. As he parried another tik'leth *strike and then moved onto the offensive, his mind was ravaged with but one thought:* T'Pring will be avenged! *The right of vengeance would be fulfilled.*

Duras made a last, desperate parry, but it did him no good. Spock knocked him to the ground and then slammed his family's bat'leth *into his enemy's chest. The light died in Duras's eyes.*

Victory was his. . . .

(. . . to your thoughts . . .)

There were many days in Worf's life that he would have defined as *happy,* though he doubted he would have admitted it aloud to anyone. But to stand there on Vulcan's Forge and to marry Saavik right there with T'Lar officiating and all of his crewmates from Deep Space 9 present was one of the moments he would treasure until the day he died. . . .

There were many days in Spock's life that he would have defined as happy, *though he doubted he would have admitted it aloud to anyone. But to stand there in Quark's bar and to marry Jadzia right there with Sirella officiating and Sarek, McCoy, and Uhura present was one of the moments he would treasure until the day he died. . . .*

(. . . our thoughts . . .)

It was small comfort as Worf stood there in the caves beneath Romulus, but at least Jean-Luc Picard was there by his side—his lone support when he was discommendated from the Klingon Empire.

* * *

It was small comfort as Spock stood there in the Great Hall on Qo'noS, but at least Jean-Luc Picard had been able to mind-meld with Spock—his last connection to his now-dead father, Sarek.

(. . . are becoming . . .)

Worf had thought that studying *Kolinahr* on Vulcan would be the answer to what had ailed him since the *Enterprise*-D was destroyed on Veridian III. But then came the siren call of V'Ger, and he knew he had to go back.

Spock had thought that studying under the clerics at Boreth would be the answer to what had ailed him since he resigned from Starfleet at the end of the Enterprise's *five-year mission. But then came the orders to report to Deep Space 9, and he knew he had to go back.*

(. . . one.)

The news that Jim Kirk had been lost on the *Enterprise*-B to some kind of energy ribbon had saddened Worf more than he thought it would. At least Kirk had sacrificed himself to save the people of Bajor. . . .

The news that Benjamin Sisko had been lost in the fire caves on Bajor had saddened Spock more than he thought it would. At least Sisko had sacrificed himself to save the el-Aurian refugees they'd rescued. . . .

"It is done."

B'Oraq stared at Worf and Spock. They'd only been "connected" for a minute or so, though it had felt like hours. "Are you both all right?" she asked.

Spock nodded. "I am well. I cannot feel Malkus's influence."

"Good," B'Oraq said.

Worf also nodded. "We shall have to hope that we will be able to continue our resistance."

"Great," McKenna said, stepping forward, "let's go, then."

"No," Spock said, putting a hand on McKenna's shoulder, "you must stay here. As soon as you leave this shuttle, you will once again be attacked by Malkus's psionic blast."

"The ambassador is correct," Worf said. "Logically, the best course of action would be for you to remain here."

"Agreed," Spock said.

It took all of B'Oraq's willpower to keep from laughing. Worf was now standing in a much more relaxed posture than usual, with his arms resting in front of him in a serene manner. In other words, the body language of a Vulcan. Spock, on the other hand, was like a coiled spring. He no longer had the haggard look he had come in with, and he seemed ready to attack at a moment's notice.

Spock turned to Worf. "I don't suppose you have any weapons?"

"No," Worf said. "We were forced to cannibalize all of our weapons in order to overload the forcefield earlier."

"A wasted effort," Spock said with disdain. "Our tactical position is much weaker."

"It was our best course of action at the time," Worf said calmly. "What kind of resistance can we expect?"

"Most of the planet's population has been mentally enslaved by Malkus. He could, in theory, turn them all against us."

One of Worf's eyebrows rose. "Then we shall have to use guile."

"So it would seem," Spock said.

"Indeed." Worf turned to McKenna. "Ensign, remain vigilant. I will take Davok's communicator and use it to contact you should we feel that it is safe." McKenna was the only one of the two Starfleet officers who still had a combadge, since Falce's was used for the device.

Impatiently, Spock said, "Let us go."

"*Qapla',*" B'Oraq said.

"Good luck," Falce added.

Again, Worf raised an eyebrow. "I do not believe in random chance."

This time, B'Oraq couldn't hold in her laugh.

"I did tell you, did I not?" Rodek said to Toq. "B'Elath sang that wretched song yesterday, and today we go into battle."

Toq looked up at Rodek. It took him a moment to focus on the gunner's presence, much less what he had said. He had been completely focused on the energy readings that he'd been studying for so many hours now. Stealing a glance at the chronometer on his console, he saw that it was time for the morning duty shift, which meant Rodek was reporting back to the gunner's position. In theory, Toq would have been doing so now as well, had he ever actually departed the bridge since returning here after last night's dinner.

"Oh, yes, of course," he said distractedly. "B'Elath."

"You've been on duty all night?" Rodek asked. The question was asked matter-of-factly.

"Yes. I still have not learned what these strange emissions are."

Rodek took up his position to Toq's right at the gunner's station. Toq was back at his operations console, since the ship was on alert status as they headed to Narendra.

"Take heart, Toq," Rodek said as he checked over his own console. "The famous android of the *Enterprise* has not figured it out, either. In fact, there is still the chance that you may find it first. *That* is a victory worth celebrating."

Toq laughed bitterly. "At this point, I would be just as happy if he did find it—just so it would be *found*."

"Interrogations are always easier when you know that the subject will talk eventually."

"Good point," Toq muttered. "The universe is usually much more reluctant to talk than your average prisoner."

Tereth walked by just then. Toq had been worried that she might reprimand them, but she said, "The universe is not our prisoner."

Rodek regarded her. "Are you saying that we are prisoners of the universe, Commander?"

"We are *Klingons*," she said quickly and with a menacing undertone, "we are no one's prisoner. We bend the universe to *our* will—which is why we will always be victorious. We do not succumb."

Toq entered a new scan into his console. "I wish the universe *was* our prisoner right now." He laughed. "In the old days, we could use the mind-sifter on—" He cut himself off. *"toH!"*

"What is it?" Tereth asked.

"Computer!" he bellowed, not answering the first officer directly. "Call up complete specifications for a mind-sifter."

A security override flashed in front of him. Viewing such files required a clearance he didn't have.

"Why do you want to know about mind-sifters, Lieutenant?" Tereth asked in her most serious tone. "They were banned by the Khitomer Accords."

"Yes, but if I'm right, those readings are similar to the emissions given off by a mind-sifter."

Rodek gave him a look. "Mind-sifters don't give off emissions."

"Everything electronic gives off an emission of some kind. You just have to know how to look for it." Toq did not look at Rodek as he replied, as he was still looking at Tereth. "Please, Commander, I think this is it."

"Since such knowledge is restricted, how did you even know to recognize a possible connection?"

Toq had been hoping the commander wouldn't ask that. "I cannot say, Commander, except that I gained the knowledge before I joined the Defense Force." That much, at least, was true. Living in the House of Lorgh for four years had been a—complex experience, to say the least.

Tereth gazed at Toq for three seconds with an impenetrable expression. Then she looked up. "Computer, grant Lieutenant Toq access to mind-sifter files, by authorization of Commander Tereth."

The computer recognized her voice pattern and the screen showed what Toq had asked for.

"Thank you, Commander," he said, gazing hungrily at the readings. "If I am right, this may be the solution to our problems."

"What problems?" Rodek asked.

"Colonel Kira told us that Malkus was able to take over the minds of the entire population of Narendra III. If we can identify how he controls people, we might be able to defend against it."

Toq then studied the readings. The waveforms were very similar, as he had thought, but . . .

"Commander," he said, suddenly looking up at Tereth, "permission to contact the *Enterprise*. I would like Commander Data to verify this and confer with him on a possible solution."

"Granted."

Within minutes, Data's face occupied the bridge's viewer, and Toq had filled him in. Tereth had, in the meantime, left Toq in charge of the bridge while she briefed the captain.

"An interesting theory, Lieutenant," Data said with enthusiasm. *"However, we do not have any records of the mind-sifter apparatus, as your government never shared them with us."*

"I am sending along the relevant portions of the schematics now," Toq said; having anticipated this request, he had partitioned out the portion of the schematics that dealt specifically with the emissions. Even the famed android wouldn't be able to construct a mind-sifter with the limited information Toq was transmitting, so there was no security breach. "It is a very close match."

"Datalink established," Data said, looking down at his console. *"Information incoming."* He looked up. *"If I may ask, Lieutenant—what led you to this train of thought?"*

"An accident," Toq said with only mild embarrassment. Several chuckles went around the bridge, prompting Toq to add, "Most of the greatest discoveries ever made were accidents."

"Indeed. Zalkatian ruins have been found on many Klingon worlds over the centuries. It is possible that the mind-sifter was created from technology adapted from one of those sites." Something grabbed his attention on the console. *"Data transfer complete. Accessing."* A pause. *"I believe you are correct, Lieutenant."*

The screen changed to a more general view of the bridge in response to another speaker: Picard. *"What does this mean in practical terms, Commander?"*

Data turned to face his captain, leaving his back to the viewer. *"I believe that we can modify the tractor beams of both the* Enterprise *and the* Gorkon *to emit a psilosy-*

*nine wave that matches the amplitude and frequency of
the energy emissions from Narendra III."*

Klag chose that moment to walk on the bridge, Tereth
behind him. "You're assuming, Commander, that such
emissions *are* coming from Narendra."

"Yes," Data said, turning back to the viewer, *"but it is
a reasonable assumption under the circumstances."*

"Can't we make a portable psilosynine wave guide?"
Toq asked. "Then we could bathe individuals in the frequency—it would modulate their electroencephalogram
to make them resist Malkus's control."

Klag smiled at his second officer before taking his
command chair. "That would give us the advantage we
need."

"Agreed," Picard said. *"Mr. Data?"*

*"It can be done, sir. I believe that Commander La
Forge and I can replicate such a device by the time we
reach Narendra."*

"Good," Klag said. "Then, when we arrive at the Oort
cloud, you can beam over here and test it on Colonel Kira.
If it frees her from Malkus's control, then it will work."

Picard nodded in agreement. *"Make it so, Mr. Data."*

Getting up from his station, Data said, *"Aye, sir,"* and
moved out of the viewer's range.

"We will speak again when we arrive, Captain Picard," Klag said. "Screen off."

Toq deactivated the viewer. Then he looked up to see
Klag smiling at him from his command chair. "Well
done, Lieutenant. A true warrior goes into battle with
the proper weapon—and you may have given us the best
possible one."

Beaming with pride, Toq said, "Thank you, sir."

Rodek leaned over. "And if we live this day, we will
celebrate your victory over the android."

Laughing, Toq said, "Oh, the bloodwine will flow *very* freely tonight!"

Vralk was late for his shift. He had overslept, like a fool. It was all well and good to think poorly of one's commanding officers, but it was better to proceed from a position of moral certitude. If Vralk was to get any kind of support from the crew for his planned overthrow of the *Gorkon* command structure, he'd need his own record to be above reproach.

Today, in fact, was when he intended to begin his campaign. He'd spent his time aboard getting the lay of the land, and he knew that there needed to be a change.

Vralk's father had raised him to be a better Klingon than one who simply stood by and let such deterioration of values go unchallenged—unlike Toq and Rodek. And Vralk knew that there simply *had* to be others who supported him. Lokor, for one. He was a Housemate of Vralk's, so he knew—

"Vralk! I will speak to you!"

The deep voice that halted Vralk in the corridor was Lokor himself, the chief of security for the *Gorkon*. Vralk had always admired Lokor growing up.

"It is good to see you, Lokor, but I am late for my shift, and—"

"Then *be* late."

Finally, Vralk realized just how furious Lokor was. His black eyes smoldered, his long, elaborately braided hair seemed to cover his head in a black flame, and all his teeth were bared. If it were anyone else, Vralk would fear that he'd be challenged. "What is it, cousin?"

Lokor spit. "Cousin—pfagh! You are no cousin of mine, you are an idiotic *petaQ* of a child!"

Vralk found his mouth falling open in shock. "I—I don't understand!"

"What kind of idiotic things are you saying to the rest of the bridge crew, boy?"

"I—"

Lokor leaned in close. Vralk could smell the *raktajino* and *gagh* on his breath, and he imagined he could hear the blood roaring in Lokor's veins. "I just had a talk with Lieutenant Rodek. He wanted to know if there was dissatisfaction with Captain Klag in the ranks. If there was concern about having a man such as him in command and having a female as his first."

Vralk let out a breath in relief. "I assume you told him the truth, cousin." He turned to continue walking toward the bridge, assuming Lokor would accompany him. "You of all people know that this kind of perversion has to be stopped before—"

His words were interrupted by Lokor's meaty hand punching him in the back. Vralk stumbled forward onto the deck. Lokor then picked him up and slammed him into the bulkhead.

"I—I don't understand," Vralk managed to cough out. It was suddenly very difficult to breathe. "You—you grew up with—with Grunnil just as—as I did! You're the only thing that has made assignment to this cesspool tolerable!"

"In that case," Lokor said—and now he was smiling, but it was a smile that filled Vralk with tremendous dread—"this cesspool is about to get much much worse." He leaned in close, his arm pressing Vralk against the bulkhead, making it even more difficult to breathe. "Understand something, Vralk. You're only still alive right now because of me. And the only way you're going to stay alive is to—"

Vralk knew where this was going. "Betray Grunnil's teachings?" He couldn't believe that a *Klingon* was saying these words to him.

"No, *toDSaH*—the only way for you to stay alive is to get off this ship as fast as you can. Trust me, you will find no allies to rally to Grunnil's antique causes here. You're in the real world now, boy, and it's time you acted like it. Trust me—keep your head down, your mouth shut, and I will see to it that you are transferred before your hearts become targets for *d'k tahg* practice."

With that, Lokor stood up straight, relieving the pressure from Vralk's chest. However, since that was also all that was holding him up against the bulkhead, he fell to the deck.

"This is the only warning you'll get, boy. And do *not* expect being part of my House to protect you any further."

Lokor walked back down the corridor the way he had come. Vralk coughed once and struggled to his feet.

As he now ran to the turbolift, he thought, *This place is worse than I imagined. My work is cut out for me. . . .*

No, I cannot afford to be the idiot Lokor thinks me to be. I am in no position to effect change—yet. I must be patient. He entered the turbolift. *I shall take that transfer, and work my way up the ranks. Eventually, I will be able to show everyone what it truly means to be Klingon.*

Kira was having a strange dream.

She was walking all over Deep Space 9, but it had been abandoned. Yet every once in a while, out of the corner of her eye, she saw someone familiar. First there was her father. Then Commander Vaughn. Then Kai Opaka. Then Quark. That led her to run into Quark's Bar, where she found Jake Sisko, Odo, Morn, and both

Jadzia *and* Ezri Dax all drinking through straws from a vat of *kanar.*

Jadzia looked at her and said, "Colonel, you awake?" But she said it in a man's voice.

Then the bar started to congeal and melt into an amalgam of random colors and lights that, after a second, coalesced into the more familiar sight of the *Gorkon* medical ward.

The last conscious thought she remembered having was the unpleasant face of Nurse Gaj standing over her. Now, though, there were four different people gazing intently at her. She knew all of them: Klag and Toq from this ship and Data and Geordi La Forge from the *Enterprise.* In fact, in her dream Jadzia had spoken with La Forge's voice.

"You all right?" La Forge asked.

What is going on here? "I'm fine—I think."

Toq asked, "Do you feel the influence of Malkus?"

Kira was about to instinctively answer in the affirmative when she realized that, in fact, she didn't feel Malkus at all. She hadn't noticed it until Toq mentioned it, but— "No, he's—he's gone." She broke into a smile. "It's nice to have my head to myself."

"It worked!" Toq said.

"What worked?" Kira asked.

Klag smiled. "You, Colonel, are the beneficiary of the genius of the other three men in this room. We have found a way to combat Malkus's telepathic influence."

"That's the good news," La Forge added.

Frowning, Kira asked, "What's the bad news?"

"We are presently in the Narendra system's Oort cloud," Klag said. "Sensors are detecting seven Defense Force ships and one Federation civilian ship in orbit of Narendra III—and they are in defensive formation. The civilian ship is a part of the formation, which leads us to think—"

"That they're all under Malkus's control," Kira finished. "Dammit."

Klag nodded. "Three of the ships are birds-of-prey under the command of Captain Huss. I know for a fact that they were at Ty'Gokor only yesterday."

"It is likely," Data said, "that they came to Narendra III and were also enthralled by Malkus."

"So it's four-to-one odds," Kira said. "Assuming Malkus doesn't enslave the rest of us."

La Forge smirked. "Well, thanks to Toq here, that won't be an issue for us. The thing is, we can neutralize Malkus altogether with our modified deflector—we're gonna rig it so that it broadcasts a large-scale version of what we hit you with. I was hoping to modify both ships, but the *Gorkon*'s deflector won't take to the modification, at least not in the time we've got. But if we're under fire . . ."

"Reinforcements?" Kira asked.

"The seven ships in orbit comprise all the Defense Force ships assigned to this sector," Klag said bitterly. "Others are en route, as are Starfleet ships—including the *Defiant* and the *Hood*—but no help will arrive for at least two more days. And we cannot afford to wait."

Data said, "Dr. Crusher has replicated the cure for the disease, based on the records from the *Constellation* and the *Enterprise* a century ago, but we cannot administer it until Malkus is neutralized."

La Forge put a hand on Data's shoulder. "I need to get back and rig up the deflector."

Nodding, Data said, "Lieutenant Toq and I will inoculate the *Gorkon* crew against Malkus's influence. Then I shall return to the *Enterprise* and do the same for our crew."

"How long will that take?" Klag asked.

"About an hour," La Forge said. "And at that, we'll be pushing it, but Beverly said we can't afford to wait much longer than that if we're going to have any chance of curing those people."

"Get to it, all of you," Klag said, and the trio departed the medical ward.

Kira got up from the biobed. Klag shot her a look. "What are you doing?"

Standing at attention, she said, "Colonel Kira Nerys, reporting for duty, Captain."

Klag threw his head back and laughed a loud, hearty laugh. "You are not a member of the Defense Force, Colonel."

"No, but I'm sure as hell not gonna sit around and let you do all the work," she said with a smile. "I'm ready, eager, and damn willing. So give me a post, Captain."

Still smiling, Klag touched his communicator. "Klag to Rodek. Lieutenant, has a new fore port gunner been assigned?"

"Bekk *Lojar was to be assigned, sir.*"

"Is there some reason why he shouldn't be?"

"He is a half-blind yIntagh *with the gunnery skill of a* grishnar *cat. Otherwise he is perfectly adequate for the job. Sir."*

Kira smiled. This Rodek person spoke in a very simple tone, conveying none of the invective of his words.

"We have someone else for the position, Lieutenant. Out." Klag cut the connection. "The *Gorkon* has four secondary gunnery positions for the twelve rotating disruptor arrays. One of the warriors assigned to the position died in a duel a week ago, and—as you heard—his replacement is inadequate."

Breaking into a grin, Kira said, "Not anymore, she isn't. I'll report to the bridge right away."

"Good," Klag said, leading her out of the medical ward. "Our controls may be strange to you. I suggest taking the next hour to familiarize yourself."

"Captain, I've flown Bajoran sub-impulse raiders, Starfleet starships, Klingon birds-of-prey, and Jem'-Hadar strike ships. I think I can handle a rotating disruptor array."

"Then report for duty, Colonel," Klag said as they arrived at a turbolift. "I will see you on the bridge."

Kira entered the lift and headed to her temporary new post.

Chapter Sixteen

MALKUS SEETHED—AS MUCH AS A disembodied mind could seethe, in any case.

It was impossible for one consciousness to maintain control over thousands of minds. But if the Instrument could allow control over only a few people at a time, it was functionally useless to Malkus. So Aidulac's team had hit upon a way of sending out shards of the user's telepathic essence to the person being controlled. That sliver of Malkus—independent, yet connected—provided the control. Malkus himself could monitor assorted shards and make adjustments as needed, but it was not required that he himself maintain constant oversight.

That ability had many good points. It meant that he was able to imprint shards of himself in the other three artifacts, and it enabled the number of people he could enslave to be in the thousands. The one bad point was that pawns could sometimes slip out of his control without his knowing it right away.

Most frustrating was his inability to hold on to Spock. The ambassador had been able to resist control practically from the beginning, and it had taken Malkus a great deal of effort forcing the shard of his consciousness to maintain its grip.

Then, when he checked on Kira Nerys, he found that his shard was nowhere to be found in her mind. Somehow, she had managed to expel it.

Unfortunately, until he was able to attach the fourth Instrument to the Great Rectangle, he did not have sufficient power to reestablish his control over her. As it was, he barely had enough to control the people on this planet and the ships in orbit. The former were busy constructing new buildings and structures and weapons for Malkus's use, as well as an android body for him to transfer his consciousness into.

When Spock had yet to return from dealing with the people in the shuttle, he connected with the shard in the ambassador's mind—only to find that it, too, was nowhere to be found.

No, wait—it was there, but it was cowering in an astral "corner" of Spock's consciousness, helpless. Malkus tried to take direct control, but he could not. There was something—different. The mental impression from Spock should have enabled Malkus to have complete control.

Then he realized that the mental impression was divided—split into two beings. Spock had performed some kind of telepathic trickery with the other ambassador he had traveled with in order to gain an advantage.

At that moment, Spock and his fellow diplomat—Worf—became more trouble than they were worth. As useful as they might have been, they now needed to die—as did their fellow prisoners in the shuttle. In retrospect, Malkus never should have let them all live in the first place.

Malkus sent out ten Klingons.

He also maintained personal control on one of them—J'lang was his name.

Through J'lang's eyes, Malkus observed the Klingons moving toward the shuttle. Six of them broke off to take care of the four in the shuttle. The other four could take care of two diplomats with ease, Malkus was sure of that. . . .

Malkus was able to use his pawns' natural abilities for himself, so the Klingons he had enthralled all did what came naturally—they unholstered their weapons as they moved through the tree-lined route between the hill where Malkus had been uncovered and the shuttle. They all had at least one bladed weapon, and some had energy weapons as well.

The six continued onward to the shuttle, while J'lang and the other three held back. Spock and Worf were nearby, Malkus knew that much. But he could not pinpoint where. They were not in sight, but the trees and bushes provided plenty of cover. It had been a long time since Malkus had coordinated a ground campaign—before his rise to power, in fact, since after that, he had generals to do the work for him—but he remembered enough to know that the two ambassadors were probably hiding behind one of the larger trees or one of the bushes. It was only a matter of flushing them out.

He split the foursome up, each taking a compass point for direction. At a certain distance beyond the field in which Malkus knew Spock and Worf had to be, they would turn back.

J'lang was carrying a weapon that was apparently used for the sculpting of rock into artwork, but it would work just as well to rend flesh. He also had a dagger of some kind—apparently, most Klingons carried one; they called it a *d'k tahg*. Both were one-handed weapons, so Malkus had J'lang have both at the ready.

Unfortunately, a search through the bushes and trees to the west revealed nothing. He turned J'lang back. When he arrived at the starting point, he saw two of his other pawns. Making contact with them, he learned that they had found nothing, either.

So where can they—?

Before Malkus could complete the thought, a bottle of some sort flew through the air and broke apart upon impact with the ground. When it did so, it burst into flames—and the fire quickly spread around the clearing.

Spock swung down from one of the branches in a kicking motion, his feet colliding with the back of one of the other Klingons' heads. As he fell, the other Klingon turned to fire his disruptor on the ambassador.

Before he could take the shot, however, a dark hand gripped his right shoulder. The Klingon convulsed and fell to the ground. Only then did Malkus see that the other ambassador had used the flames as cover to sneak up behind him and apply the same maneuver to the Klingon that Spock had used on Worf earlier.

I had thought that to be a Vulcan technique.

Then the fourth Klingon, who was named Roka, returned, and immediately charged Spock. He had instinctively attacked with his *bat'leth*—an edged weapon, but one favored by some Klingons over energy weapons. With astonishing speed, Spock grabbed one of the branches that had caught fire, and used it to hold Roka off.

Meanwhile, Malkus instructed J'lang to charge Worf. The sculpting tool could indeed be deadly, but it was not a distance weapon.

The Klingon that Spock had downed also had a *bat'leth,* and the half-breed was able to keep Roka at bay with his torch long enough to grab the weapon and use it to parry.

Malkus noted that Spock was using a fighting style that he recognized from the other Klingons he'd possessed—it was based on their form of combat called *mok'bara.* Malkus also knew that Spock had never studied the *mok'bara.*

Then again, he thought as Worf calmly dodged and weaved out of the way of J'lang's two-pronged *d'k tahg* and sculpting-tool attack, this Klingon ambassador had likely never learned the nerve pinch.

Malkus enjoyed a worthy foe as much as the next tyrant, but enough was enough. He needed to end this and get back to the business of rebuilding his empire.

It was then that he discovered that two ships were approaching Narendra III: a Starfleet vessel and a Klingon Defense Force vessel. Both were large—considerably more powerful than any of the eight ships Malkus had in his power. He reached out to the two new ships' captains—while he could not enslave the entire complements of the vessels, if he could at least take over their leaders. . . .

But he could not. Somehow, the minds of *all* the people on both ships were unavailable to him. That had never happened before.

So he sent his ships off to attack and destroy the vessels, then turned his attention back to J'lang—

—just as Worf knocked the sculpting tool out of J'lang's right hand with a chopping motion. He then converted that motion into a jab with his elbow to J'lang's face. As J'lang stumbled backward, Worf grabbed J'lang's left wrist, effectively neutralizing the *d'k tahg,* then yanked J'lang forward. J'lang stumbled toward Worf; Malkus tried to put up some kind of defense, but Worf then stopped J'lang's forward motion by grabbing J'lang's right shoulder with his left hand.

Malkus retreated from J'lang's mind as the sculptor lost consciousness, another victim of that be-damned Vulcan attack. He transferred his active control to Roka.

Spock and Roka seemed to be evenly matched with the *bat'leth,* at least. Roka had mostly been on the offensive, but Spock had parried each blow with the ease of the expert that Malkus knew full well he wasn't.

With a downward slash, Roka managed to entangle Spock's *bat'leth* and drive it to the grassy ground. He used his left elbow to jab Spock in the jaw, then disentangled his weapon from Spock's and swung upward.

However, Spock was able to duck backward and not be struck. Then he raised his own *bat'leth* in defense of Roka's next thrust.

They sparred for a moment, neither side gaining the offensive. Roka used Kilog's gambit against Spock, followed up by B'Arq's defense. According to Roka's memories, B'Arq's defense was impenetrable.

With an underhanded swing, Spock penetrated Roka's use of B'Arq's defense, knocking the *bat'leth* out of Roka's hands. Spock then slammed the leading edge of the *bat'leth* into Roka's side.

Malkus cursed as Roka fell to the ground, unable to move. He gazed upon the two ambassadors with fury as they stared at each other.

Worf raised an eyebrow. "Fascinating. Your penetration of B'Arq's defense was—familiar."

Spock half-smiled. "It should be, since I learned it from you. An excellent technique, if I may say so."

"Thank you. We should continue. Malkus may send more of his thralls against us."

You don't know the half of it, Klingon, Malkus thought angrily. He reached out to the pawns that had gone to the shuttle—

—only to find that five of the six were still engaged with the quintet from the shuttle. The sixth was dead, a *d'k tahg* having slit his throat. If the remainder broke off their attack to go after Spock and Worf, they too would be cut down.

Then Malkus laughed to himself. The solution was simple: the four Klingons who had been defeated here and the one dead at the shuttle were of no use. So Malkus sent those shards of his consciousness to B'Oraq, Davok, G'joth, Matthew Falce, and Hilary McKenna.

That gave him a full ten pawns to send after Spock and Worf.

Soon they'll all be dead. . . .

"New course, 287 mark 9—execute!"

"Train disruptors on the *Rikmok*."

"Weapons locked."

"Vralk, execute course *now!*"

"Prepare to fire on my mark."

Kira heard the voices in the background, but barely focused on who was talking. Her primary concern was the field of range belonging to the fore port disruptor array. There were three of them, each had four view-screens, one large and three small. Each screen showed a ninety-degree field, with the large one showing the ninety-degree area that the disruptor was currently trained in, the other three showing the remaining two hundred and seventy degrees. Her job was a simple one—identify any targets that came in range of any of the three disruptors under her purview, train the weapon on that target, and fire. Of course, with the speed at which ships moved and the comparatively limited range of the disruptors, that didn't leave her—or her three counterparts—many opportunities to fire, but they were only a small part of the *Gorkon*'s arsenal.

She tried not to think about what the Bajoran Resistance could have done with a ship like this against the Cardassians. *Hell, this thing even puts the* Defiant *to shame.*

Klag's deep voice penetrated the wall of sound that the bridge had become. "Remember, shoot to disable, not destroy. There is no glory in defeating mind-controlled warriors, nor any honor in dying in such a state." A pause. "But don't be fools, either. No matter what, we *shall* be victorious!"

Tereth said, "Captain Huss's ships are entering range. I suggest waiting—train weapons at 185 mark 9. She's likely to attempt a *bIng* manuever—it was a favorite of hers when I served with her."

Kira realized that one of her disruptors fell into that range. She immediately trained her number-three disruptor on that area—currently bereft of any ships.

Toq said, *"Nukmay, Khich,* and *Jor* changing course!" A pause. "A perfect *bIng* maneuver."

All three ships came right into Kira's sights, just as predicted.

"Fire!" Klag bellowed.

Kira trained her array on the wing of the *Nukmay,* the lead ship. It, combined with the disruptors fired by Rodek, slammed through the bird-of-prey's shields and tore a hole through the wing. That sent the ship into a spin that caused it to collide with the *Khich.* The latter ship's shields were disrupted into oblivion, though there was no hull damage.

A cheer went up from around the bridge, and the gunner closest to Kira—a *bekk* named Klorga—said, "Well done for a first shot, Bajoran."

"You ain't seen nothin' yet," Kira muttered. There was still the *Jor,* which fired its dirsuptors at the *Gorkon. Looks like they're aiming for the engines,* Kira thought.

"Shields down to eighty percent," Toq said.

Kira fired on the *Jor,* taking the ship's shields out with three shots before it left the range of her disruptors.

"We're being hailed by the *Enterprise,*" said the ensign at the communications console.

"On audio," Klag said.

"Klag, we need you to draw off some of these ships," Picard said. *"We can't use the deflector modification without lowering shields."*

Kira stole a glance at the tactical display on the main viewer. The *Enterprise* was more than holding its own against the other four ships—the *Sovereign*-class vessel had only suffered minor shield damage, whereas two of the Klingon ships were in pretty bad shape and the other two were on their way to more of the same. But that wouldn't last forever, especially since the *Enterprise* and *Gorkon* were doing their best to minimize casualties and their foes were working under no such constraint.

"Vralk, change course toward the *Enterprise,*" Klag said.

Tereth added, "Rodek, give us covering fire on the birds-of-prey."

That instruction, Kira knew, would be passed on to the two at the aft disruptor arrays.

A part of Kira liked the simplicity of it—all she was responsible for was three small three-hundred-and-sixty-degree fields of fire. No more, no less. Given the awesome responsibilities she had as the commanding officer of one of the more strategically important starbases in the quadrant, accountability for so little came as a relief.

But a part of her hated it for the same reason she hated what Malkus did to her. It was Klag who directed the battle, Tereth who commanded the troops, Rodek who carried out those commands, and only then did Kira get involved if those commands happened to relate to her tiny area of control.

And Kira Nerys never liked having limited control.

It had taken Aidulac two days to work her way across Narendra III.

With the aid of the component she'd found from the third Instrument, she had been able to trace the final Instrument to this planet, but frustratingly, not to *where* on this planet. She had to wait until someone unearthed the Instrument before she would be able to locate it more precisely.

So she settled on a remote island, converted the *Sun* to a shelter, and used its resources to survive. Her ability to influence men's minds was sufficient to keep prying eyes away from her—especially given the location she'd chosen in the middle of Narendra III's largest ocean—and she waited.

She'd waited ninety thousand years. She was prepared to wait another ninety thousand.

As it happened, she only had to wait for five years. A major war was fought in the interim, though the fighting never actually reached Narendra despite its position near both the Romulan and Federation borders.

Aidulac continued to wait.

Then, finally, the Instrument was exposed.

Naturally, it was on the other side of the planet.

From here on, Aidulac had to be careful. She could not afford to use the *Sun*, as it would be detected. Besides, Malkus's consciousness had, as she had feared, been imprisoned within the Instrument. Now he planned to rebuild his empire.

The fools. The unmitigated fools. The thought was directed at the well-meaning rebels who had overthrown Malkus. *They should have just killed him and had done with it. But no, they had to teach him a lesson, to imprison him, to make him suffer.*

They don't understand him. No one ever did. Not even me.

Especially not me. If I had, I would have just killed myself when he came to me.

First she took a boat to the mainland. Then she needed to find a groundcar to take her to where the memorial was being built. That had proven difficult, but not impossible. Her own immunity and invisibility to Malkus's telepathic control enabled her to move freely, but avoiding visual detection was a lot harder. Her own talents for persuasion were helpful, but not always reliable.

Now, though, she was less than an hour away on foot from the memorial site where he'd been uncovered.

Then, she thought, *this will all finally be over.*

Vralk maneuvered the *Gorkon* into position, hoping to draw fire away from the *Enterprise* so they could use their device to neutralize Malkus.

It doesn't surprise me, Vralk thought with disdain. *Klag would leave the glory to the weaklings of the Federation, even though it was we who learned the secret for defeating this Malkus thing.* He turned to glance at the secondary gunner positions, specifically the one where the Bajoran woman sat. *He even lets inferiors serve on his bridge. He is so unworthy of this vessel, it makes me ill.*

"Bring us around," Tereth shouted, "187 mark 9. *Now,* Lieutenant!"

Vralk changed course to 187 mark 9 and restrained himself from telling Commander Tereth to stop blathering at him. As Rodek had said, she *was* the first officer, even if she didn't deserve it—after all, as Lokor had said, he would find no allies for his cause on this ship.

"Hard to port," Tereth said. "Try to get the *Rikmok* off the *Enterprise*'s saucer."

"Shields failing," Toq said. "The birds-of-prey are continuing to fire!"

"Covering fire," Klag said. "Drive them off with the rear weapons, but try not to destroy them."

Vralk could not help himself. "We show weakness before the enemy?"

Klag turned angrily on Vralk. "They are *not* our enemy. When a Klingon *truly* takes up arms against me, then I will kill him or die without hesitation, but I will *not* destroy mind-controlled slaves unless I have to. And I do not have to—yet."

Disruptor blasts and torpedoes continued to slam into the *Gorkon*'s shields. Vralk found he could not avoid all of them, especially now that they were close to the *Enterprise*—some of the Defense Force ships simply fired on both targets. While the *Enterprise* and *Gorkon* were far more powerful, they were also larger and less maneuverable than their eight foes.

"The *QaS DevwI'* have all reported in," the ensign at communications said. "All ground troops are standing by."

"Good," Tereth said.

Again, Vralk found he could not help himself. He turned to Tereth, who was standing between the com console and Vralk's own helm control. "The *QaS DevwI'* will not be able to lead the troops into battle if we are blown up before they can be deployed!"

Another impact. Several consoles went down.

"Shields have failed!" Toq cried.

"You are a fool to continue this!" Vralk said, getting up and walking toward Tereth. "We must—"

Tereth suddenly leapt at Vralk, tackling him.

As Vralk fell to the deck his heart sang out with joy. *At last, the fool woman has tipped her hand! She feels the need to silence me in public! Now I can truly challenge her and show everyone that she is unworthy!*

He clambered to an upright position, unsheathing his *d'k tahg.*

Tereth remained on the deck, with a very large chunk of what was once a piece of the ceiling bulkhead now embedded in her back.

She had not been challenging him, she had saved his life at the cost of her own.

He dropped his *d'k tahg* to the deck.

Had he remained at his post, the shrapnel would not have hit him or Tereth. But because he abandoned his post in a conflict, a superior was dead.

What have I done?

"Vralk, you're relieved," Klag said. "I will kill you later. Koxx, take the helm! Bring us around, 241 mark 6. Rodek—full weapons!"

Turning toward the turbolift, his *d'k tahg* still on the deck, Vralk thought, *I suppose now he has to use deadly force. If he had done it sooner, Tereth might not be dead now.*

And if I had not been such a fool, she would not be dead, either.

Aidulac checked the readings on her scanner. She had less than an hour's walk to where Malkus was keeping himself. And then—one way or another—it would all be over.

This was parkland now. Aidulac had never been to this world when it was part of the Zalkat Union, nor in the millennia since, so she had no idea what it might have been like then. *Probably some backwater—otherwise, why hide the Instrument away here?*

She hadn't expected to be tackled by a crazed Klingon in military garb.

The Klingon knocked her to the ground, knelt down on her chest, then swiped at her face with some kind of edged weapon. Aidulac raised her arm to defend herself, and the blade sank into her forearm. She cried out in pain as the Klingon yanked the blade out and started to take another swipe.

Before he could, a hand gripped the Klingon's shoulder, and he fell to the ground, unconscious.

Another Klingon, this one wearing a floor-length coat that, from what Aidulac knew of Klingon traditions, meant he held some kind of high office, rolled Aidulac's attacker off her. "Thank you," she said. "I wasn't aware of any Klingons who knew the Vulcan nerve pinch."

"It is a long story," he said. "I am Worf, son of Mogh. You do not appear to be in Malkus's thrall."

"No," she said, putting pressure on her wound. "I am Aidulac, and I'm here to stop Malkus."

Worf's eyebrow rose—another Vulcan gesture. "Fascinating. How do you intend to accomplish this?"

Before she could answer, a Vulcan approached, wearing once-elegant robes that had not weathered travel through this forest particularly well—the black cloth was spattered with dirt and grass stains. Bloodstains were present as well, but they were not green, so they did not belong to him. His movements were also odd, for a Vulcan—and he was carrying a Klingon weapon.

"Two of our foes—" the Vulcan started, then noticed the other one on the ground. "Three of our foes have been defeated. We must hurry, before the others catch up." He looked at Aidulac and then spoke irritably. "Who is this?"

"I am Aidulac. I am here to stop Malkus—forever. I've waited ninety thousand years for this day." She frowned. "You two have mind-melded?"

"Yes," Worf said. "It was the logical way to resist Malkus's control."

"Very wise."

"I am Spock," the Vulcan said. "We don't have much time. The mind-meld will start to fade soon, and both Ambassador Worf and I will be helpless if that should happen. Do you have a method of neutralizing Malkus?"

Aidulac nodded. "I believe so. I have had many millennia to construct the device, but no way to ever test it. My attempts to do so with the previous artifacts met with resistance."

Spock raised his eyebrow in the exact same manner that Worf had done a moment ago. "I do recall a report of a woman named Aidulac attempting to land on Alpha Proxima II when the first artifact was found there. Are you the same woman?"

"Yes."

"Fascinating," both Worf and Spock said simultaneously.

Worf continued, "But not relevant at this time. We must press forward before Malkus's thralls catch up to us—or he sends more."

"We don't have far to go," Aidulac said. Keeping the pressure on her wound, she started walking.

After a moment, the Vulcan and the Klingon followed.

Within a few minutes, they had arrived. They took up position behind a large tree that overlooked the hill. Aidulac saw two humans—a younger one in a Starfleet uniform, and an older one in a variation of the same—standing near a table on which sat all four Instruments.

Three of them, Aidulac noted, were connected. The fourth was separate. She smiled. "I see he tried to construct the Great Rectangle."

Worf turned to her. "We have received no resistance since we met you. Why is that?"

"I am invisible to Malkus thanks to this." She removed the component from the third Instrument from her belt.

"That is the missing component from the third artifact," Spock said.

Aidulac nodded. "I found it five years ago. Then I waited here for the final Instrument to be unearthed."

Just then, two humans and three Klingons approached Malkus from the other side of the clearing.

"You were right," Worf said to Spock. "He did enslave our fellow prisoners."

"It seemed a reasonable hypothesis," Spock said. "How close do you need to be to the artifacts in order for your device to work?"

"Closer than this," Aidulac said ruefully. "We shall have to go out into the open."

"Wait," Worf said. "Look."

The humans and Klingons all left—including one of the two Starfleet officers who had already been present—leaving only the elderly human to guard Malkus.

"They've probably gone to keep searching for you two."

"Indeed," Worf said. "Leaving only Dr. McCoy—and as the admiral himself might say, he is a doctor, *not* a fighter."

Worf unsheathed a disruptor pistol, and Spock hefted the Klingon blade. They exchanged a nod, and then charged, Aidulac behind them.

Unsurprisingly, by the time they reached the Instruments, some of the thralls had returned. Worf, however, took two of them out with his disruptor, and the one that charged in at close quarters was dealt with by Spock. They covered her approach to Malkus quite well.

McCoy made a halfhearted attempt to attack Worf, but the human was far too aged to be any real threat. Worf grabbed his neck and said, "Sorry, Doctor, I have no time to discuss this logically."

As Worf gently set the elderly human on the ground before turning his attention to other mind-controlled foes, Aidulac deactivated the component from the third Instrument. She no longer needed its protection from Malkus's influence. "It's been a long time, Mighty One."

You! Then she felt his laughter in her mind. *Of course, you survived. I should have known.*

"I only survived for one reason, Mighty One—to see you and the Instruments I made for you destroyed."

She switched on the device. In theory, it would neutralize all four artifacts.

NOOOOOOOOOOOOOOOOOOOOOOOOOOOOOOOO OOOOOO!

Both the Klingon warrior that Spock was sparring with and the Starfleet officer that Worf was wrestling with stopped fighting. Spock was able to disarm the Klingon, and Worf knocked the Starfleet officer to the ground.

The Starfleet officer frowned. "What happened? Ambassador Worf? What the hell's going on?"

"My apologies, Captain DeSoto," Worf said, offering the man a hand up.

The Klingon warrior stared at Spock. "Why am I fighting a Vulcan?"

"All will be explained in due course," Spock said, then turned to Aidulac. "It seems you were successful. Malkus's telepathic hold appears to have been broken."

Aidulac smiled.

"Captain, the birds-of-prey have broken formation!"

Klag whirled around at Rodek. "What?"

"The other ships as well—they have ceased firing."

Toq said, "Sir, we are being hailed—by all the ships. They wish to know what is going on."

Getting up out of his command chair—once again no stumbling—Klag thought, *Something must have happened to Malkus.* "Get me Picard, *now!*"

"Channel open," Toq said.

"Activate your deflector now, Picard!"

"Understood, Klag."

Klag watched the viewer as the *Enterprise* lowered its shields. Then its deflector dish lit up with a harsh light as the Starfleet vessel changed position.

To the new pilot, the captain said, "Koxx, keep us between the *Enterprise* and any threats, in case Malkus reasserts himself."

Toq said, "The *Enterprise* is firing!"

The device exploded in Aidulac's hands.

Unfortunately, the explosion took Aidulac's hand with it.

She screamed in pain and collapsed to the ground.

Never, in all her millennia of life, had she ever felt anything remotely like the agony she felt now.

But the physical pain was as nothing compared to the mental anguish of her failure. *All my work for naught. I was a fool to think I could defeat the Mighty One. I never could then—why would it be different now?*

She heard Malkus's laughter in her mind.

It was a brave attempt, Aidulac, Malkus said to her. *But I am Malkus the Mighty. With but a gesture, I destroyed entire solar systems. You are as nothing to me. The galaxy is as nothing to me. Soon, I will—*

Then she heard nothing. It was as if someone had simply turned Malkus off in midsentence. His presence was completely gone from her mind, as much as it was before she deactivated the component.

Looking over at the table that the four Instruments sat on, she saw that they had suddenly gone dead.

The voice of the android Data sounded over the *Gorkon*'s speakers. *"I am reading no emissions from the Malkus Artifacts. They have been rendered inert."*

Toq added, "Confirmed. None of the mind-control readings are present, and neither are the Malkus emissions."

The ensign at the engineering station cried, "Victory!" Several others followed suit.

Klag ignored the cries. Instead, he walked over to the body of Commander Tereth, still lying on the deck next to the helm control. Turning her body over, Klag pried open her eyes.

She had been the best of them, serving him well, working with the crew, being his eyes and ears and hands on the *Gorkon*. He doubted he would ever be able to properly replace her.

And how did she die? In battle, covered in glory?

No. She died saving the life of an undeserving animal.

Rearing his head back, Klag screamed.

Next to him, Koxx did the same.

After a moment, so did everyone on the bridge—almost a score of warriors, screaming to the heavens. Klag's ears rang with it, and it prompted him only to scream louder.

The Black Fleet in *Sto-Vo-Kor* now knew that Tereth, daughter of Rokis of the House of Kular, was crossing the River of Blood to join them.

The screams finally subsided. Klag looked down at the empty shell that was once his first officer. Then he looked up to see Colonel Kira standing over them.

"I would have liked to have shared that drink with her," she said.

"You and I shall share it in her honor," Klag said as he got to his feet.

He did so by bracing himself with his right arm, and got to his feet gracefully.

Chapter Seventeen

WORF TOOK A LONG SIP OF PRUNE JUICE, wishing that the human beverage were more useful for driving out splitting headaches.

The ambassador sat in the Ten-Forward lounge of the *Enterprise,* perusing the report that Giancarlo Wu had sent along from Qo'noS. Wu had attended to the difficulty on Mempa V with his usual efficiency—the Tellarites were freed after paying a hefty fine, and escorted out of the Empire with all due haste—and the fifth draft of the Klingon/Tholian resolution had apparently met with approval by both sides.

"May I join you?" said a familiar voice.

Worf looked up to see Ambassador Spock, looking much as he had when Worf first saw him on the *St. Lawrence.* He had cleaned up and put on fresh robes to replace the blood-and-dirt-stained ones from the surface. In addition, he was walking like a Vulcan again instead of the ready-to-fight demeanor that Worf himself favored.

Keith R.A. DeCandido

"Of course," Worf said, happily putting the padd down as Spock took the seat opposite him.

"Forgive the intrusion, but I wished to inquire after your health. The mind-meld can sometimes be difficult even for native-born Vulcans, much less outsiders."

"I am fine," Worf said. "Although—" He hesitated.

"Yes?"

Worf took a bracing sip of prune juice before continuing. This wasn't easy for him to say. "I would like to apologize for my behavior on the *St. Lawrence*. I should not have questioned your motives. The mind-meld has given me—a new perspective on your position. Your thoughts are not of the Romulan government, but of the Romulan *people*—the ones who lost their brothers and sisters to the war. Those are—noble goals."

"I have spent a great deal of time over the last few years with the Romulan people. They should not be punished for the shortsightedness of their government— or of someone else's. However," Spock said quickly, "I too feel the need to offer an apology. I now understand the crux of your argument: that, while the Klingon Empire and the Federation went to war with the Dominion in order to preserve the Alpha Quadrant, the Romulan Empire went to war to preserve the Romulan Empire. A subtle distinction that I, in my zeal to protect the Romulan people, lost sight of."

Worf shook his head. "Not at all. I believe that both arguments have merit."

"Indeed. And we shall have many opportunities to present them at Khitomer." Spock paused and regarded Worf with a penetrating gaze. "You have led a most— intriguing life, Mr. Ambassador. If you have time—and the inclination—I would like to discuss certain elements of it with you."

Had anyone else made the request, Worf would have refused. But, just as Spock had obviously been intrigued by Worf's life, so too was Worf by Spock's. The man was truly a living legend, and Worf had gained some—there was no other word for it—fascinating insights into the man behind that legend. It left him with a great desire to learn more.

Then he remembered something. "Computer, time?"

"The time is 1105 hours."

"I am sorry, Mr. Ambassador. I would like to have those discussions—but not at the moment. I have an—appointment on the *Gorkon*."

Spock inclined his head. "Of course. We will have ample opportunities to converse over the next few days in any event."

Worf stood up and drained the rest of his prune juice. "I look forward to it." Truly, he did—had he not made the promise to Klag, he would have stayed to talk with Spock for as long as the Vulcan ambassador wished. Leaving aside his interest in discussing the things Spock had seen, the battles he had fought, it was also an infinitely preferable alternative to the mindless drudgery of Worf's life as Federation Ambassador to Qo'noS. Khitomer promised plenty of that as it was—talking with Spock would be a welcome palliative.

Leonard McCoy was tired.

Less than a year from his hundred and fiftieth birthday, McCoy got tired fairly easily these days. On top of the usual fatigue of daily existence as a cranky old man, he had to put up with Malkus invading his cranium. Admittedly, dealing with it was less of an issue than it might have been for a younger person. After all, your limbs not doing what you intend them to do was a fact of life the longer you spent on the wrong side of the century mark. Still, it wasn't usually the whole body.

McCoy sat in the *Enterprise*'s Ten-Forward lounge, sipping a syntheholic mint julep that tasted about as dreadful as he expected. But his cardiovascular system couldn't really handle the real thing all that much these days—especially after the exertions Malkus put him through.

"How are you feeling, Doctor?"

The sudden voice at his back almost made McCoy drop his glass. He turned around to see Spock standing behind him. Only a few minutes ago, McCoy had noticed Spock sitting with Worf. The doctor looked over to see that their table was now empty.

As his old comrade sat down across from him, McCoy said, "I hate it when you do that. And to answer your question, I was fine until you scared the daylights out of me. How 'bout you?"

"The effects of the mind-meld have almost faded. There will always be a residue of Ambassador Worf inside me and of me in him, but that is to be expected."

McCoy chuckled. "After all the melds you've done in your time, your cerebral cortex is probably more crowded than Paris on Inauguration Day. As for me, I like to keep my head to myself, thanks. It was bad enough when I had to share my brain with you way back when. Malkus was a helluva lot worse. One thing I don't get, though."

"Only one thing?" Spock asked in his usual deadpan.

"Don't start with me, bucko, we're both too old," McCoy muttered. "Back when you core-dumped your brain into mine before you died, I couldn't do that damn neck pinch of yours. Worf only had some of your marbles, and he was distributing neck pinches right and left."

"The mind-meld is not a precise tool, as you well know, Doctor. It would seem that Worf was simply luckier than you."

"Got that right," he said, taking another sip of the julep.

"However, that experience from ninety years ago is a primary reason why I was able to resist Malkus's control enough to perform the mind-meld in the first place. My death and resurrection on Genesis altered my brain chemistry sufficiently to make Malkus's grip on my mind tenuous at best."

"As opposed to your grip on reality, which is completely tenuous," McCoy said with a smile.

Spock's eyebrow shot up. "I thought we were too old for this sort of thing?"

McCoy shrugged. "I lied."

Before Spock could reply, Picard entered the lounge and headed to their table. "Gentlemen, may I join you?"

"Of course, Captain," Spock said, indicating one of the seats between them.

"How're things dirtside?" McCoy asked.

"Settling down. Captain Klag's ground troops have been able to restore order. Dr. Crusher was able to cure as many of the Klingons imprisoned in the sports arena as were still alive."

"Still alive?" McCoy frowned. "There wasn't time for the virus to— Oh, hell. A virus that pumps adrenaline into Klingons."

"Yes," Picard said gravely. "I'm afraid that the virus combined with the enclosed space to cause no small amount of violence, even by Klingon standards."

McCoy shook his head, thinking about all those who died before he and Lew Rosenhaus came up with the cure the last time it reared its ugly head on Proxima a century earlier.

"How is Aidulac, Captain?" Spock asked.

"Dr. Crusher has fitted her with prosthetic hands. She has requested that she be allowed to take the artifacts into her personal custody."

"Makes sense—she helped build the damn things," McCoy said.

Picard's head tilted to one side slightly. "Unfortunately, she also has several warrants out for her arrest—some dating back over two hundred years. For obvious reasons the Federation is not very interested in turning over four powerful weapons to her—and very interested in fulfilling those warrants."

"Understandable," Spock said.

"In any event, the artifacts will be returned to the Rector Institute—with security heightened, obviously," Picard added with a wry smile.

"DeSoto's not gonna get in any hot water, is he?" McCoy asked.

"I doubt it," Picard said. "There will be a hearing for formality's sake—"

McCoy muttered into his julep. "Right, 'cause heaven forfend there not be paperwork for the bureaucrats to play with."

"—but I'm sure he'll be cleared of any theft charges. The *Hood* is still en route to pick him up—as is the *Defiant* to retrieve Colonel Kira. We've loaded the *St. Lawrence* into our shuttlebay, and we shall convey you," he glanced at Spock, "and Ambassador Worf to Khitomer this afternoon, along with your pilots. You'll be happy to know that the opening meetings have been delayed until our arrival, despite objections from the Romulans. Captain Klag will remain behind with the *Gorkon* to oversee putting Narendra III back together. Apparently he has also offered to repair Captain Butterworth's ship."

"Who?" McCoy asked. *That for damn sure doesn't sound like any Klingon name I've ever heard.*

"The civilian freighter that was part of Malkus's fleet," Picard said. "They sustained heavy damage during the conflict."

"What the hell was a Federation civilian freighter doing here anyhow?" McCoy asked.

Picard gave a half-smile. "They were providing marble for the Dominion War memorial that is being built on Narendra—in fact, it was the groundbreaking for that memorial that led to the artifact being unearthed."

"Figures," McCoy muttered.

"In any event, Admiral," Picard said, "I believe Klag is arranging for you and Dr. B'Oraq to travel to Qo'noS as soon as you're ready. The High Council doesn't like to be kept waiting," he added with a smile.

Snorting, McCoy said, "Hell, they're probably teed off that I made it through this alive. Now they're stuck with me giving them their lecture."

"Surely a fate worse than death," Spock said dryly. Turning to Picard before McCoy could reply to the jab, he said, "The arrival of yourself and Captain Klag was most timely. It was greatly appreciated, since eventually Ambassador Worf and I would have succumbed—either to Malkus's thralls or to his telepathic attack when the mind-meld deteriorated."

"Your interference also gave us the opportunity to use our psilosynine wave, Ambassador, so I'd say we're even."

"Actually, Captain, it was Aidulac who truly provided the distraction."

Picard's eyes widened. "Did she? Well, perhaps that will be a mitigating factor in her defense. In any case, you should be thanking Colonel Kira more than anyone. She was the one who led us here."

"Where is the colonel, anyhow?" McCoy asked.

"I believe she had some final business on the *Gorkon*."

Lokor sat at the desk in his quarters, reading over the daily reports from his guards. The reports were shorter than usual by dint of most of the *Gorkon*'s ground troops being on-planet. The biggest security headache on a ship this size was when the ground troops went for an extended period without actually being put to use. Of course, they had drills and exercises and tasks to perform, but unless they were off the ship and doing their jobs—which boiled down to fighting and dying for the Empire on a planet or base or enemy vessel—they tended to go stir-crazy.

And stir-crazy troops meant difficulties for the person in charge of maintaining order.

But Lokor had done his job well, he thought. The incidents were kept to a minimum—little beyond the usual maimings of daily life in the Defense Force. And, with the Narendra situation, a comparatively quiet day for a change.

His door chime rang. "Enter."

The door opened to the smell of *adanji*. At first he thought one of his deputies had confiscated some incense. He looked up to say that he didn't want that foul-smelling stuff in his quarters, when he saw that it wasn't one of his deputies, it was Vralk.

As if that wasn't bad enough, he was wearing not his uniform but the ceremonial robes of the House of Grunnil. A *mevak* dagger was holstered in his belt.

"What is it you want, boy?" Lokor asked, though he could guess the answer.

Vralk hesitated, then spoke in a solemn voice. "I have dishonored our family name—our House. I know that Captain Klag will condemn me for my dishonorable actions, and so I wish to reclaim my honor in the next life. I have come for *Mauk to'Vor.*"

Lokor stood up and walked around his desk. He was a full head taller than Vralk. He put his hands on the boy's shoulders and looked solemnly down at him

Then he burst into hysterical laughter.

"Truly you are the biggest imbecile in a House of imbeciles."

Vralk looked like he'd swallowed dead *gagh.* "You—you're not—" He shook his head. "You *must* fulfill my request to kill me honorably! It is your duty as my cousin!"

"And what of your duty to your ship? In case you have forgotten, boy, you got the first officer killed. A first officer, I might add, who was a great deal better liked by the crew than you. If by some miracle the captain does *not* have you killed, you still won't live to see your next duty shift."

"I—I don't understand." Vralk shook his head. "I have lived an honorable life. I have striven to be the best Klingon I know how to be. I do not deserve to go to *Gre'thor!*"

The sight of Vralk was pitiful, and Lokor couldn't help but laugh again. "If this is the best Klingon you know how to be, than it is preferable that you die quickly and make room for someone who can do it right." He shook his head and turned his back on his cousin. "Now get out of my sight—and take that odoriferous *taHqeq* with you."

Lokor waited until he heard the door open and the scent of the *adanji* faded from his nostrils before he turned around.

Then he sat back down at his desk and looked at his security reports.

* * *

Robert DeSoto stared at the Go board game. The replicator in his guest quarters on the *Enterprise* had been happy to provide one. It would have been equally happy to provide him with the stones, but DeSoto hadn't been able to bring himself to ask for that as well.

The door chime rang. "Come on in," he said.

The tall form of Will Riker stood on the other side of the door. DeSoto couldn't help but smile broadly. "Hey, Will. How's everything going?"

Riker came into the quarters, an equally broad smile on his beardless face. "That was going to be my question for you, Captain. After all, I wasn't mind-controlled by a ninety-thousand-year-old tyrant."

"Good point."

"Just by the way," Riker said, pointing at the Go board, "I've already warned the crew about you, so if you're planning to hustle anyone—"

"No, I'm not," DeSoto said, unable to keep his tone jovial. "In fact—honestly, this is the first time I've even *looked* at a Go board in a year and a half. Ever since Chin'toka." He sighed. "It's funny, the last time one of those Malkus Artifacts got dug up was five years ago. Since then, I've pretty much lost everyone who was on the *Hood* then—the only one who didn't die in the war or leave Starfleet is my old security chief, and he's got his own ship now. But the worst was losing Dina."

"She was your first officer?" Riker asked.

DeSoto nodded. "She actually used to beat me at Go."

"You're kidding."

At that, DeSoto did actually laugh, just from the sheer incredulousness in Riker's tone. "Yup. She went from a handicap to whupping my tail in less than a year. I've taught lots of people to play—including, if memory serves," he added with a look at Riker, "a young lieutenant commander who said he didn't like games where he couldn't bluff—but she was the only one who got to be as good as me. Hell, she was probably better."

DeSoto got up from the desk and walked over to the replicator. "You want anything?"

Riker shook his head.

"Water, cold." As the replicator provided the glass of water, DeSoto said, "The worst part is, she wasn't even supposed to still be on the ship. For Chin'toka, I mean. Her promotion'd come through, but her post, the *Tian An Men*, was still in the yard for repairs. She insisted on coming along for one last hurrah on the *Hood*." He took a sip of the water. "It was a last hurrah, all right. It's funny, she died the same way that first officer on the Klingon ship went. A plasma conduit blew, and the shrapnel would've shredded one of the junior officers. She knocked the ensign out of the way, took it all herself." He gulped down the rest of the water. "I haven't played Go since."

Riker didn't say anything for several seconds. Then: "You doing anything right now, Captain?"

DeSoto shrugged. "Just waiting for the *Hood* to show up and take me to a starbase so they can do my disciplinary hearing."

"I'm sure that'll be fine."

"Yeah." DeSoto sighed. "You know, Malkus sat in that artifact for ninety thousand years—and that Aidulac woman wandered around the galaxy for ninety thousand years waiting for him. That's a helluva long time to basically do nothing. And you know what? I'm not going to be like that." He smiled. "How'd you like a game?"

"Much as I would love to humiliate myself before your Go prowess, Captain," Riker said with a grin, "I have another engagement. And I'd like you to join me."

* * *

Aidulac stared at the four walls of her cell.

Well, three walls, truly. The fourth was a forcefield.

She was no more concerned now than she was the last time she'd been put in prison after a defeat to Malkus. Her skills weren't what they once were, but she still had them. She would be able to escape.

The cries of the dead continued to haunt her. It had been ninety thousand years, and still the corpses that Malkus had created with Instruments she helped create would not leave her mind's eye.

Not to mention the corpses of her team.

A very large part of her thought that it was time to simply end it all. She'd waited for ninety thousand years, traveling the galaxy in a variety of ships waiting for the Instruments to be revealed and Malkus to be reawakened, only to fail utterly in her endeavor to destroy both Malkus and the Instruments once and for all.

On the other hand, she knew precisely where they all were now. And they'd already been stolen once. . . .

Klag sat alone in his office, staring dolefully at the bottle of bloodwine and the six empty mugs on his desk, when the door chime rang. "Enter," he said.

Kira, Riker, Worf, B'Oraq, and DeSoto all came in.

"Ah, good," he said. "Come in, all of you."

The quintet gathered around Klag's desk. Klag himself remained seated, the others remained standing, even though there were two guest chairs. Klag suspected that they were all too polite to take a seat over one of the others. From Riker, DeSoto, and Kira he'd expect such— *though the ambassador was raised among humans, and the doctor studied with them, so they no doubt picked up bad habits, too,* he thought with an internal smile.

"When she first came on board the *Gorkon*, Commander Tereth gave me this bottle of bloodwine. It was made by House Ozhpri."

Only DeSoto seemed confused—the others, even Kira and Riker, knew the name of one of the Empire's best vintners and looked suitably impressed. And at those looks, DeSoto seemed to guess what Klag meant, and he nodded.

"I asked her for what occasion she honored me with this bottle. She said when the time was right, I would know. Now she is dead, and while it is not the death I would have wished for so fine a warrior, she died in uniform. She died in battle. She died defending the Empire." As he spoke, he poured the bloodwine into each of the mugs, ending with the quote, " 'In death there is victory and honor.' " He looked at each of them. "The time is right now. And you are the right people to share it with."

Klag held up a mug as he addressed each person without getting up from his chair. "Worf, son of Mogh, whose actions on taD enabled me to find an excuse to get rid of Drex, thus paving the way for me to bring Tereth to the *Gorkon*."

Worf nodded as he took the mug from Klag's outstretched hand.

"B'Oraq, daughter of Grala, who gave me a new right arm and helped me to restore my own family's honor, and to whom I never gave proper thanks. I thought I'd take this opportunity to do so before you are once again kidnapped by a ninety-thousand-year-old megalomaniac."

Laughing, B'Oraq accepted the mug and said, "An understandable precaution, Captain."

"Riker, my old comrade-in-arms—at last we have been reunited in battle, and been victorious. And we lived, giving us another chance to fight and die together."

Grinning, Riker took the mug. "Let's hope for lots of those chances."

"DeSoto, Riker tells me that you lost your own first officer during the war. He thought this would give you an opportunity to celebrate the releasing of her spirit."

DeSoto nodded and took the mug. "He thought right. Thank you—both of you."

"And Kira. As promised—the drink you and Tereth pledged to share."

"Thank you," the colonel said, taking the mug.

Klag raised the last mug and cried, "Raise your drinks! Today a new warrior enters *Sto-Vo-Kor!* May her battle be endless, her glory be eternal—and may we all join her in due course! To Tereth!"

Together, they all cried, "To Tereth!" Then they each gulped their bloodwine—Worf, B'Oraq, and Klag enthusiastically, Riker, DeSoto, and Kira somewhat more cautiously.

Klag felt the oily liquid coat his mouth and throat. It was a marvelous sensation—as one would have expected from Ozhpri bloodwine. It was the finest vintage he'd ever had.

Worf took a second gulp, finishing off his mug, then started to sing in a deep bass voice. *"Qoy qeylIs puqloD. Qoy puqbe'pu'."*

B'Oraq joined him for the next line. *"yoHbogh matlhbogh je SuvwI'."*

Klag threw his head back and bellowed out the next: *"Say'moHchu' may' 'Iw. maSuv manong 'ej maHoHchu'."*

Together, the three of them—joined here and there by Riker, DeSoto, and Kira, who obviously did not know the words, but got into the spirit as best they could—sang the rest of the Warrior's Anthem in Tereth's memory.

Klag drained the last of his bloodwine. "Thank you all, my friends. You have honored me with your presence, and honored Tereth as well—not to mention," he added with a look to DeSoto, "Commander Voyskunsky."

"It was my pleasure," Kira said.

"Oh, Colonel," Klag said, reaching into a drawer in his desk, "Tereth left something for you." He removed an optical chip and handed it to Kira. "A recording of 'The Battle for Deep Space 9.' "

Kira grinned and took the chip. "I look forward to hearing it."

Riker set his mug down on Klag's desk and looked at Worf. "We need to get back—we still have to get you to Khitomer."

"Yes. It is good to see you again, Captain," the ambassador said to Klag.

"Qapla', all of you," Klag said.

They all returned the salutation: *"Qapla'!"*

With that, the four of them departed, leaving Klag and B'Oraq alone.

"Have you requested a new first officer yet?" B'Oraq asked.

"No," Klag said. "In truth, I fear for what Command will send me this time." He stared at the now-empty bottle. "We shall never see her like again."

"Perhaps," B'Oraq said. "Perhaps we will see better."

Klag threw his head back and laughed. "Ever the optimist, Doctor?"

"Naturally, Captain. I'm trying to improve Klingon medicine—if I weren't an optimist, I'd have given up years ago."

"An excellent point." Klag braced his hands on the arms of his chair and got up.

Then he stumbled to the right, not adequately compensating for his shorter right arm.

"Qu'vatlh!" he cursed in anger.

Malkus had been in the middle of excoriating the hapless Aidulac when he was interrupted.

His sensory input was, of course, limited to telepathic contact, but that contact included an entire world and beyond. Suddenly, without any kind of warning, that contact just stopped.

He no longer felt the presence of his pawns.

Worse, he no longer felt the presence of the other Instruments.

In fact, he couldn't even feel the presence of the Instrument he was trapped within.

How, he did not know, but he had been cut off from everything.

For ninety thousand years, he had been trapped with only the most minimal contact with the galaxy.

Now it seemed he was trapped once again with even less than that.

Desperately, he reached out, trying to find some connection to another mind, another Instrument, Aidulac, anything.

Utter silence was his only answer.

Malkus started to scream a silent scream that no one would hear.

A scream that would never end.

THE BRAVE AND THE BOLD

Technical Specifications of the *Qang*-Class Vessels in the Klingon Defense Force

by Tammy Love Larrabee

Statistics

Classification	Heavy Cruiser
Class	*Qang* (Chancellor)
Number Constructed	***Classified***
Number Destroyed	***Classified***
Ship's Complement	2725 crew
Brigs	110
Transporters	35 6-person
Holodecks	1

Ship Size

Length	479.40m
Width	364.44m
Height	105.24m
Displacement	1123.0102mt

Weapons

Disruptor Arrays	12 360o
Disruptor Output	$9.0x1011w/x4.0x1011w$ Continuous
Disruptor Cannon	1
Cannon Output	$7.8x1012w/3.7x1012w$ Continuous
Photon Torpedoes	102
Quantum Torpedoes	36

Defensive

Shield Holdoff	$8.87x1012w$
Shield Refresh	$3.45x1012w$
Reactive Armor/ Damage	Deflective Plating

Speed

Optimum Speed	Warp 7
Cruising Speed	Warp 8
Maximum Speed	Warp 9.82

ECM

Cloaking Device	
Electronic Jamming Equipment	

Hull Separation Capability

Emergency separation of the primary hull section from the secondary hull is possible. The secondary hull houses the disruptor cannon and is able to function at sublight speeds. The main bridge section is also capable of separation from the primary hull, and is maneuverable at impulse speeds using emergency impulse engines.

Weaponry

The *Qang* class has one forward-facing disruptor cannon, mounted in the "head" of the ship, with an output of 7.8×10^{12}w/3.7×10^{12}w continuous. There are 12 360° disruptor arrays on the *Qang*. Six are top-mounted and six are bottom-mounted with an output of 9.0×10^{12}/4.0×10^{12}w. All disruptors are set for a variable modulation every 10–12 seconds with a repetition rate of 300,000 cycles; this feature was added to combat the Borg. The photon-torpedo tubes are located on the bottom of the ship. Standard complement of torpedoes for this ship is 102 photon and 36 quantum torpedoes.

Deflector Shields and Plating

Advanced deflector emitters create an energetic deflecting shield around the ship. Emitters are located in various sections of the ship and provide overlap shielding, causing attacks and collisions to "glance off." When the deflector shields fail, the ship relies upon its damage deflective plating, which enhances standard hull integrity to absorb damage until the deflector shields can be reengaged.

Cloaking Device

The cloaking device utilizes a gravitational field to bend light around the ship, while using warp-bubble technology to bend space-time, making the ship appear invisible. The field generators are located in the lower midsection of the ship.

ECM

The ECM hampers enemy communications, scrambles sensors, and even creates false images to confuse enemy craft and installations.

Tractor Beams

The tractor-beam system utilizes an energy field generator to either surround and pull, or push against objects the ship needs to capture/move. The inertial dampers and impulse drive must be online for this system to work during flight, inertial dampers for unexpected bumps and collisions and the impulse engines so that when the ship is moving something larger than itself the object moves and the ship does not. The tractor beam is located in the lower fore section of the ship.

The tractor-beam inflight sequence is as follows:

- Tractor beam activated
- Inertial dampers to 100%
- Impulse engines engaged
- Tractor beam charged and ready

Holodeck

The holodeck uses a combination of holographic, replicator, and transporter technology. The holocomputer calculates the three-dimensional divergent patterns of light that would be cast from any given hypothetical or real object submitted by the person writing the program, and projects it as a hologram. Simultaneously the holodeck matter replication and transport beam utilizes "holodeck matter" to form a holobeing or object with substance. Holobeing personalities are preprogrammed and controlled by the holocomputer as defined by the program. Projected holograms are used on the walls of the holodeck to give the illusion of a three-dimensional environment that extends to the horizon. Holodeck matter owes its form and solidity to the pattern held within the holodeck replication and transport buffer and therefore is disassembled when the emitters are turned off or the holomatter is removed from the holodeck. Klingon holodecks are used to heighten hunting and fighting skills. There are no safety protocols; any damage done is the real thing.

Transporters

There are 35 six-person transporters with three separate molecular/informational signature pattern buffers per transporter. The transporter platform is slightly raised to reduce the chance of occasional static discharge. Destination coordinates are relayed via computer from the destination or are directly input by the operator. Targeting scanners located in the sensor arrays determine the coordinates and provide environmental information on the target site. A standard transporter has a range of 40,000km.

The annular confinement beam (ACB) creates a spatial matrix from the primary energizing coils overhead, four redundant molecular imaging scanners in the overhead pads make the memory file of the transporter's quantum state. An individual's molecular/genetic pattern is scanned and old records are updated with current information. Or, for a first-time transport the new individual's molecular/genetic patterns are stored, allowing for emergency molecular reconstruction during subsequent transports. The pattern is stored in the buffer as a retrievable trace, while a transporter log records the beamout. All signatures are stored until purposefully purged by transporter personnel.

Using a widespread quark manipulation field, the phase transition coils in the lower pads disassemble the body by unbinding the energy at a subatomic level; once converted to a subatomic matter stream the transporter is diverted into a pattern buffer. This is due to the Doppler effect (any relative motion between transporter and target must be taken into account). The pattern buffer is used for Doppler shift compensation. A buffer may hold the entire matter stream for up to 420 seconds before permanent pattern degradation occurs. Once beamout is secured, an ACB "carrier" directs each pattern's matter stream through an emitter array on the hull of the ship, toward the target coordinates. A booster set of coils and scanners then work in reverse within the ACB to reassemble each pattern into its original form. These arrays work in such a way as to provide 360° coverage in all directions, as well as intraship transports. The ACB can be used to remove weapons and other "non desirable" items from incoming transporters, and the transporter's biofilter automatically detects and removes all active forms of known harmful viruses and diseases.

THE BRAVE AND THE BOLD

Propulsion (Impulse)

The impulse engines utilize collector arrays, situated in the foresections of the ship's wings, to gather available energy of any type from the surrounding space, which is then filtered through a series of energy replicators, where it is changed into the deuterium atoms needed to cause the fusion reaction that powers the impulse drive unit.

At full impulse speed, the ship is traveling at ¼ light speed, or 125,000 km/sec. If it wasn't for the inertial damping systems, at those speeds most creatures would be torn apart . . . including Klingons.

Inertial Dampers

This system uses warp technology to generate a limited "soap bubble" effect, which falsifies a planetary atmospheric environment. There are set openings in the "bubble" at the impulse ports, allowing the impulse engines to push the ship along without gravitational/impact damage to the interior and crew.

Inertial dampers are on a continuous setting of 50% to allow for unexpected impacts, advancing as the impulse engines/tractor beams are activated, or impact happens.

Impulse sequence is as follows:

Impulse Engines	0%	25%	50%	75%	100%
Inertial Dampers	50%	70%	90%	100%	

Propulsion (warp)

The warp drive unit allows for faster-than-light travel without the time dilation and matter density problems involved in traveling "near light" to light speeds. Inside the warp core, deuterium gasses and antimatter in the form of antihydrogen, regulated and controlled by dilithium crystals, are forced together, causing a small controlled matter/antimatter explosion, which is contained within the reaction chamber of the main warp core. The explosion creates an energy stream, which is collected by power converters and routed via conduit to the warp nacelles. Inside the nacelles the routed plasma is used to energize the verterium cortenide warp field generators. Verterium cortenide causes the plasma frequencies to shift into subspace, creating fields of warped space. The field coils inside the nacelles are arranged in rows, each layer exerting controlled force against its outermost neighboring coil. The cumulative force of the nested fields drives the ship on a spatial wave. The coils are energized in sequential order, the number of times each coil is energized controls the overall warp speed factor of the vessel.

Acceleration is as follows:

Speed	KPH	x light
Standard Orbit	9600	0.00001
Full Impulse	270 million	0.25
Warp 1	1 billion	1
Warp 2	11 billion	10
Warp 3	42 billion	39
Warp 4	109 billion	102
Warp 5	230 billion	214

Speed	KPH	x light
Warp 6	421 billion	392
Warp 7	703 billion	656
Warp 8	1.10 trillion	1,024
Warp 9	1.62 trillion	1,516
Warp 9.2	1.77 trillion	1,649
Warp 9.6	2.05 trillion	1,909
Warp 9.9	3.27 trillion	3,053

Dilithium Crystals

Dilithium is currently the only matter known to be porous to antimatter. Each individual crystal is a crystalline latticework composed of dilithium, diallosilicate, and heptoferranide. When diverted through the crystal, antimatter remains at a centralized distance from all sides of the latticework. Sonic vibration is used to expand and contract the crystals, regulating the flow of antimatter into the reaction chamber.

Qang Bridge

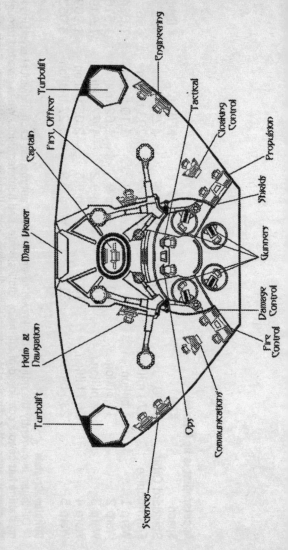

Turbolift

First Officer Turbolift

Captain

Engineering

Tactical

Cloaking Control

Propulsion

Main Viewer

Shields

Gunners

Helm & Navigation

Damage Control

Fire Control

Turbolift

Ops

Communications

Sciences

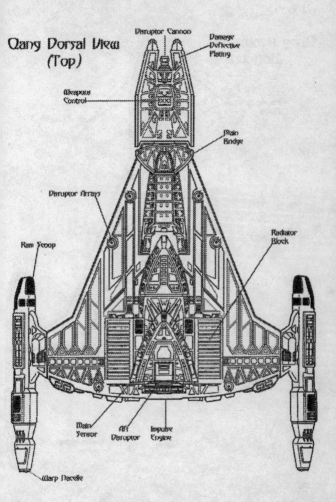

Qang Dorsal View (Top)

Disruptor Cannon

Damage Deflective Plating

Weapons Control

Main Bridge

Disruptor Arrays

Ram Scoop

Radiator Block

Main Sensor

Aft Disruptor

Impulse Engine

Warp Nacelle

289

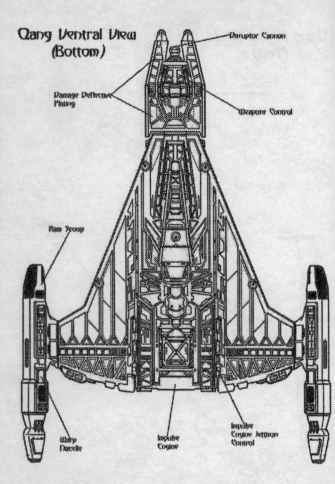

Qang Ventral View (Bottom)

Disruptor Cannon

Damage Deflector Plating

Weapons Control

Ram Scoop

Warp Nacelle

Impulse Engine

Impulse Engine Jettison Control

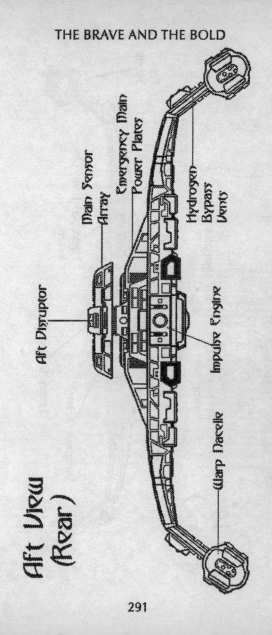

Aft View
(Rear)

Aft Disruptor

Main Sensor
Array

Emergency Main
Power Plates

Hydrogen
Bypass
Vents

Impulse Engine

Warp Nacelle

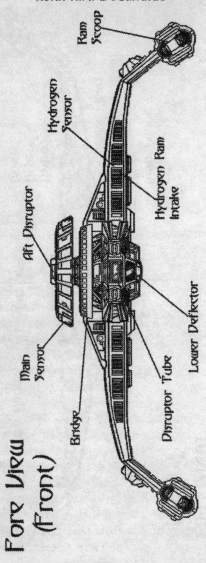

Fore View
(Front)

Ram Scoop

Hydrogen Sensor

Hydrogen Ram Intake

Aft Disruptor

Main Sensor

Bridge

Disruptor Tube

Lower Deflector

AFTERWORD

I first got the idea for *The Brave and the Bold* in 1999. It had its origins in the 1967 *Star Trek* episode "The Doomsday Machine." I always liked the character of Matt Decker—William Windom's layered performance had a lot to do with that—and I wanted to know more about him. He and Kirk obviously knew each other— they were on a first-name basis—so I started thinking about the idea of a previous adventure that had Kirk and Decker working together.

This got my brain going on the idea of "starship team-up." Wouldn't it be cool to pair up the familiar crews with some unknown—or barely known—other ships, and do it from the POV of the other ships? Goodness knows we've met enough other captains in guest shots. Why not see how they view Our Heroes? Having already had the jones to put Kirk and Decker together, I used the settings of *Star Trek: Deep Space Nine* and *Star Trek: Voyager* to answer more questions. With *DS9* there was the intriguing dislike between Jadzia Dax and Captain Keogh of the *Odyssey,* as seen in "The Jem'Hadar." That episode made it clear that the *Odyssey* had just stopped over at Deep Space 9 recently and that Dax and Keogh didn't exactly hit it off—so why not chronicle that adventure? It also gave me the opportunity to bring back one of the first Bajoran terrorists we ever met, Orta, from *Star Trek: The Next Generation*'s "Ensign Ro." And, while several novels (*Double Helix: Quarantine* by John Vornholt, *Pathways* by Jeri Taylor, and the *Voyager* segment of Susan Wright's *The Badlands*) dealt with the *Voyager* crew prior to "Caretaker," none of those tales told the story I was curious about: How and why did Tuvok infiltrate Chakotay's Maquis cell in the first place? The "team-up" motif necessitated setting the story prior to the *Voyager*'s disappearance into the Delta Quadrant in any case, and to my mind, that was the most compelling untold tale from that time period. It also gave me the opportunity to show more of *TNG*'s Captain DeSoto, Riker's former CO, and considered a good friend of Picard's as well. We'd heard good things about him in "Encounter at Farpoint," met him briefly in "Tin Man," but hadn't gotten a good look at him. This was a chance to do so, and also take another gander at the first Maquis we ever met, Cal Hudson (from *DS9*'s "The Maquis Parts 1–2"), and have him join forces with Chakotay.

With the *TNG* segment, I had the opportunity to revisit a crew I'd developed—that of the *I.K.S. Gorkon.* In my *TNG* novel, *Diplomatic Implausibility,* I'd established the *Gorkon,* commanded by Klag (first seen in *TNG*'s "A Matter of Honor"). Reader response to the *Gorkon* and its crew (made up of both original characters and past *TNG* and *DS9* guest stars) was outstanding, so I was given the go-ahead to use them again in this duology and continue their stories forward (look for the first two books in the *Star Trek: I.K.S. Gorkon* series, *A Good Day to Die* and *Honor Bound,* in late 2003).

And, naturally, I couldn't resist the best team-up of all: the "fighting ambassadors," Worf and Spock.

This duology also has the distinction of being the first story to feature all five *Trek* TV franchises. The story called for a prelude to get the story going, and what better place to set it than on Captain Archer's *Enterprise?*

Several people require thanks and praise for their help in writing these two books:

Top of the list are the nifty-keeno folks at Pocket Books, particularly John J. Ordover, who not only said yes but told me how to make it better, and Carol Greenburg, who molded the shapeless mass (or should that be "mess"?) of my first drafts into good pieces of work, as well as Scott Shannon, Marco Palmieri, Jessica Mc-Givney, Margaret Clark, John Perrella, and most especially Pocket's unsung heroine, Elisa Kassin. Not far behind them are Paula M. Block and John Van Citters at Paramount, who are truly deities among licensing folk.

As always, Gene Roddenberry, who got this whole schmear started; Gene L. Coon, Rick Berman, Michael Piller, Jeri Taylor, Ira Steven Behr, and Brannon Braga for keeping it going; and the screenwriters who gave us the guest captains: Norman Spinrad (Decker), Ira Steven Behr (Keogh), James Crocker (Hudson), Dennis Putman Bailey & David Bischoff (DeSoto), and Burton Armus (Klag).

You can't do a TV tie-in without thanking the actors—or at least you shouldn't. They provide the voice you use to write the characters. So hearty thanks to (deep breath): Rene Auberjonois (Odo), Scott Bakula

(Archer), Majel Barrett (Chapel and Lwaxana), Robert Beltran (Chakotay), Jolene Blalock (T'Pol), Avery Brooks (Sisko), LeVar Burton (La Forge), Bernie Casey (Hudson), Michael Cavanaugh (DeSoto), Stephen Collins (Will Decker), Roxann Dawson (Torres), Michael Dorn (Worf), Brad Dourif (Suder), Terry Farrell (Dax), Jonathan Frakes (Riker), Martha Hackett (Seska), Jeffery Hayenga (Orta), Michael Jace (Shabalala), Scott Jaeck (Cavit), Dominic Keating (Reed), DeForest Kelley (McCoy), Sterling Macer (Toq), Derek McGrath (Chell), Colm Meaney (O'Brien), Kenny Morrison (Gerron), Kate Mulgrew (Janeway), Leonard Nimoy (Spock), Stephanie Niznik (Perim), Natalia Nogulich (Nechayev), Alan Oppenheimer (Keogh), Linda Park (Sato), Richard Poe (Evek), Tim Russ (Tuvok), Armand Schultz (Dalby), William Shatner (Kirk), Armin Shimerman (Quark), Brent Spiner (Data), Patrick Stewart (Picard), George Takei (Sulu), Brian Thompson (Klag), Tony Todd (Rodek), Connor Trinneer (Tucker), Nana Visitor (Kira), and William Windom (Matt Decker).

David Henderson for timeline assistance with the prelude.

The University of Colorado's *Hypertexts for Biomedical Sciences* on the Web (http://arbl.cvmbs.colostate.edu/hbooks), especially their section on the adrenal gland, and the directory of compounds at http://www.allatoms.com/CompoundWebSites.htm.

Dayton Ward, Dave Galanter, and Allyn Gibson for reassuring me that I got Kirk's voice right.

Roy L. Post, for setting me straight on how to make a moon into arable farmland.

Mindy McAdams for all her help with the details of the Game of Go. For more on this ancient game of strategy, check out the American Go Association's Web site at http://www.usgo.org.

The Maquis Index at Janet's *Star Trek: Voyager* Site (http://www.star-trek-voyager.fsnet.co.uk) for help in identifying the Maquis members of *Voyager*'s crew. (Also thanks to Todd "Scavenger" Kogutt for pointing me to it.)

John M. Ford, for his seminal *Star Trek* novel *The Final Reflection*—still the definitive Klingon novel—and S. D. Perry and Robert Greenberger, for giving Captain Klag a couple of cameos in *Avatar* Book 2 and "The Other Side" in *What Lay Beyond*, respectively.

Michael A. Martin for useful and handy editorial guidance.

Tammy Love Larrabee for taking the vague idea of what the *Gorkon* looked like in my head and turning it into an actual set of specifications.

GraceAnne Andreassi DeCandido, aka The Mom, aka Editorial Goddess The Elder, who worked her usual magic on my drafts.

The Magical Starbucks of Good Writing in midtown Manhattan. Thanks to owning a laptop, I can write pretty much anywhere, and *The Brave and the Bold* was written in a variety of locations across the United States (not to mention Montréal)—but, for whatever reason, I was most productive at this particular Starbucks. Go fig'.

CITH, the best writers' group ever, who kept me on track and gave invaluable feedback that made the book far better than it would've been without them; the Malibu Group and the Geek Patrol, just 'cause; the Forebearance, for decades of encouragement; and the ever-encouraging fans on the assorted Internet bulletin boards, but most especially those at Psi Phi's *Star Trek*

novels board (www.psiphi.org), the *Trek* BBS's *Trek*
Literature board (www.trekbbs.com), Simon & Schuster's *Star Trek* novels board (www.startrekbooks.com),
and the Yahoo! *Star Trek* Books group.

Most of all, though, to the love of my life, Terri Os-
borne, who makes it all worthwhile.

—Keith R.A. DeCandido
somewhere in New York City, 2002

About The Author

After a trip to the galactic barrier in order to save an injured Klingon, Keith R.A. DeCandido found himself seventy thousand light-years from home and put on trial for the crimes of humanity, after which he was declared Emissary. Eventually, after switching bodies with an insane woman, he was able to become one with the Prophets, stop an anti-time wave from destroying the multiverse, and get home with the help of his alternate future self. These days, he writes in a variety of milieus. His other *Star Trek* work ranges from the *Star Trek: The Next Generation* novel *Diplomatic Implausibility* to the *Star Trek: Deep Space Nine* novel *Demons of Air and Darkness* to the *TNG* comic book *Perchance to Dream* to the award-winning *DS9* novella "Horn and Ivory." In addition, he is the co-developer of the *Star Trek: S.C.E.* line, and has written or cowritten over half a dozen eBooks in this series of adventures featuring the Starfleet Corps of Engineers (some reprinted in the volumes *Have Tech, Will Travel* and *Miracle Workers* in early 2002). The year 2003 will see the debut of *Star Trek: I.K.S. Gorkon,* books starring Captain Klag and his Klingon crew—the first time Pocket Books has published a series focusing on *Star Trek*'s most popular aliens. To say Keith is thrilled at this opportunity would be the gravest of understatements. He will also be contributing to the summer 2003 *Star Trek: The Lost Era* series.

In addition to all this *Trekkin*', Keith has written novels, short stories, and nonfiction books in the worlds of *Gene Roddenberry's Andromeda, Farscape, Buffy the Vampire Slayer, Doctor Who,* Marvel Comics, and many more. He is also the editor of the upcoming anthology of original science fiction *Imaginings* and the author of *Dragon Precinct,* an original fantasy novel to be published in 2004.

Keith lives in the Bronx with his girlfriend and the world's two goofiest cats. Find out even more useless information about him at his official Web site at the easy-to-remember URL of DeCandido.net, or just e-mail him directly at keith@decandido.net and tell him *just* what you think of him. You can even join his fan club at www.kradfanclub.com.

Look for STAR TREK fiction from Pocket Books

Star Trek®

Star Trek®: The Original Series

Star Trek: The Next Generation®

Star Trek: Deep Space Nine®

Novelizations
> *Caretaker* • L.A. Graf
> *Flashback* • Diane Carey
> *Day of Honor* • Michael Jan Friedman
> *Equinox* • Diane Carey
> *Endgame* • Diane Carey & Christie Golden

#1 • *Caretaker* • L.A. Graf
#2 • *The Escape* • Dean Wesley Smith & Kristine Kathryn Rusch
#3 • *Ragnarok* • Nathan Archer
#4 • *Violations* • Susan Wright
#5 • *Incident at Arbuk* • John Gregory Betancourt
#6 • *The Murdered Sun* • Christie Golden
#7 • *Ghost of a Chance* • Mark A. Garland & Charles G. McGraw
#8 • *Cybersong* • S.N. Lewitt
#9 • *Invasion! #4: The Final Fury* • Dafydd ab Hugh
#10 • *Bless the Beasts* • Karen Haber
#11 • *The Garden* • Melissa Scott
#12 • *Chrysalis* • David Niall Wilson
#13 • *The Black Shore* • Greg Cox
#14 • *Marooned* • Christie Golden
#15 • *Echoes* • Dean Wesley Smith, Kristine Kathryn Rusch & Nina Kiriki Hoffman
#16 • *Seven of Nine* • Christie Golden
#17 • *Death of a Neutron Star* • Eric Kotani
#18 • *Battle Lines* • Dave Galanter & Greg Brodeur
#19-21 • *Dark Matters* • Christie Golden
> #19 • *Cloak and Dagger*
> #20 • *Ghost Dance*
> #21 • *Shadow of Heaven*

Enterprise®

Broken Bow • Diane Carey
Shockwave • Paul Ruditis
By the Book • Dean Wesley Smith & Kristine Kathryn Rusch
What Price Honor? • Dave Stern

Star Trek®: New Frontier

New Frontier #1-4 Collector's Edition • Peter David
> #1 • *House of Cards*
> #2 • *Into the Void*
> #3 • *The Two-Front War*
> #4 • *End Game*

Star Trek®: Stargazer

Star Trek®: Starfleet Corps of Engineers (eBooks)

Star Trek®: Gateways

#1 • *One Small Step* • Susan Wright
#2 • *Chainmail* • Diane Carey
#3 • *Doors Into Chaos* • Robert Greenberger
#4 • *Demons of Air and Darkness* • Keith R.A. DeCandido
#5 • *No Man's Land* • Christie Golden
#6 • *Cold Wars* • Peter David
#7 • *What Lay Beyond* • various
Epilogue: Here There Be Monsters • Keith R.A. DeCandido

Star Trek®: The Badlands

#1 • Susan Wright
#2 • Susan Wright

Star Trek®: Dark Passions

#1 • Susan Wright
#2 • Susan Wright

Star Trek®: The Brave and the Bold

#1 • Keith R.A. DeCandido
#2 • Keith R.A. DeCandido

Star Trek® Omnibus Editions

Invasion! Omnibus • various
Day of Honor Omnibus • various
The Captain's Table Omnibus • various
Star Trek: Odyssey • William Shatner with Judith and Garfield Reeves-Stevens
Millennium Omnibus • Judith and Garfield Reeves-Stevens
Starfleet: Year One • Michael Jan Friedman

Other Star Trek® Fiction

Legends of the Ferengi • Ira Steven Behr & Robert Hewitt Wolfe
Strange New Worlds, vol. I, II, III, IV, and V • Dean Wesley Smith, ed.
Adventures in Time and Space • Mary P. Taylor, ed.
Captain Proton: Defender of the Earth • D.W. "Prof" Smith
New Worlds, New Civilizations • Michael Jan Friedman
The Lives of Dax • Marco Palmieri, ed.
The Klingon Hamlet • Wil'yam Shex'pir
Enterprise Logs • Carol Greenburg, ed.
The Amazing Stories • various